CORRUPTED HEARTS

J.E. & M. KEEP

DEDICATION

To our friends who didn't judge, readers of The Keep back when we were first starting out, and Darknest Fantasy Erotica who encouraged us to keep going.

CONTENTS

CONTENT WARNING

J.E. & M. Keep recognize that erotica can be very personal, and that everyone has their limits on what they wish to read. Because of this, we provide content warnings for all our erotica so that you can avoid any **triggering material** – or find the story you most want to read. If you want your book spoiler free, please skip this section!

This particular story contains polyamory/open relationships, all manners of sex, and some violence.

CHAPTER 1

As the slaver's caravan rolled along, the wagon in which Glaurakos was held bumped and jostled wildly. The make of the transport was clearly designed for security, not comfort. It was enough to send someone with poor balance toppling to and fro. He was in a different world from the chaotic realm he'd escaped, but the confinement... that was familiar.

The terrain was rough, following the road less travelled along the path from Sho'ar into the smaller trading camps. It was also more private, which was what the slavers needed. Glaurakos could see the thick forest as they slowly made their way past it, the hot sun beating down on them. It didn't bother him, though.

An odd mix of the beautiful and the terrifying, Glaurakos was born a Fae-Demon. His elven blood manifested in his bright, golden hued skin, handsome facial features and orange-gold hair that fell down around his back and shoulders, straight and silken-smooth. The other half of him was that of a hellish demon, with massive back-swept horns, leathery bat-like wings, glowing red eyes, sharp teeth, clawed fingers and six-and-a-half-foot height.

He was a rare beast on the surface world, a prize for any slaver smart enough – or stupid enough – to try to capture.

He was not bound in the caged wagon, but he was kept there alone, and a crisscross of metal mesh kept him from summoning his sword to him and fighting back against his captors. The damnable humans knew what a price they could fetch for him, and they hungered for it. Any demon, even a half-breed, fought with mastery in battle that a human could never obtain.

Glaurakos seethed as he plotted his escape.

It had been a while since the newest addition had been added to the caravan: a beautiful winged woman who was chained to the back of the caravan, but a few feet from him. She was walking with her head down, following closely after the wagon. Her slender form looked even smaller against the manacles around her hands, their enchantments no doubt keeping her from casting spells. These slavers weren't the usual, trading in grunt workers. They were seeking the big wins.

She looked to be an angel with her large, feathery wings and her delicate features. An innocent, someone easily manipulated and trusting. Even for a fiend like him. She was tall and svelte. Her body was naturally slim, but she looked like she had recently shed some weight, leaving her cheeks a tad more hollow than usual. She tried her best not to move her manacled hands to draw any further attention to herself. Her wings were bound behind her, the tips pressed together painfully, enough to cause a constant cringe to taint her otherwise attractive face. Her porcelain white skin was framed by a black shock of hair, and he had no doubt that this was how she looked at her worst.

These slavers were exceptionally clever, or terrifically lucky, to have found and captured two of the rarer species of humanoids around.

The slavers spread out after a time, keeping a wide sentry on the moving caravan. He managed to fight them off before they could shed him of his thick and intricate armour, a series of chest and leg plates with a short cloak draped about his shoulders and back. Perhaps they figured that once they got him to their destination they could better steal his earthly goods. He had to act fast, and Glaurakos shifted to move onto his knees.

"Angel. I can break us free if you help me," he whispered, his voice preternaturally deep and raspy. There was a terrifying sense of command that permeated his words, not by practice, but by natural inheritance.

Lilah raised her freshly bruised eyes to him, clearly having taken a couple of blows in the struggle to get her to go with the slavers. Her expression was sour and cruel, though it brightened at his promise. She glanced around at her surroundings briefly with her eerie, green eyes.

"What do you figure?" she asked, her voice nearly ethereal, a practiced combination of sweet and tantalizing with an undertone of hidden promise.

"They haven't stripped me of my magic. They think me a mere warrior," he grinned, baring his sharply fanged teeth slyly. "But without help outside, my spells are useless. So..." He paused, some reluctant doubt tingeing his voice as though he didn't expect her to agree to his plan. "With your agreement, I will shift us, summon my sword and free us to escape to safety."

She averted her eyes from him, keenly on the lookout for any who may notice her speaking to him.

"What do you need me for?" she asked. Her voice was skeptical, but still filled with hope.

"These bars prevent me from magically passing through," he rasped, licking his lips briefly with his bizarrely pointed tongue.

"However, with a spell I could switch our places. It's not the same, you see? An eventuality they are not likely to have prepared for." He smirked mischievously at her. "Once I'm outside this wagon, I will be able to get us out of here without issue. They only caught me by dumb luck in the first place. So, what say you?"

His large, leathery wings twitched upon his back anxiously. He had not nearly enough room to unfurl them.

She opened her plush lips to argue before shutting them. Whether she was chained helpless to the wagon, or captured within, there were few options for escape. She looked at him for as long as she'd dared before her eyes flicked away from his harsh gaze.

"If you leave me, I will find you," she said finally, jutting her jaw in annoyance at the reluctant and tentative agreement. "I know my way from here."

Pursing his lips for a moment, he smiled widely, giving her a stern nod.

"I will free you," he said, eyeing her wings. "Do they work still? Or did they just bind them? I want to know before I try to free us. Things will move fast once I'm out, I don't have time to figure out how to break your chains once we start."

"They are bound without magical means. Though I will need to be freed of it before I can fly," she replied.

Glaurakos nodded sternly. "Chain or leather straps?"

"Leather. I'd do it myself if I had time. I don't imagine I will, if you're able to do this."

"Get ready," he said with finality. His voice was preternaturally rich and deep that everything he said sounded commanding and authoritative.

Glaurakos stood as well as he could in the caged wagon, focused and determined as he prepared his gambit. It was a fairly simple spell, but required her consent to be dragged through the ether.

Without further delay he muttered the profane words.

CHAPTER 2

In a disorienting moment, the two strange beings were switched in place. The angel didn't even have to do anything, simply allow it to happen. The manacles, thankfully, didn't hinder magic being done *to* her. She closed her eyes as she landed within the wagon, her knees a bit weak as she got used to the jostling rhythm. She had to crouch down in order to make room for her large, feathered wings.

Standing free behind the wagon, the half-demon began to cast another spell. The caravan guards were too spread out to notice until his confiscated blade magically flew back into his hand. A cry went up for help and two guards hopped down from one of the wagons at the front of the caravan.

She watched him from behind those bars, dry curiosity on her face as she awaited her inevitable betrayal. He was a demon. The only reason she even accepted his deal was she knew that she was trapped. She was desperate.

His wings spread wide, as if about to take off, but instead he gave a flourish of his blade and an arc of lightning caught the two foes, holding their paralyzed forms in place. With just a cursory glance, he turned to the lock on the back door to the wagon.

Broad and tall, the hulking demonic-elf focused his concentration, holding out a clawed hand to utter another spell. A blast of force shot from his partly scaled hand, throwing the lock on the door open. He kept his word, much to her surprise. The demon held out his free hand to her.

"Come on!" he growled urgently.

Lilah took his hand, her soft, alabaster skin a bright contrast to his hard, dark grasp as she leapt from the back of the wagon. As soon as her feet hit land, standing on her tiptoes, she turned her back on him. Her wings ruffled in an attempt to break free of the constraints.

Reaching his free hand to the top of her wings, Glaurakos grasped the thick appendage before carefully slicing the leather restraint away with the massive, two-handed blade.

Her wings rippled as soon as they were free, parting and spreading. With her hands still manacled, she fled. She flapped her large wings a few times, her slender body easily lifted to the sky, as she watched her saviour becoming smaller and smaller below her. When finally she could see nothing, she laughed, gleefully. She was free again!

On the ground, Glaurakos saw more guards approaching, one lifting a crossbow to fire. He flung his sword into the air and a fiery crescent emanated from the blade as it spun toward the man. It missed the bowman, but only after he fumbled his shot and fell back. The sword then continued spinning, striking another slaver squarely, slicing open his neck. Without delay, the horned Fae-Demon took to the sky, his bat-like wings carrying him into the air without another word. His sword returned to his hand as he traveled toward the tree line north of the caravan.

Lilah spotted him, her laughter dying as she took flight after him, gliding with natural ease while glancing down at her chained hands in disgust.

Some arrows followed the pair, but with the chaos below and the swerving, deft flight above, no arrows struck true, and before long, they were safely over the canopy of the forest.

Flying for some time, the air whipping his golden-orange hair back, he glanced back to see the angelic figure still following him. Lowering himself, he descended into a dark area of the trees, a small clearing allowing him to slip beneath the canopy and land. He kept his sword out, turning and waiting for the fellow captive to meet with him.

She paused above him, looking down on him and trying to read his intentions. She could try to find someone else to help her with the manacles, but the slavers had stripped her of what little valuables she held. They had even taken her clothes, leaving her in a pale pink slip with no undergarments. She had clearly made a better captive than the hulking half-demon, no doubt helped by how quickly they had stripped her of her magic.

She could barter in a nearby town, of course, though it may be just as well to barter with the devilish male below her. After all, he had followed through on his word to save her, beyond her expectations.

She fluttered down in a graceful motion, her right leg extending and softening her slow decent as it caught the ground, her left leg touching the grass shortly thereafter. She wore nothing on her feet. Her long, raven hair trailed down over her shoulders ethereally as the wind died out in the clearing. She smiled at Glaurakos, her plush lips pursed.

Glaurakos looked at her, his handsome beauty framed in menace; his soft face lined by large, thick horns and a powerful jaw. He gave her a careful once-over, his reddish eyes intense as they studied her form. He had not, until now, been able to get a clear look at her. The criss-cross of metal bars had been too thick to allow it. His large gold-and-red wings flapped before settling around his back, almost like a second cloak as he towered there, feet placed widely apart.

"I kept to my bargain, so why do you push your luck following me, angel?" His heavy-set brows furrowed as he continued to study her.

"I need the use of my hands. I can offer you a trade, or I can travel to the next town to find someone more interested in what I may offer," she said, her voice calm and studied, still with the tinge of something deep and primal lacing her words. She offered out her hands in demonstration and her wings fluttered, as though readying herself for takeoff.

Glaurakos arched his brow, his eyes still on her. He slowly lifted his weapon and slid it deftly into a series of clasps down his back between his wings.

"And you know the area well enough to make it there safely in the nude?" he asked, humour edging his voice, a curl upon his lips. "Pray tell what, angel, would you trade in your current state should you get there alone?"

"My uncertain safety is the reason I chose to proposition you, first," She smiled, lowering her gaze and bowing her head in a show of trust, though she was still quite alert, tension running along her spine. She righted herself quickly. "As for what I may offer, well..." Her wings receding to a relaxed position along her spine, her hands still held in front of her pelvis, "I'm sure there are many things a man in the wilds may want for." Her green eyes caught his briefly as she took demure steps towards him, her toes touching the ground first, letting herself down softly as she approached the half devil.

The words of the woman were strange to him. Not at all what he was expecting from an angelic figure. He made no move, though, not the slightest flinch at her approach. He was confident in his own defense and not at all worried about what she could do to him.

"You are no angel," he said, a slight smirk curving the corner of his lips. "Or else you are the most practical one I have ever met." His raspy, unnaturally deep voice was a light boom even as he spoke softly to her.

"I believe in being practical," she smiled coyly at him, letting her head tilt to the side as she subtly pressed her chest forward, her breasts only barely hidden behind the light garment, the bottom of it rippling.

"How did you come to be caught?" Glaurakos asked, his voice filled with curiosity, and a tinge of something more; an instinctual interest in her.

"I was resting and, I suppose in my exhaustion, I let my guard down." She pouted, pressing her lush bottom lip outward, a pleasant peachy-pink against her pale flesh. "If you could undo me, I will repay you."

Lifting a hand up to her face, Glaurakos took hold of her cheeks, pinching her chin firmly, but avoiding pricking or cutting her with his clawed digits.

"If you truly meant it, you'd have offered me your services earlier," he said, a cocky grin spreading across his face. He leaned in a bit closer, lowering his voice further still, his breath warm and pleasant on her flesh. "I've proven my word already, haven't I?"

Though it had just been pragmatic to release her. With two captives free, the slavers would scatter, distracted in their search for two quarries rather than just the one.

"You have," she replied, her voice honeyed and seductive. "Though without my hands, I can't promise it will be all it could be." She held his gaze, her posture neither begging nor pleading in nature, but insistent.

He loosed his grasp on her face, his nose twitching as he sniffed at her, nostrils flaring. He shifted his wings, the hooked claws upon each one curved in around his arms, and back around his shoulders.

Lowering his hand, he let the back of one thick finger trail along her tiny pink slip, grazing her breast lightly as he stepped back further into the shadows of the tree. Her body responded instantly, hardening against the soft material. His wings clung to him, giving him the appearance of a haughty arch-devil, a lord of the Pits of Hell vanishing into the black of shadow.

"Come," he ordered, turning and moving through the trees without looking behind. He led her to a small clearing beneath the completely dark canopy, the foliage thick above them from the large, towering trees. A massive stone sat in the middle of the clearing, and he walked around it, checking the area, his fiendish eyes inspecting the dark keenly before turning back to her.

Her footsteps were light, and she stayed on her toes as she danced after Glaurakos, her slip clinging to her torso as it billowed backward with her swift movements. A few moments passed before her eyes adjusted to the forest's dark.

"I doubt anyone would have stumbled upon us there, though I respect your desire for privacy," she said.

"Those slavers won't come into the woods," he answered in a gruff rasp, his stance firm and tall, legs still positioned into the ground wide apart like metal pillars. His hands moved from beneath his wings to his belt, and he began to unbuckle it casually, gazing on her with a stern look. "But we'd be fools to stand around in a clearing for long." The metal clasp of his belt clinked as he pulled it open.

She took a step towards him.

"Fair enough." Her eyes trailed from his face to watch his hands work at his belt, a flash of hunger showing for a fleeting moment in her eyes as she forced herself to look away, a teasing smile curling up her lips. "We'd be very unlucky to be caught twice."

"We'd be very dumb is the word," he said gruffly, undoing his pants but not pulling them open. The tight leather beneath the armour clung to his form, even without the belt. He stepped in toward her, meeting her as she casually sauntered closer. He grasped her slender shoulder, taking a firm hold. Strong, even for a half-breed of his size, he twisted her form to push her toward the large rock, the stone taller than she. He pressed himself against her backside.

She raised her chained arms to brace herself, showing no resistance to his touch. The heels of her palms impacted against the stone, her manacles rattling. Her wings parted from her back, allowing him to pull himself closer, his unnatural heat smothering her.

He moved a powerful hand down to her waist, holding her firmly. He pinched her thin stomach as he reached between them, his hand pushing back the leather of his pants to reach in for his member. Leaning over her back, he smelled at her hair and neck again.

"Something tells me such a trade isn't so uncommon for you," he growled as he pushed her slip up over her hips. Her breath caught in her throat. He freed his cock from the tight confines of his leather pants and pressed it against her bare slit, the bulging head broad and massive. It was a true reflection of his fiendish nature it pulsed large and hard against her.

His voice cut in with an edge to his words, "You're no angel at all."

Poised on her tiptoes, she felt the hot flare of his member press against her equally hot nethers, perpetually slick and craving. She had a mild tuft of hair above her slit, leaving her bare around the lips. Her body bore back toward him, encouraging and inviting.

No, she certainly didn't act like an angel.

With a loud grunt he jabbed himself into her wet and willing body in one motion, her slick cunny walls tight but still drawing him in as he delved into her depths. Groaning, he brought his other hand against her hip, taking a firm hold of her hips, grinding himself inside her, his voice a throaty groan.

"You're a deceptive little thing. A deceiver to the core," he said, pulling his hips back and ramming them forward again, hilting himself in her.

She didn't refute his charge as her womanhood clung to him tightly, her elbows and forearms bracing for each impact. Held in place by his powerful grip, her skin prickled with need.

Her white flesh gleamed in contrast to the darkness of the forest, the grey-black of the rock, her body pure and pristine with no flaws or blemishes but for a small beauty mark just below her left wing. Her ass curved, but didn't offer much padding against his powerful motions. He slammed into her again and she moaned a sound of genuine relief and pleasure.

One of his hands moved up her side as the rough, carelessly hard thrusts continued, sliding up her smooth flesh. He raised the pink slip as he neared her breast, a sharp claw prodding and pricking it before his rough palm encompassed and squeezed it fully.

The half-breed brute grunted and groaned freely as he rammed into her, his own eyes heavily lidded with his desire. The pain collided with the pleasure, enriching the sensations, she felt alive with her need.

She was delighted to be manhandled, moaning just as openly as he with each thrust. He slid his other hand up her spine towards her hair, coiling the dark strands about his powerful fingers and tugging her head back with a firm grasp, bucking into her, utterly lost in his own gratification.

She gasped, her throat exposed, eyes fluttering open to see if there was a weapon above waiting to kiss her pure flesh. Seeing none, she shuddered with pent up delight, the rush of the fear coursing heavily through her, throbbing in her tiny pink nub.

Glaurakos bent his knees, bringing himself down to her height, even as she stood upon her toes to meet him, and his bucks came wild and harder. His pointed tongue licked his lips, his cock swelling inside her.

Her eyes fluttered open and closed again, not quite knowing whether to look for danger around them or revel in the danger buried within her folds and enjoy him to her fullest.

His hand tugged harder on her hair while he squeezed her breast and painfully pressed a nipple between two clawed digits. She let out a tiny squeak while he pinched her nipple; the erect, pinked flesh sensitive to the half-devil's touch. He released her raven locks only to grab at her neck, his fingers curling around and clenching her throat, pounding fast. Her eyes widened in shock and her nails clawed into the stone as she began to lose breath and struggle with alarm.

His strong fingers clutch tightly, closing off her breath as his claws jab at her flesh like threatening daggers. But all the while, his hand continued to grasp her breast, clenching and molesting its pale white flesh as he thrust frantically and erratically. A low, raspy moan built into a loud growling groan, signaling his impending climax. His unnaturally large cock swelled within her, burning with impending release.

With one last thrust he threw back his head and unleashed his load, the only movements now the reactive twitches of his hips and the bulging throbs of his dick within her.

Her hands pounded flatly on the rock, manacles jangling, her cunt twitching with her fear, the tiny spasms of breathlessness lingering throughout her body as she struggles for precious air, her wings fluttering with annoyance.

Feeling her jerk forward in an attempt to free herself, he moved with her, his large body staying close and trying to prevent himself from slipping free. He failed, and a few strands of his pearly semen trailed across her slit.

Breathing heavily, he released her neck, his hand upon her breast keeping her from falling forward.

She leaned against him, letting his rough grasp hold her steadily as she struggled to regain her breath. She coughed.

Licking at his lips with his pointed, reddish tongue, he eyes her through narrow slits, admiring his handiwork laced across her ass and back. He reached his hand to her head again, stroking it over her long dark hair, his clawed tips trailing through her long flowing mane.

"What are you? Tell me the truth," he demanded in a husky, rasping voice.

Her head tilted toward him as he stroked her hair. "I'm sure you've guessed," she said hesitantly, her voice laced with awkward residual pain.

Letting his hand move down through her hair, he continued petting her.

"You look angelic..." he said matter-of-factly, but with a bit of appreciation. His fingers slid from her hair, tracing her spine, and he let one clawed finger move across her wing a bit. "You're a half-angel" he said in a light whisper. It dawned on him then, "No... You're an avian, aren't you?"

She shrugged her shoulders, her feathers ruffling in the night air, soft to his flawed touch, the muscle flinching at the unexpected sharpness. She turned to face him, never leaving her tip toed position.

"Partly," she admitted softly. "We aren't so different, then."

His sharp elven ears, almost hidden beneath his horns, twitched at her voice. His eyes narrowed, though not in irritation or anger, just curiosity as he inspected her face closely. His thumb idly stroked the curve of her breast. The avians were an elusive species, innocent yet beguiling. They could be more similar to demons than angels with their hedonistic ways, though their appearances offered great camouflage.

It also meant that she would be far more useful than he imagined. Though he hadn't thought much of it earlier, there hung a faint smell of certain herbs in her hair. He had to wonder if she'd had some training in spell craft and potions.

"So it seems. I'm glad I didn't ask and you hadn't told me until I finished," he smirked.

"I wouldn't tell at all if I were not at your, ah, mercy," she said softly, her voice still touched with the after effects of his tight grasp. She sucked her lower lip, not bothering to correct her disheveled outfit. She offered her wrists to him.

"Mercy indeed." He let his red glowing eyes move down over her form once more, his finger trailing up over her neck which he rudely grabbed and choked. His brow arched as he noticed the red marks of his heated hands, her angry red flesh burning most with his fiery nature. Glaurakos tucked his member back into his pants before he stepped back, buckling his belt.

Her gaze passed briefly over his disappearing member, lingering there long enough for him to notice.

"Hold them apart and as steady as you can," he commands gruffly, reaching for his sword and turning his attention toward her hands.

Her pale, slender wrists part as her body shrunk away from the manacles, her slip fluttering down properly over her body and hiding her glossy folds. She held her breath, waiting for the sword's impact.

Glaurakos swept his two-handed blade in one smooth, heavy arc. A dull clank filled the air as it broke through the bonds, severing them entirely with one blow. Though it jarred her arms downward, he didn't nick her.

"Can you pick them now? Otherwise, put it to the rock there," he pointed to a high, sharp corner of the stone, "and I'll bust each part open."

She did as he ordered, and he placed his large, coarse hand over her wrist and manacle, holding it firmly in his grasp. He nudged her hand away from the extended part of the steel mechanism, where the loose broken chain links dangled and two bolts held it together about her wrist.

"Keep your hand away. This'll hurt," he warned

Despite his words, he forcibly pushed her hand out of danger and swung his weapon again, damaging the weapon with a rough impact that jarred her painfully as he warned, but it wasn't enough to break it. He repeated the motion again, bashing it open for the manacle to be pried free by his strong hands, grunting as he opened it enough for her to free her wrist.

She breathed an audible sigh of relief in the eerie stillness of the deep forest, her eyes finding his, filled with warm gratitude as she flexed her freed hand. A light spark of arcane energy flowed between them before it dissipated, a little more than a brief shock of purple light.

"Thank you," she said gratefully.

Eyeing her with a certain air of caution at first he nodded to her. Pointing to the other manacle still remaining he said, "Can you free yourself of that one now that your one hand is free? I can do the same to that, but..." He smirked a little, reaching out his free hand to stroke at her long hair with the backs of his fingers lightly, "I'd imagine it'd be softer if you had a spell for such a thing."

She nodded, looking up at him and took a brief step backwards, still on tiptoes as she brought her legs together. Standing straight she began a quiet incantation, short and with few words, but each one crackled with the promise of power as the manacle quickly dropped from her wrist, just barely missing her foot as it collided with the moist ground.

She flexed both her hands in triumph as she stepped closer to him once more, giving him a polite bow of respect. "I am indebted to you, Master..." she looked to him for his name.

With his broad great sword in one hand, the tip tilting down towards the ground but not touching, his free hand raises to her jaw to lightly cup it.

His voice rolls out throaty and raspy, "Master, is it?" A light grin forms on his lips, "Glaurakos. And you, winged vixen?"

"Consider it an honorarium to one who has indebted me so. You could have killed me many times over. Or, well, you could have tried. In earnest," She looked at him once more, eyes scanning across the full of his face. "Lilah, at your service."

His beautifully elven features marred by his fiendish heritage stared down at her stoically before his grin returned. His fingers twitched and move along her cheeks and chin, stroking lightly, the rough edges of his digits scraping along her skin.

"A lovely name for such a deceptively lovely woman." He licked his full lips once more with his pointed, red tongue. "You're right, I could have killed you. But there had been nothing in it for me, and I made quite a bargain." He adds, "Both times," with a smirk. "Where were you headed when they caught you?"

"North," she said simply, staring at him with wide eyes, her pale cheeks flushed with an attractive pink rush of blood, her lips looking almost swollen. "Yourself?"

Continuing the light but coarse stroking of his fingers along her cheeks and chin he continued to appreciate her beauty. "Likewise. And you," he let his gaze sweep down over her slight form, so barely covered, "are as yet still in need of assistance, are you not? I feel another deal may be in order." He cracked a smile at her, barely a grin. "How well do you know these lands?"

"I've travelled nearby paths many times. On foot and by air. It has been many years since I have last passed through, but I know the lands. What did you have in mind, if you already feel this to be a bargain with your upper hand?"

"As you say, a man alone has needs you can fulfill. And these forests won't shelter us long. It is home to hostile wild elves, Lilah." He trailed his thumb from her jawline up to her lower lip, prodding the plush flesh with his pointed claw lightly. His voice takes on a more serious tone abruptly, "You will aid me on my journey north as I see fit, and in return I'll protect you. Get you some more supplies. I've had mine taken from me as well, but with my sword and armour I at least will be able to claim for us new ones much easier than you could." He tore his gaze away from her body to meet her eyes again, "Deal?"

She paused, mulling her options, her brow furrowing as she looked up at the canopy. Very little light filtered through, night slowly being cast upon their world. "I am quite capable of fighting without armour and, should I need to, I have been able to come to many amicable agreements in troubled times before." She held his gaze, her voice lowering to just above a whisper, "However, you have shown me great kindness today, which I will reward in turn."

Tracing the pointed tip of his claw along her lip carefully, he smiled down at her, raising his sword and slipping it onto his back once more, securing it firmly there. "I've little doubt you have a decent chance at it alone. But it will be an easier, safer time with me. And will cost you little to nothing you wouldn't gladly give me or want for yourself regardless."

Her eyes flickered away from him as her lips curved upwards.

"Ah, well, aren't you presumptuous," she said with a smug grin.

He chuckled, his broad-set shoulders heaving a bit. He smiled in amusement.

"We do both, after all, seek to go the same route, do we not? And one room is cheaper than two." He smirked down at her, his own smugness showing as he leaned in, muttering quietly, "And I promise I won't waste so much time on foreplay when next we rut, lovely Lilah."

She smirked deviously at his sarcasm before glancing away, her ebony hair rustling over her shoulder. She placed a hand on his chest, feeling the devilish heat emitting from him, stroking him with her thumb lightly before pulling away once more, offering her hand to his.

"Then we'll shake to our mutual aiding of one another. We will, after all, likely come to rely on my subtleties to getting certain provisions and discounts, won't we? I dare say you haven't an inkling of just how much of a bargain you may be receiving in this."

He tilted his head at her curiously, his eyes glancing to her hand. He smiled quickly, his grin widening across his golden face. He extended his own large hand, wrapping it around her slender digits and squeezing. Much to her surprise, he bent forward courteously, and kissed the back of her hand as he twisted it around, some of his long golden-orange hair spilling down and tickling her skin before he rises back up.

"An interesting woman you are. We have a deal."

Lilah's face remained blank, though she was secretly pleased he thought to kiss her hand. She would not give much away to her mysterious new 'friend' if she could help it.

He puffed out his chest, but didn't relinquish her hand.

"However, to barter and discount we will need something to do it with. And for that, I shall procure us our first bounty." He peered up through the canopy, noting the darkening sky through the limbs. "You will grow cold wandering about in nothing," he stated plainly, looking back to her. "If we can't make it to some farm house or traveller in time you will likely have to huddle close for warmth this eve."

"I'm not unused to spending an eve in the wilds with less comforting company, and they didn't radiate such a, ah, masculine heat," she paused, looking at him through her long, dark lashes. "But if you would be more comfortable within the confines of a building, I'll support that notion as well."

Smiling smugly down at her, he enjoyed Lilah's candor. Though intelligent, he was by no means a particularly charming man himself. He was more suited to cunning.

"Very well," he pulled her closer to him, tugging her into his chest, "Let's not have it be said I wasn't accommodating to a lovely woman's wishes. Not yet anyway."

His two hands moved around her, feeling over her slender form through the thin fabric of her slip. One moved down to cup over the round swell of her rear.

CHAPTER 3

Lilah blinked in the early morning break of light, her green eyes adjusting slowly to the strange forest around her. Glaurakos' heated body warmed her through her core. She moved only slightly, the leaves beneath her rustling as she propped herself up on her hand. The half-demon had kept her company for the evening, and she truly looked at him for the first time.

Her eyes glided over his slumbering face, down his bare chest, and over his lower limbs. A soft, pleased smile formed on her lips. She brought her nose to his neck, inhaling his scent before lightly nuzzling him to wakefulness.

Glaurakos had rested rather still and peacefully, one arm about the woman, unperturbed by the cool forest air, as his own natural heat was exhaustless. He was aware of her rising, but paid it no heed as she observed him.

He grinned, turning his conscious eyes upon her, and he rubbed a coarse hand on her lower back. With a long, rumbling exhale he turned his head to her, kissing beneath her ear.

Their clothes cast aside, her skin responded eagerly to his touch.

Lilah's eyelids fluttered lightly at his affection, smiling gently as she roused him.

"We should be on our way..." she said slowly, trying to convince herself to get up. Her limbs stretched outward, rejecting the notion.

Glaurakos growled in response and rolled atop her, his face buried in her neck still. His sharp fanged teeth kissed and suckled her flesh. Powerful, trunk-like arms support him as he shifted his bulky frame over her. His golden-orange hair spilled over her neck and chest, and he undulated with the motions of his mouth, hips slowly joining the rhythm, moving to take her once more on the forest floor.

Lilah was only too willing, her legs splayed before him, her honeyed mound ready for him. She inhaled as she felt him press to her sex and her hips moved to beg him in. Once more she clasped him in her embrace, her carnal warmth paling in comparison to his radiant heat. Her pelvis thrust toward his as she met him full on, accepting him easily even with the lack of pretense.

No foreplay. There was no need for it.

Supporting himself on one thickly muscled arm, he brought the other to her bare chest. Grasping her breasts, he arched his spine and pushed his shoulders back, plowing into her tight valley once more. The coupling lasted longer still than their rutting the night before, until once more he carelessly spilled himself into her with a loud groan of satisfaction and a few final motions of his hips.

She muttered contentedly, as though she had hungered for years before finally being fed her fill, her pelvis and hips roiled with pleasure at the forceful demon. As he finished she leaned back with an arched spine and broad smile, looking quite happy.

"Well then," she breathed.

With heavily lidded eyes and a pleased, smug look of satisfaction, he pulled himself from her and rolled away, pushing himself onto his haunches. He started to put on his armour. The gold hued skin of his muscular body was edged with red. Scale-like flesh spattered along parts of his body.

"We'll head east," he said, his voice huskier than usual from the early hour, "I believe there is some sign of farmland that way."

She rolled to the side, seeming quite content in the nude and not altogether too interested in putting her slip back on. She rose to all fours, looking up at him curiously.

"And then what?" Lilah asked.

Glaurakos' eyes slid down to her body as he watched her move on all fours with great amusement. He tugged one thick bracer on, then the next.

"And then I'll move in and acquire us some provisions," he said, reaching down to pick up his chest piece and pulling it on, strapping it into place carefully. "You do wear clothes, right?"

She stared at him blankly, tilting her head to the side without expression. "If I have to," she replied, watching him dress with some amount of disdain. "I'm surprised they let you keep your stuff."

"They weren't going to let me keep any of my gear. I was still fighting when they trapped me, and they judged it not worth some broken noses or worse to get it off me once they had taken my sword away." Grinning cockily, he stood up, his thickly muscled lower legs on display.

His limbs were red and rough, becoming more heavily scaled closer to his feet, which were darkly clawed just like his hands. He pulled on a loincloth, followed by his leggings. He shrugged, clamping the leg armour on, "My best guess is they were betting they'd get a wizard to incapacitate me back at their camp."

She reluctantly picked up her slip, pulling it on below her wings and tying it in front.

"Why would they even bother trying to capture someone like you? They should know better than that," she said flirtatiously.

Slipping his boots back on, he smirked, looking a bit full of himself as he strapped them into place. Standing straight, he looked to her. Her words were fake and sycophantic, he thought, but he enjoyed them nonetheless.

"For their trouble they made off with some valuable items. Even with the slaver guards they lost, I dare say they made a tidy profit from messing with me."

He held out his cloak to her, which was long enough to drape over her completely. "Had I the time and patience I'd make them pay for daring. They can keep their luck at catching me in such a trap."

Her lips furrowed to the side thoughtfully as she accepted the cloak.

"Yes, I lost my pack. Which, gladly enough, only contained everything of value I had left," she said icily as she moved to drape the cloak over her, grateful that the fiend had tailored it to his specifications, allowing it to fit between her wings. "However, as you can tell, I'm not in any state to get it back yet."

He sneered sympathetically at her tale of her loss while checking his armour once again.

"There will be more valuables along the way ahead, I am certain," he reassured, "When we hit the farmhouse, we will have to leave no survivors," he said casually, testing her. "If any know of us having done it, they will send hunters after us up north and without end."

"Most of the people around here have bigger things to worry about than us, though that would just make us a more convenient target," she hummed lightly, "And we do tend to stick out in a crowd." She moved toward him on her light feet. "I doubt they'll have much of value, and farmer's wives rarely have any attractive clothes," she purrs, "What do you hope to attain there?"

He comfortably slipped an arm around her waist, resting his hand upon her hip as he looked down at her.

"Something for you to wear... just for now," he said, "Perhaps some farming families' savings and heirlooms to buy us a little something in the town ahead. And," he added, "Food. Have you not felt hunger set in yet, Lilah?"

She shrugged her shoulders with a smile, bringing her cloak in around her.

"I suppose," she cooed at him modestly, looking at him through her lashes. "Perhaps one of the ladies will be a very wild woman in private, spoiling their meagre life's savings on that one, perfect corset...." she stared off wistfully.

Chuckling again, he stroked his heated hand over the small of her back.

"If you prefer it like this, very well," he said, resigned, "But do keep in mind the lands north of here are cold and barren. The Karn live upon mostly tundra. Even I would have trouble keeping you warm throughout that all, especially in the air." The Karn were great, furred beasts that walked upright and rutted constantly. They definitely knew how to stay warm.

He looked around the clearing, and spotted their entrance from hours before. "Come" he directed authoritatively, his arm remaining about her waist.

Lilah allowed Glaurakos to lead her, and she pranced along with him, heels never hitting the dirt.

"I understand the need for warm clothing. I just would rather not arrive looking like an old bag. I have some skills on my own, and some may be entranced by a woman such as myself, even if she were wearing a sack. But, should I barter on your behalf, it would befit me to dress the part, dear master Glaurakos."

Smiling with smug pleasure, he moved along until the dim light of the waning night could be seen through the clearing. Pausing before stepping out into the starlight, he looked down to her.

"It's only a temporary solution. As soon as we hit a real town, you can barter all you like. I've no doubt your skills with charm are in some way linked to your skills at dress... or undress," he laughed, stepping out into the clearing and unfurling his leathery, bat-like wings.

She followed his motions, her own feathery wings opening to their full span, flexing and elongating. She stretched her lithe body, working the awkward kinks from her neck.

"Lead the way, handsome," she chimed.

With a quick bend of his knees, Glaurakos flapped his wings and kicked his strong legs, propelling himself up into the sky. Flying upward, he glanced around into the distance, his leathery wings beating the air to hold him up as he sought direction. He paid her another glance before setting off.

Soaring over the treetops, his red eyes scanned the horizon, peering through the dark for any signs of habitation.

Lilah followed closely, holding her position just above his, eyeing his ass as he flew. Her feathered wings rustled in the breeze, her sheer clothing and his thick cloak clinging to her tightly.

"If we make it there quickly enough we can catch them before sunrise. It will make things easier," he said loudly through the din of the wind blowing past them, his long, golden-orange hair streaming through the air.

He sized her up once more, "How are you feeling? Capable of fighting if need be? I should have no issue, but you never know in such matters."

"As long as you keep them off me, there are a few things I can do without my trinkets. The quicker we can resupply on ingredients, the more useful I'll be. We'll be in and out, take everything of value, as few deaths as possible."

He pondered her words. "No more than are necessary. But there can be no witnesses." He had been right. If she needed ingredients, then certainly she could cast some spells. Maybe even more. It excited him to know how much they had in common, even as he kept his gaze straight, his large body bobbing and swaying in the air as his wings carried him.

"Stand back, let me handle things. But be on alert. I don't want some guard patrol to stumble upon you as I do the work," he said, pointing off in the distance to a home visible in their dark vision. "There. We're nearing."

"I'll be able to handle them," she smiled darkly, heading toward the point in the dark, pulling the cloak in around her tighter as she prepared to land.

Soaring a little lower, he began to approach the ground, remaining at a distance from the farmhouse as he landed quietly. With as much silence as he can muster he pulled his large leathery wings in around him once more, trying not to make more of a rustling than necessary. "Defend yourself and call to me if it comes to that. Let us approach cautiously; they likely have a hound."

Lilah moved, barely making a sound, her body so light on her feet, her motions so graceful and fluid that she was able to saunter on quietly. Her keen eyes darted around to ensure their concealment.

Their mutual elven heritage gave them nimble reflexes, and though he was a large and heavy set, he moved quietly. In the dark of the early morning, he spied a hound resting near the entrance to the farmhouse. Pulling his blade from his sheath quietly, he let it fly. It struck the beast and killed it before it could do more than give a startled noise. Stained with the animal's blood, his weapon returned to him and he flicked away the mess, nodding back to her over his shoulder before they moved on.

He crept to the doorway and nodded to her, standing aside and waiting.

She turned her back to him as she quickly studied the lock. Her thick lashes hide her eyes as she muttered a few words softly, her hands glowing an eerie green. The lock popped open before her. She smiled toothily, pleased with her work.

Cracking a slight smile, he placed one of his large palms upon her slender shoulder heavily, carefully moving her aside. He opened it carefully, quietly stepping inside after giving her a final silent motion for her to stand watch. Creeping forward, he looked about, the home completely dark inside but his night-sensitive vision granted him sight all the same.

Cautiously he made his way toward a closed door, opening it with care and seeing nothing but supplies. The house was a decent size, but older, and he made note to step lightly to avoid making the floor groan. He crossed the stairs to the open room. He peered into the pantry with his great sword in hand. He paused as his pointed ears twitched at the sounds of motion.

CHAPTER 4

Lilah remained poised at the doorway, watching both the exterior and the interior alternately, her breathing coming to a near halt as she played watchdog.

She tried to remember charms, sleep spells, memory spells. Full-on attack spells. Her ears twitched at the sound of motion. Her eyes glanced towards the stairs.

CHAPTER 5

In the moments before entry, Glaurakos thought back to his many years in confinement. The ensorcelled dungeons that had held him in check for so long, locked away with mad demons. Those creatures were unpredictable. Cruel. Merciless. In the beginning he loathed them. Then he came to understand them.

That understanding made him loath them even more.

Standing at the precipice of a simple home of the mortal realm, he imagined that the beings inside were like those foul creatures of his imprisonment: unpredictable. Treacherous. It was no loss to take from them what he needed. Humans were no different from demons in that way.

Cautiously he turned and crept out when he heard the creaking sound of a door opening, followed by a click of locks. Slinking through the kitchen as quickly and quietly as he could, he stepped outside the door and looked up the steps.

He saw nothing there or above; just a single, closed door. Studying it a moment he looked toward his accomplice. Glaurakos caught sight of a human man outside, holding a spear and inching toward his companion's back. Focusing his eyes on the enemy he glowered and vanished. Instantly he appeared beside the human, his sword cutting downward in an arc, slicing through the unarmoured man's torso and severing him in half with one motion.

Lilah spun around just in time to see the two halves of the human slick to the ground.

"We'll have to make this quick," she said, her wide, astonished eyes studying the dead man's features before she moved back into the core of the house.

His strike was so quick that little blood splattered, but he huffed a bit from the exertion, and the mess pooled upon the floor, flowing around the body. The man's spear lay carelessly on top of it like a discarded toy.

His red eyes glowing intensely, Glaurakos looked to Lilah and said, "Yes. I was hoping to avoid bloodshed. He must've circled down from the windows in back."

He looked around outside, closing the door after him. Pointing upward, he said quietly, "The family must be barricaded upstairs. See if you can find any of their valuables down here while I check on them."

She nodded, quickly moving into the uninspected room, her footsteps still light. Lilah glowered sourly as she entered the kitchen, flicking through the pantry for food.

She knew any valuables they had would likely be upstairs. She filched a cooled loaf of bread and a small bag of prepared meat. It was enough to feed them a couple days, provided they would be able to find water, she thought. She hefted it before she checked the rest of the room for anything else that she should take.

She didn't have a larger bag, but managed to hold what she had in under her arms as she snooped about.

All the stealth he could muster could not prevent the aging wood from groaning beneath Glaurakos' weight. Flicking blood from his weapon he moved to the single door, cautiously trying it in a prepared stance, ready to fight. When the door swung open unlocked, he saw two other doors beyond a short hallway, one shut, the other slightly ajar.

Stepping in, he tried the closed one, finding it locked. Cautiously he snuck into the open room, finding a single large bed, wardrobe and washing basin. Picking up a handcrafted chair, he jammed it beneath the other locked door, eliciting a cry from a young child, as he barred it shut. The noise made the inhabitants panic.

"Come here," Glaurakos called to Lilah.

Upon hearing the Fae-Demon's call, Lilah traipsed up the stairs quickly, her light steps bounding as though she expected trouble, almost tripping over the chair in her hurry. She balanced herself quickly, and followed after him.

Grabbing a cloth sack near the door, he dumped out a bundle of thread spools, holding it open for her as she dumped the food in.

"In here," he gestured at the wardrobe, "see if the lady has anything worth a damn, if you care to." He cracked a slight smirk at his waifish accomplice.

She hoped against her logical hope for something beautiful, glamorous, and, yes, warm. She opened it, but to her frustration it only contained frumpy outfits with itchy fabrics.

She sighed, downtrodden, as she pulled out the least repugnant item. A brown, simple dress that was long in the sleeves and legs, and modest in the chest. She held it up to her to find it too large, though she accepted it with disdain. Moving toward the dresser, she opened the top drawer, hoping for lingerie, but found none of that either.

Lilah spotted a small jewelry box in the back corner, hidden by some socks. She pushed the legwear aside and removed the box, opening it to find a modest gemstone attached to a thin chain. She smiled at Glaurakos, dangling it in front of him.

He smiled back at her, mirroring her smugly pleased look. He nodded to her, leaving the bauble in her keep. He pushed past her and shoved the dresser over with a crash, causing another scream from the other room. Checking behind it he found no hidden compartments or fake board, much to his chagrin.

She frowned at the screams as she draped the necklace around her neck, fastening it and letting it drop below her throat.

"Anything?" she whispered to Glaurakos, helping him search the other drawers quickly, her fingers nimbly moving through the meagre clothing of the residents.

"No," he grunts gruffly.

Peering around the room for any signs, his eyes spotted the bed. With his massive strength, he grasped the end and shoved it across the room. He crouched down and inspected the floor, his red eyes alight as he spots a floor board, irregularly short and scratched at one edge. Glaurakos dug his sword point between the wood, prying it open and exposing an empty space beneath where a tiny wooden box laid. Reaching in, he plucked the object up and stood, grinning triumphantly at Lilah.

Carefully he pried the box open, and inside they saw what must have been the family's entire wealth; an altogether unimpressive bundle. Glaurakos plucked out coins and a weathered old ring, leaving behind the parchments inside, none appearing to be enchantment scrolls of any kind. Dropping the box he put the contents into a pocket on his greaves.

"It's not much, but at least you won't freeze or starve on our way to the next stop," he said, reaching out to lightly graze Lilah's cheek with a claw.

She nodded in agreement, turning slowly to gaze out the door.

"We should go before they get brave," she muttered, looking back at him with her wide, innocent eyes, smiling gently.

He grinned, letting his coarse, devilish hand linger upon her smooth, pale skin. Glancing toward the barred room, he concurred, "Very well. No need to lay waste to more of them; they saw nothing."

"Come," he said, tying his satchel to his belt and pushing Lilah toward the doorway.

She didn't really need the push, she thought, but she accepted it all the same. Lilah was smiling to herself, a private look hidden from her companion. She glided down the stairs, opening the door and stepping over the halved body quickly.

Glaurakos plucked up a pair of woman's shoes he spotted as he walked out.

"Do you wear shoes at all?" he asked inquisitively.

"If I have to..." she sighed, "I should, if we're headed north. This is why I hate traveling north."

"You can shove them in the sack for now if you please, along with whatever else, if the cold's not bothering you yet," he added, handing over the shoes and grinning wryly. He looked to the east, then back at the farmhouse.

"Keep your wings down; we'll walk until we're out of view. We don't want them to peek out and see us flying away. It'll only help any pursuers track us," he warned.

Lilah's wings vanished and she looked just like an elf even though she felt them flutter behind her. It was a simple illusion, a trick of the eye. As an elf she was still foreign and exotic to the lands, but without the feathery wings, she was less conspicuous.

Still, she seemed unsettled with having to walk and hold up her disguise. She kept a brisk pace as the farmhouse fell further and further into the background. Lilah's heart thumped in her chest. "If I had seen him, I could have charmed him," she said softly, as though embarrassed.

"He was quiet. And likely smart. He timed it just right so we were distracted with the noises upstairs," Glaurakos grunted. "He was a fool to attack. Had he hid in the room with the rest there'd have been no need for his death," he said, sneering.

There was a long silence spread out between them.

"He didn't know that. I checked outside just before I looked upstairs, you know," she said, her soft voice breaking Glaurakos' reverie.

"Of course you did. And you would have killed him without my help, but not before he nicked one of your lovely wings, or worse," he shot back, continuing their brisk pace. He spared her a slow sidelong look.

She looked mildly troubled, her face deeply contorted with her reeling thoughts. "There's only going to be so many times you'll be willing to save my lovely wings," she sighed.

"As long as you're not a burden I don't see why. Regardless of what the circumstances are, you are not that. Had you not been there, he might've jabbed me before I saw," he said, shrugging his broad shoulders and sliding his blade into the sheath upon his back as he spoke, his voice its usual preternaturally deep rasp.

There was a long pause as she digested his words.

Shaking off her unease, her voice lilted and became excited.

"I'll race you!" she exclaimed. Her invisible wings began to shimmer into existence and flapped, bringing her high off the ground in one bounded leap. She rose higher above the treetops, moving forward quickly.

CHAPTER 6

With a few bounds of his own, Glaurakos unfurled his wings, letting the air catch the leathery flaps before rising up to meet her. Flapping his wings to catch up, he called out, "Do you know the nearest or best town from here?"

"Twin Stars!" she shouted back to him, not slowing, quite serious about their race. "It's a supply town; we'll be able to get what we need!"

Lilah glided on the wind, letting it carry her forward quickly before she flapped her wings again, her skin rising in goose bumps in the flight.

Flapping his own wings much more slowly, but with stronger pushes, Glaurakos swayed and bobbed in the air, not able to fly faster than the winged woman, but uninvested in her race.

"Very well," he called. He inspected her from behind as they soared, "I trust you'll have no issue bartering with what little we have?"

She laughed joyfully over her shoulder, smirking brightly. Already she was over the loss of the human life, and felt her spirits return. "I could barter with nothing more than you found me in, couldn't I? And I imagine you're a harder sell than some of them. Though not all!"

"I've no doubt about that. Though I'd rather avoid waiting for you to screw the township if it could be helped. It will take a lot of time from our journey northwards," he said.

"I suppose... " she said disappointedly. "Though I would only screw those that could help us in the quickest way possible. It's more time-effective."

"Do as you wish, Lilah. Though if your plan is to seduce some other fool to replace me, spare me the wait and tell me ahead of time," he growled.

"I doubt any there would be any bit as useful," she said with sincerity. "And until they start rescuing me left and right, I'm afraid they're going to have to do something wildly amazing and unexpected," she purred, her rhythm slowing enough so that she flies closer to him. She grinned at him, looking sincere.

The wind blew past his face, sending tendrils of his long golden-orange hair whipping and flailing behind him. He watched her, his red gaze fixated thoughtfully.

"True enough," he said at last, his lips forming into a grin. "About how far from here do you say it is then?" He peered off to the horizon, the sun peeking over and filling the dark sky with light as they soar along.

She shrugged her angelic shoulders, smiling at him. "We'll be there in time before night fall. Always the best time to barter. What types of things will you need?"

Teetering back and forth in the air as if the act of pondering set him to such motion, he grinned over at her.

"Nothing even you could buy in this place, I don't suppose," he said, "Except a quality satchel and some basic supplies. The grand trinkets and regents I carried before are too pricey and rare to find the likes of which here, even had we the coin. Or," he let his gaze trail over her slowly down from her face, "other assets."

"Well, it is a merchant town, though it is fairly small. Where were you travelling, anyway? Will they have what you seek?" She tilted her head back, unfazed, as he gazed at her lewdly.

"Up north." He paused, assessing her and arching a brow before adding, "To Lar'nef. And I won't know until I get there. But I imagine they shall, in some form or another." He looked ahead, "And you, my lovely companion? Where do you head, and will they have what you seek once you arrive?"

"I doubt you'll find anything rare there," Lilah said, tilting her head again and looking at him.

"You doubt my destination then? Why? What's changed?" Glaurakos asked, disturbed. He flew closer.

"I don't doubt your destination; I just doubt you'll find anything rare there. And I was headed to Mesh'her, originally, though I haven't much reason to go there without my supplies. I curse myself for letting my guard down. I should have known better. So no, they won't have what I want because I can't provide what *they* want."

"What are you seeking to offer them then? I'm curious," he smirked.

She paused, looking at him and deciding whether or not to tell him. She had nothing to lose, she thought.

"People seek me out for pleasures of all kinds. I was bringing them a more herbal remedy to ease their burdens," she said softly.

"I see," he replied, unfazed. Wetting his lips with his pointed tongue, he looked back to her, "What do you know of my destination then? Other than that it's not likely to have rare things, that is."

"Mostly bandits roam there. I haven't ever been, personally, but I've never had cause to want to, either," she blinked, quickly wiping the confused look from her face.

Furrowing his brows slightly he asked, "Are you certain? Where, then, do our kind find themselves welcomed here? I've no intention to wander the wilds for an eternity, amassing no power or wealth beyond the increasingly ragged clothes on my back."

"As I said, I've never been there," Lilah repeated, "But I've never heard of it being anything but. As for welcome, well, some of us have been moving to Mesh'her from Sho'ar."

"Come with me," he suggested, his tone gruff, "Join me on my journey. We will see for ourselves what awaits us in Lar'nef, and should it be nothing we will turn aside and look elsewhere. Perhaps we'll seek this Mesh'her you speak of. What do you say? You have no mission of your own anymore." Glaurakos tilted his strong chin upward.

"I have nothing better to do," Lilah replied thoughtfully, "Though I'll be flying as blind as you. We'll need a map or some guidance to get there. I hope you won't plan on taking advantage of me."

"Often and regularly," he answered without meeting her curious gaze, his voice steady and sure, perfectly casual in its deep gruffness. With a slow slide of his gaze over to her, a grin spreads across his face.

She flutters her lashes flirtatiously. "I didn't mean like that..." Lilah replied coyly, with a brief swipe of her tongue over her lips, "My intent was neither enjoyable nor fun, I'll have you know."

"I've made my offer, and shown you repeatedly the value of my word," he dismissed. Holding her gaze with his red eyes he added, "I'll not take advantage of you in such a manner, as long as you hold the same bargain with me. Do we have a deal, my angelic friend?"

"I have no need nor benefit from harming you," she assured sincerely, looking at him briefly before glancing at the horizon. She navigated them a slightly westward, ensuring they stayed on course.

"People have a way of finding benefit in such things, dear Lilah. That's the way of it," Glaurakos said.

She looked at him curiously, a bit of a smirk to her full lips. "You think I'm going to find someone who will give me the world if only I do away with you?" she asked.

Chuckling deeply he glanced at her, "You amuse me, but no. However, perhaps we come across some great bounty, and you think leaving me to die and making your way out with it would be better for you." Glaurakos looked away slowly, "But I'm hoping you realize better. Putting up with me is more profitable in the long run than a big payoff in the short. You look smart enough to see that."

"I don't leave those for dead when I can," she smiled, giving him a teasing quirk of her neck. "I have lived a long time. Fleeting treasures do very little for me. Especially when they are so fleeting that I can be left with nothing after but a few days."

Nodding firmly he peered off to the east as he spoke, looking confidently self-assured, "Then it's agreed. We'll be travel companions on this journey, much to our mutual profit and growth. I feel we should settle this new arrangement with some act, but our destination is still so out of reach." He smirked and chuckled gruffly, looking back ahead.

"I'm sure you'll make time for that once we arrive, hmm?" Lilah suggested, "Though I'll insist on some privacy at first, to make a few deals. If we arrive around supper hour, they'll be prime for... bartering."

With a loud snort he sounded almost offended at first, but then broke into a chuckle. "Go work your charms, my feathered harlot," He smirked slyly at her, "I'm sure I will be amazed by the fruits of your efforts once it's done."

Lilah dove on ahead, slowing once more to say, "We'll need supplies: a bag for you, some more rations, because I cannot eat just gruel for weeks on end, and I'll need a new outfit," she stated matter-of-factly.

"Get whatever you desire. My own needs are simple and inexpensive for the time being. If, as you say, Lar'nef is bereft of much luxury, but then again, that might change when we reach a decent city," he added.

"Larger cities are always more fun to barter in anyways," Lilah giggled, with a bit of a flourished twirl in the air, showing off for him. "How did you obtain your armour?" she asked.

"It was taken from an old grey elf who taught me much about swordplay. He died before he could teach me all he knew, but regardless, I benefited in other ways," he reminisced, enjoying Lilah's aerial show, her lithe frame twirling before his red gaze in a manner his larger body and wings could never match.

"I'm surprised it fit," she said coyly. "Did you have to get it customized to your frame?" her eyebrows perked as she complimented his bulk.

"Indeed I did, my aerial beauty," he nodded. He soared up a bit before pulling his wings in and letting himself fall. Then, extending his wings once more, he arced back up to her level with a smooth bob in the air.

"It allowed me to strengthen it, which only helped it. Though," he grumbled, "I do lament the loss of my old robes in my pack."

"Robes?" her eyebrows rose, looking a little devilish, "I wouldn't have taken you for a robe man. Though it has its appeal," she said.

"I practiced wizardry for a long time, before I found my body as useful as my mind," he grinned smugly, his body swaying back and forth from side to side in the air as if swaggering, his red eyes lasciviously watching her in return.

"Oh hey. I never would have figured," she said, her eyes widening, "What made you change? Let me guess, got sick of them trying to cram you into a box you didn't fit, right?" She cooed, flying as close to him as she could.

Watching her response with some amusement of his own, he replied, "You could say that. Much of it had to do with the events that transpired after my return... being absent. The War of Binding as they're calling it, made me consider new paths. Something more... versatile to circumstances, so I'm not so reliant upon one form of combat. Like you said." He smirked. He rather liked feeling impressive.

CHAPTER 7

Swooping down from the sky, just outside the small travellers' town, Glaurakos wrapped his wings around him like a cloak before turning to Lilah and plucking his actual cloak from her back. Placing the garment over his head and shoulders, he raised the hood to cover his horns and forehead before nodding to her quietly and making his way into the village.

Lilah prepared as well, casting a spell to render her wings invisible once more. Her beauty, though, made her stand out from the crowd. Her long, glossy hair and big eyes drew stares from the busy townsfolk.

The town bustled with traders at this time of year, and the tall, broad Fae-Demon made his way through the people with little notice because of the commotion. Pressing his way through the most crowded inn, he moved to a dark booth in the back.

A frumpy barmaid came to serve him, proving more discourteous than one might imagine as she sloshed the liquid over the rim of the mug. Her perpetual scowl must have been born from years of working in the dingy place, serving vagabonds and ruffians. Glaurakos watched the room quietly, nursing a single drink as she walked away, slapping another hand away from her ass.

CHAPTER 8

Having left all their recently acquired goods in Glaurakos' care, Lilah stood nymph-like and barely dressed. She pouted as she walked toward a more genteel tavern, peering at the place nervously.

She wasn't too picky, of course, but the gruff looking human that approached her had a glowing smile and that made the way her fingers worked over his tunic a little more eager, a little more genuine.

"Come upstairs with me," he husked in her ear, and her body tingled with excitement.

"I'd love to," she replied.

CHAPTER 9

A few hours later she returned to her companion, a new bag in hand. Within it were various small travellers' supplies, a map, and a new outfit for her.

Lilah tapped Glaurakos on the shoulder and he twisted his head to the side, glancing at the new satchel a moment before nodding and sliding up from his seat. Towering over her, he offered her a seat on the inside of the booth, speaking to her in a gruff, raspy whisper, only as loud as it takes to carry over the din of the tavern.

"It went well I trust?" Glaurakos asked.

"Well enough," Lilah shrugged, sliding into her seat. She still was not wearing her new outfit, choosing instead to traipse around in her flimsy pink slip. "He didn't have as much gold as I'd like, but what can you do about that, really. Regardless, you have your new bag!"

"You didn't get yourself the clothes you were after? Will that mean you'll be busy again this evening then?" he asked, sliding in beside her and blotting out his view of her as he turned inward. Up so close, he eyed her with his red gaze.

"They're in here," she said, tilting her head toward the bag. "Oh, did I mention the bag is enchanted?" She smiled toothily, quite pleased with herself. "It's larger on the inside than on the outside."

"Very well done, Lilah," Glaurakos admitted, arching an impressed brow. A grin formed upon his face, flashing some of his sharply fanged teeth, "I thought it would be a while before I could arrange to replace my old satchel." He reached a hand over, placing his coarse palm upon her smooth shoulder.

"Well, good thing we're in a trade town, hm. Oh, it may or may not have been used. By him. He was all too happy to give it to me, though, once I told him of my terrible plight."

"But of course," Glaurakos said, grinning widely, his large hand rubbing at her slender shoulder, a gruff laugh rolling up from deep within his chest. "Do you want anything? A drink? More food?" He peered around, looking for the barmaid once more, "I have not been completely idle either." He looked back to Lilah with that expression of smug confidence again.

"A drink would be great. And what'd you do?" she tilted her head to the side, enjoying the closeness of his body and the preternatural heat it gave her.

Lifting his free hand, the fingers tucked down to hide his claws, he flagged the barmaid's attention.

The woman looked as though she wished to avoid serving him, but his intimidating glare forced her to reconsider. She came over to the dark booth, and before she could speak, Glaurakos said gruffly, "A fine glass of wine for my little lady friend here. Good stuff."

Lilah ignored the other woman, instead using the distraction to look at her companion with longing and need. She was quite like him, and his body was already making her squirm. Even though she was back from being so recently debauched.

Biting her lower lip, the barmaid gave a half-bow and went away to fetch the drink.

"I managed to glean some tales of our destination while I waited." Glaurakos said, turning back to Lilah, his fiendishly heated body close to hers as he continued to rub at her slender shoulder.

"Oh?" her ears perked up, leaning in closer to him as she returned her gaze from his groin.

Catching her look momentarily, he flashed a grin — a wider, more lascivious one — and continued on, his free hand moving over to stroke the back of a finger along her chin.

She luxuriated in the sensation, looking like a cat being lovingly stroked.

Returning with the wine, the barmaid sat it on the table and Glaurakos handed her the coins, waving her off immediately.

"Thank you, sir," the barmaid muttered, unable to steal Glaurakos' eyes from Lilah for half a moment.

"I have heard tale of some powerful wizards of Sho'ar having gone there in search of certain artifacts," Glaurakos rumbled.

Lilah's mouth widened into a perfect "O," her slender fingers touching her glass, eyes not leaving his. "Well then, I'm ashamed that they of Sho'ar would not have told me of such things. But then, they do covet their precious information."

"So our journey has more promise than we feared, Lilah." Glaurakos chuckled, trailing his eyes to her fingers along the glass then back again. "With some work and good luck, you and I could perhaps find ourselves fortunate enough to return wealthy and more powerful from our expedition." He tucked his chin down, his handsome elven features bearing a big grin, cheeks dimpled as his devilish eyes lit up.

She watched his reaction in somewhat of a stunned silence. The idea of returning back to anywhere in a better state than she left, at this point, was utterly unthinkable, she thought.

"I see. And if the wizards get there first?" She took a sip from her glass, contemplating.

Tilting his chin up, he stroked hers, nudging it up and leaning in to mutter quietly, "Then it's unfortunate for them should we cross paths." There was a silence.

"We'll come back wealthier one way or another. Times could not be so bad such powerful beings as ourselves couldn't find something to increase our fortune upon the way," Glaurakos suggested.

She considered his words carefully. Then said, "We will fly at dawn, after a good eve's rest, I imagine," she smirked.

Glaurakos' expression showed agreement and he said, "We will set out after the night's rest. There's nothing else holding us back, is there?"

Leaning in closely, his unnaturally heated breath washed over her slender, porcelain ear.

She shook her head daintily, her breath baited. She leaned forward to meet him in kind, her hand resting against his chest. "We have enough food to last us until we get there," she cooed. "And enough supplies."

With his hood up and his lips pursed, he looked like a handsome elven fighter. His golden-orange hair flowed out of his hood around his smooth, deeply hued skin as he pressed in closely to her.

"The room here is already taken care of. It's the biggest they had available," Glaurakos said, his voice heavy with suggestion.

"I imagine it'd have to be, with the way you play," she teased coyly, pressing herself against him, "I hope you didn't pay a deposit for any damage you might... incur."

Giving a low, rumbling noise of approval he leaned in, his lips parting as he nipped at her delicate, pale ear teasingly, his mouth hot to her flesh.

"That'd be foolish of me," he whispered, "Had I my old things I could've made us a lovely pocket dimension for travel lodgings, where such things wouldn't be a concern at all. Pity."

She uttered a low, impressed noise, thinking of all the possibilities. "I wish we could get it back. I had a good quantity of, ah, materials that would make it feel... even more..." she trailed off. She pushed him backward, her chest pressing against his.

"Hrrmm, the fun we could've had then, no? Cooped up in a comfortable room wherever we went with all the... enhanced stimulation we could desire," Glaurakos grinned, his smooth golden hued skin grazing her face as he brought his free hand down to her thigh just above her knee. Gripping her there, he rubbed at the soft flesh.

"But there's something rugged about roughing it, slumming it in some inn, wrecking up the place and taking off, never to be seen again," she laughed, a light, tinkling sound, delighting in the idea before lowering her voice with seductive huskiness.

"Oh yes. We'll destroy that room and be gone before sunrise," He chuckled, his chest heaving as he nodded. Licking his lips he let his hand creep up her thigh, squeezing and roughly massaging her flesh. "If anyone asks we'll just say we were attacked by a group of bandits in the night."

"It wouldn't seem too out of the ordinary, given my luck," she said airily.

With a rasping chuckle he squeezed his powerful arm about her back protectively. The woman was so like himself, Glaurakos thought, yet so deceptively fragile-looking.

"And these... enhancements you had. Do you make them yourself?" he asked, "Is that your... trade?"

"I can make some," she purred into his golden ear. "Others I trade. I like to have a variety to sell, but I specialize in making those I know I can do better than anyone." She gives his hot lobe a slight kiss, followed by a tug. "I figured you were going to leave me back there, stuck in the wagon."

Pursing his lips, a soft shudder passed through him.

"I'm glad I didn't. It's proved… most fruitful," he added, his powerful hand nudging her creamy thighs apart, prying beneath her skimpy slip. "The company and support on my journey will be a welcome addition."

Lilah's legs parted subtly, allowing his thick hand a squeezed passage between her thighs. Her heat was already radiating as she toyed with his ear.

"Or that you would have left me in the forest, stained and chained, for any passers-by," she suggested.

"Mmm, I prefer you like that for myself, I do think. What a folly it would be to waste such a beauty," he lamented, squeezing at her thigh so near to the source of her own radiating heat. He trailed the tips of his claws lightly against her flesh, little more than a teasing tickle compared to the scratching of his coarse skin on hers. He gave a low, rumbling groan of his own as she continued to toy with his ear.

She gave a light, airy titter, fully enjoying their flirty play, though she knew she wouldn't be able to handle much more of it. She turned slightly, toppling her almost-full glass back through her peach-colored lips. Her bottom lip was stained darker for a moment before she sucked it into her mouth, staring at him pointedly.

Sliding back from the seat Glaurakos stood and held out both hands. He grasped her slender fingers and held them as she reached for her satchel. Her wrist was exposed, the white underside of her arm pulsing with her rushing blood.

"Come," he urged in his familiar, husky voice, pulling her in his powerful grasp from the seat.

She managed to stand gracefully, her movements careful and smooth. She bounded after him on her tiptoes, seemingly pleased to be seen with him.

They were an odd pair. One a lithe, statuesque angelic figure, albeit with hidden wings, the other a broad and looming demon in a hood. Even in the packed tavern they got some stares because of it, though he paid it no mind. He walked with smug confidence as he led her through the crowds, causing people to scurry out of their way, or he gave a shove to the inobservant drunkards who didn't to make room for his co-conspirator.

Clearing the way to the hallway he smiled wryly at her before fishing the room key from his cloak. Stepping to the door he clutched the satchel in one hand and bent to unlock it.

She stood with her back to the doorframe, looking out toward where they had just came from, her hands behind her bottom as she slowly turns to look at him unlocking the door.

"So would I have burned, were I pure angel?" she asked.

He unlocked the door and pushed it open. With a glance inside, he urged her in with a gesture of his head.

"Oh, it'd sting at least." He reached out, casually placing his hand upon her hip and using his strength to gently nudge her towards the room, carefully, but forcefully, guiding her.

She followed him, paying no mind to his forceful mannerisms.

"I'd think it feels good," she muttered lowly, just loud enough for him to hear.

Stepping in after her, his feet placed widely apart, he shut the door and locked it behind them. He reached to his shoulders, pulling his cloak and hood off to shake his golden-orange hair free.

"Of course you do," he said smugly, undoing clasps on his leather armour, "Have you fucked many of our kind before?"

"Not enough," she admitted, turning to face him, her slip clinging to her seductively, ending just below her pelvis bone, the front dipping between her breasts, showing the pale outline of her chest. "What about you?"

Glaurakos undid his armour, shrugging his shoulders to loosen it, revealing his broad, muscular chest beneath.

"Almost exclusively," he said casually, dropping the armour and his sword to the floor as he stepped toward her. Glaurakos began to unbuckle his belt, his wings shifting, "but none like you," he added.

"Oh? And what were they like?" she teased, smiling up at him, letting her wings become visible once more. Lilah seemed so much smaller compared to him, he thought, even though she stood at a good height around most others.

The metal clasp of his belt tinkled slightly as it came undone. He pried the leather greaves away, unsnapping them along his outer thighs, leaving him quite nude. His member was exposed, massive and erect, nestled beneath a tuft of golden-orange hair. The organ was a shade of tan, smoothly skinned but lined with thick veins.

Glaurakos took hold of Lilah's arms, his hot chest pressing against hers.

"They were exciting at first, but ultimately selfish," he mused, diving down, pressing his lips to hers in an aggressively passionate kiss.

She opened her mouth in response, and felt his tongue probe her mouth. She allowed herself to get caught up in the moment, fervent kisses matching his as her hands ran the length of his body, stopping to rest on his hips.

A low growl built in his chest. His powerful hands brushed across her arms, one sliding down her back, cupping and squeezing the pert roundness of her ass. His member swelled and pressed to her stomach through her soiled slip. Breaking the kiss, he licked her lips and bit the bottom one briefly.

She responded with a gasp of breath, almost wishing he hadn't pulled away. Her eyes sparkled as his hands move her slit closer to his throbbing manhood. "This isn't selfish?" she asked breathlessly.

He leaned in and kissed her lips again, then again, more passionately, his hands groping, pinching.

When he breaks away again, he forcibly gripped her shoulder and ass, turning her around. She twirled on her tiptoes as though dancing. Lilah arched her back, bending forward with his motions, her heart thumping loudly in her chest. The scent of her willingness enriched the air around them.

"It is. But I think our selfish desires mesh well... don't you?" he murmured huskily in her ear.

"I do," she replied breathily.

His powerful hands traveled up her form, along her slender waist, sliding the slip up. He rounded over her, cupping a breast, bending her over the bed.

Looking down at her, his red eyes glowed as he appreciated her form and beauty. His cock throbbed and swelled with desire against her thighs. He pulled back his hips and angled himself for her loins, nudging the crest of his cock into her wet folds.

"I know you do," he muttered gruffly, his voice filled with want.

Lilah tightened her calves, easing his descent into her slippery lips. She tugged her slip up over her hips, letting it rest around her stomach as she shivered with desire for the half-devil. She wriggled her bottom back and forth with encouragement.

Pressing into her cunt he groaned, his fingers sinking into her soft skin as he forcibly impaled her to the very hilt in one smooth motion. Grinding himself against her, he let his pointed claws tease and threaten her flawless skin.

"I've met succubi less enticing than you," he murmured, giving her a quick jab of his hips, pulling out then thrusting in rapid succession.

A gasp of breath swallowed Lilah's girlish giggle, her head tilted backwards as he hit her inner barrier. Her white skin contrasted brightly against his golden-red, her complexion so flawless against his slightly scaled and clawed body. Lilah and Glaurakos looked the part of angel and devil, adding to the pleasurable experience as she ground against him, taking him in fuller.

He repeated the pendulous swing of his hips, feet planted wide, hands gripping her lithe body, ramming into her from behind. He jammed past her puffy, reddened lips and rutted into her forcefully. He moaned lowly, sharp claws nipping and threatening her skin.

"I hope that fucker paid his life savings for this," he husked through heavy breaths.

Lilah trembled at the mention of her last tryst, the hidden enjoyment of what she did gave way to a wave of pleasure. Her innermost depths tingled around him. Her head fell forward as her breasts undulated with each thrust, her body meeting his with hungry energy.

A coarse, rough hand gripped her breast, groping at her lewdly and carelessly as he continued to batter her roughly. Her slight frame seemed too small to take his force, as he grew rougher. Raking his claws down across her shoulder he grunted, his hot, devil-born flesh feeling almost searing as their mutual heat grew together in the wild rutting.

Lilah was used to rough sex, but, she thought, she still wasn't familiar with the ferocity of a partner as large as this one. Not that she was complaining. She only found pleasure in his painful thrusts, his wicked claws, his hot flesh.

She whimpered, stumbling forward half a step, leaning against the bed.

Lifting one knee Glaurakos placed his foot on the edge of the bed, bending his other leg as he lifted her body from the floor. With one arm wrapped around her waist, the clawed fingers rested atop her mons and clit. His heat traveled through to them as he held her in place, ramming himself into what would be a long night.

CHAPTER 10

Glaurakos hid his fiendish appearance with a thick cowl about his head, and a cloak that draped across his form. His large wings carried him on the chilled winds, the cloak flying out behind him.

"Do you need some rest?" he asked Lilah, who was flying next to him.

Looking north, he saw something on the horizon. The pair was well off the road and far from the town they set out from in the dark morning.

"We're nearly there, I think, but the chill wind is a burden no doubt," he said sympathetically. Glaurakos was all but immune to the cold, and his own concern for his companion surprised him.

Lilah shook her head. Curled up in her heavy, fur cloak, the black and brown material was wrapped around her tightly. It hid her new corseted top and dusty pink skirt. Her brown boots, lined with fur, dangled out of the bottom of the cloak.

"If you think we might have trouble, I'll rest," she said with a long stroke of her wings, soaring nearer to him.

He smiled beneath his cowl at her, looking fondly at her, his red eyes glowing.

"We never know what we will find there. I should think trouble would be a good sign; it would indicate another treasure hunter of our ilk is on to something," he suggested.

"We can stop there before entering, to make sure you're ready," he said, pointing to a rocky outcropping in the distance.

She nodded, beginning her downward descent, giving him ample time to catch the flash of skin beneath her long cloak. Her ankles crossed as she flew, feet ever pointed. She landed with a graceful click of her flat-heeled boots, looking up at him as he joined her. Her face pink from the cold, she immediately moved closer to Glaurakos, ever her very large, portable, furnace.

Landing beside her, less gracefully, he moved to her unbidden, the two of them meeting as his thick leathery wings wrapped, not just about himself, but her as well. His outer clothes were cool from the high upper winds, but it took a few seconds for his natural heat to build up and pass through to her.

"These lands are unnaturally cold, and getting colder ever year they say," he ruminated quietly.

She clung to him tightly, and felt pleased and comforted by his warmth.

"I had heard that, though I didn't believe it. I suppose it could be a remnant of the War, maybe..." she trailed off, "Or perhaps something else. A lich setting out to dominate the area, rid it of all natural life. They do that from time to time."

Peering to the stone outcropping beside them, he extended a hand to touch its surface briefly before bringing it up around her, holding her in his arms about the waist.

"Mmhmm," he nodded, "I think your second prediction is likely more accurate. Fallout from the war should be lessening, not worsening." He smiled beneath the cloth, "We could start a fire if you're still cold."

"I'll be fine," she said, curling into him tighter. She much preferred his natural body heat, she thought, to something so unfamiliar as a fire. She relaxed her shoulders, her heavy eyelids drooping shut.

"There'll be a few spells we'll likely need," she said, "I'm just trying to think of all possible scenarios and bring them to the forefront of my mind so they'll be ready."

His large red hands stroked her lower back and down further, comforting her with his fiendish heat.

"Good," he remarked in a light, raspy voice. "I have no idea what we might encounter in the ruins up ahead."

He looked back to the stone that sheltered them from the wind, a wind-worn relic of the Lar'en.

"Stay a safe distance, not too far, not too close. The locals back at the tavern warned of demons, but they sound like superstitious fools," he said nonchalantly.

He brushed the smooth part of his cheek against her face. He lifted his mouth from the cloak to breathe warm air across her ear.

"If all goes well though, the payoff could be enough to keep us occupied until the summer, when it's not so cold for our next expedition," he muttered. Though that was really only scratching the surface. Beings such as them were not used to having nothing, of being captured as if they were peons rather than powerful fighters and brilliant sorcerers. They both were hunting for adventure, for wealth, to regain what they'd lost.

"Demons may be the least of our problems, but who's really to say?" she purred, her eyes still closed. "It's best to visit every possible scenario, but I'll be watching your back."

She looked toward their destination, seeing nothing more than tundra and blinding light reflecting off it.

"It'd be better if we knew a more precise location to drop in on," she suggested.

Growling, he stroked her between her feathery wings, his own leather pair shifting and rubbing against her to keep her warm.

"A demon we might bargain with. You're right, a bigger danger would be another wizard or expedition who got there before us," he said. Pausing, he followed her line of sight.

"We should approach carefully and scout. I would propose a ritual to scry it out, but that was lost to me with most of my things when I was captured. I'm not sure if going in on foot or by air would be best. Either way, we leave ourselves exposed to being sighted in this wasteland," he said.

"At least in the air we can see more, and plan a bit better. Not to mention we'll have speed on our side," she paused thoughtfully, "We should stick together, though. Even in the air. We'll be able to spot trouble quicker with two sets of eyes, after all. I'm ready when you are."

He loosened his hold on her to let her step back just a bit.

"Very good. My thinking exactly. It would be foolhardy to get caught separated out here in the open. Let's try not to soar too high, so we can dive behind cover if necessary," he recommended.

Pulling his hands back from around her, trailing along her arms, he smiled at her.

"Then we go in," he said, the dimming sky announcing evening's approach. "It will be a good time for the approach for us as well."

He pulled his wings from her at last, flapping them in preparation.

She fluttered her own pair, rising up a few feet, pulling her cloak tightly around her. Nothing of her white skin was exposed but for the tip of her nose. The rest of her outfit blended into the darkening sky, her eyes intent.

Pushing himself up with his powerful legs, his leathery wings flapped in the chilly air, carrying him up once more. Soaring toward the ruins, he stayed close to his companion, pushing out just ahead of her as his keen eyes surmised the ruins.

His fiendish vision allowed him to pick up more than most in the shadows of the fallen structures of Vargath. The setting sun helped to hide their approach. As they came closer, he could make out greater details. His red glowing eyes darted around the scene. Gesturing, he directed them both down, the two half-breeds darting to a spot between two fallen towers.

Before Glaurakos landed, he slipped his sword from his back and motioned to her cautiously. He wrapped his wings around him, the two leather appendages settling around his shoulders. Pressing one hand to a stone column he peered around. Lilah landed slowly and carefully, bringing her down on her tiptoes. She gathered her surroundings quickly, moving toward him.

He gestured to her to follow and took one step out then — vanished. Lilah looked around and saw him standing behind the tumbled, decapitated body of a zombie.

She'd seen the things before, but it startled her nonetheless. Lilah sighed a deep purr of pleasured relief as he reappeared.

"To the towers?" she asked, biting her lower lip, her breathing shallow.

Seeming primed for combat, he shook his head.

"No," he replied. He inched forward to a stone slab between the two towers. He made a couple surveillance rounds of the area before looking back at Lilah, pointing at the ground.

As she moved closer, she spotted a descending stairway.

"There are more undead minions up here, but we can avoid them for now if we're quiet. We eluded their detection in approaching," he stated quietly.

Lilah's hands were primed and ready for trouble. With light footsteps, she readied herself. She allowed Glaurakos to begin down the stairs first, playing the role of the sweet, fragile angel found in the slavers' caravan, making him feel more masculine and needed.

Moving down into the dark stairwell Glaurakos kept his footfalls light. Reaching the bottom, he inspected the doorway, and found another stone slab. Turning to Lilah, he reached his free hand out to her, resting it warmly upon her slender shoulder and guiding her in by his powerful grasp.

"It's all yours," he offered casually, gesturing to the closed doorway.

She stared intently at the wall. Her fingers touched it lightly and she closed her eyes. A few long moments passed with a whispered breath of an incantation before her hand pressed on it fully. Her white hand contrasted with the dark gray stone slab, making the light that glowed from her hands all the more apparent. With a final crescendo of words, the stone door creaked open, allowing them access to the passage beyond.

Nodding in approval, Glaurakos tugged at his cowl and smiled at her. His strong hand guided her back from the door as he stepped around it and peered in. His sword was at the ready he entered the gloom.

A series of hallways branched off in various directions before him. Some were caved in and blocked. The main corridor branched off into at least eight other hallways. Glaurakos inspected the floor and noticed the shuffling motions of the undead revealed distinct paths through the catacombs that were more used than others.

"Expect more trouble," he warned.

She looked behind them, stepping in through the door before turning and shutting it gently, binding it with a magical seal that would respond to them alone. After finishing her minor spell work, Lilah looked down the hall.

"If you were something magical and rare, I bet you'd be in the deepest part," she said softly.

"Perhaps," Glaurakos replied. He pointed to one of the further hallways. Smiling wryly he set off, following the shuffling trail in the dust and debris. Rounding the corner cautiously he waved her onward, unaware of another undead shambling slowly from an opposing doorway.

Lilah began chanting quickly, the words low and airy. A bright clap of light seared toward the undead. It stumbled back a few steps, losing its footing and falling, the glowing light beaming in its chest, gaining brightness until finally it exploded, sending bits of necrotic flesh flying. She stepped back and paused before catching up with her companion.

Glaurakos watched as the zombie exploded behind him, his annoyance wiped away by satisfaction as Lilah bounded up behind him. Grinning, Glaurakos reached out and squeezed her slender shoulder, lightly grazing his fingers across her jawline. He then turned to hurry on, leading them through the dark tunnels.

The tunnels twisted and turned for what seemed like hours. The pair stopped to inspect unused rooms, all of which were empty, except for some ancient debris.

Lilah frowned in disapproval at the lack of treasure, her plump, peach lips downturned. She was on edge, even though no further undead were found. She strode behind Glaurakos cautiously, her fingers twitching with their readiness to cast another spell.

Glaurakos stopped abruptly, eyes wide as he turned to Lilah.

"A closed room ahead. Two guards," he whispered, adding, "You take the right. Try to be quiet."

Lilah rolled her eyes at his patronizing her. A chromatic orb congealed in the air before her palm, and she lobbed it at the undead guard. The orb transformed into a green ball of poison as it hit the guard on the left side of his chest. The brute cried out in rage. Her eyes widened as it moved toward her. She began casting a second attack.

Glaurakos vanished and appeared next to the remaining undead, striking it down with his great sword, the weapon bursting into flames as he attacked, searing necrotic flesh. The beast collapsed and burned.

The poison kept eating at the undead Lilah fought, dissolving what little it wore, the material dripping down its rotting body and pooling on the floor as it continued to amble towards her. She finished her second spell, a bolt of chaotic energy, striking him square in the chest where its heart would be. The undead didn't falter, and it swiped at her with a half-rusted sword.

She dodged the blow gracefully, her large eyes narrowed in annoyance.

Glaurakos growled angrily, flourishing his flaming blade and sending out a spiral of fire at the undead Lilah fought. Finally, it burned away to nothingness, the fetid stench of rotting, burning flesh lingering in the air.

"Are you injured?" he asked, turning toward the doorway.

"I'm fine. Go, before more of them come. It was noisier than I'd like," Lilah whispered urgently.

"It was. I think surprise has abandoned us." Pressing against the door, he found it unlocked, rusted away over the years. Glaurakos shoved the door open, unleashing a trap!

CHAPTER 11

A bolt of fire flew through, but it was poorly aimed and missed them both. They leapt out of the way and gazed inside the room at a woman dressed in red robes, blue etchings embroidered along the sides of the elaborately cut cloth.

Filalios, vuscoth terrinass fusith. Fusith, vuscoth raune. Raune, vuscoth felisoth, eln felisoth denistin hellios! She was speaking to no one in a tongue that was familiar to both of them. It was common in most magical texts, especially those dealing with the demonic arts.

Glaurakos snapped his sword out as though it were a whip, an arch of lightning spiralling along the blade, flinging from the tip. It reached outward, but the woman was too fast. Her eyes went wide and fiery as she darted to the side, too fast to be seen. He interrupted her mid-spell, though, and magic fizzled in the air.

"You will not interrupt my work!" she squealed, and her hands moved at an impossible pace. Suddenly the world was moving much slower, and both Lilah and Glaurakos were caught in time. The witch ran for one of her books, grabbing it and beginning to change.

Deneroth, valictor gustalf!

A black bold of something shot from her hands and hit Lilah's side, just inches from her heart, and the demonic angel toppled back. Time shifted once more and Glaurakos regained his power. Seeing his companion struck, he lashed out again with his sword, though this time the lightening whip struck true.

He grabbed the woman, pulling her toward him by the waist. She cried in shock, her next spell interrupted as he slashed at her with his sword. She twisted away, but his blade cut a slash in her sleeve, and a bloodstain crept across the fabric.

Lilah stumbled to the ground, clutching herself in shock. The tar like substance was eating into her skin and she whimpered in pain, even as she tried to regain her control. She began to cast a spiral of fire, but the agony was too much and it fizzled in mid-air.

The red witch cursed at them as Glaurakos' lightening wrapped around her tighter, the foul word echoed four times over. She created mirror images of herself that filled the room and she disappeared from Glaurakos' spell.

A single orb of light lit the chamber, casting a dim illumination upon the four wizard images. Glaurakos' red eyes darted around the room, eying each copy until he split himself. A second Fae-Demon slashed at one of the wizards, causing it to vanish.

Lilah stared at two images standing together, both casting the same spell, eyes burning with the same intensity. Lilah's mouth matched the furious speed of the wizards' spells and this time she forced herself to finish. She hit one with a dazzling light and it puffed out of sight, but she couldn't jump out of the way of the second one. She screamed as her wings were singed by the wizards' arcane blast.

The two Fae-Demons, spinning in opposite directions, struck at two of the remaining wizards. The real Glaurakos grinned in triumph as his blade took a frosted edge, slashing at the real woman. Lilah slumped against the wall with relief, her breathing ragged and pained.

Divots of frost spattered on the red witch, though the slash itself barely cut through her defenses to make her thigh bleed. The magical remnants froze her blood, travelling through her body until her face became icy-pale and cold. She struggled to move. The witch barely finished her spell, and a colourful orb formed and flew out into the room. The orb broke and struck at Glaurakos with multi-colored beams of light. He grunted as the light burned his forearms as he tried to defend himself from the magical blast.

Seeing her lover struck, Lilah gathered all the strength she had, pushing herself up. The spell was cast so much slower than usual, but the witch thought she was incapacitated. It gave Lilah a chance, and a spit of fire struck the woman's face, igniting it.

The heat burned and ate her flesh, Glaurakos safe from the flames of his birthright. The twitching of the witch's pained body subsided as the woman crumpled to the floor, the stench of burned flesh filling the room.

CHAPTER 12

Glaurakos moved quickly towards Lilah and cupped her chin, looking over her battered side. His rough hand caressed her soft, porcelain-like skin. "How bad is it?"

"I just need some salve," she groaned, fluttering her wings and testing how bad the wound was. The direst one was the black ink in her side, but the pain had lessened, though the mystical burn remained."

"The witch probably had some. And aside from some random undead, I'd say the place is ours for now," he boasted.

She nodded and they moved in to the witch's lair. Half the room was bare and gloomy, but the wizard's things were arrayed in the other half. Crates and chests of varying sizes were stacked, and a candle atop one crate shed light on an open book and some regents beside it.

Lilah went to the strange vials and bottles, plucking up the one she needed and applying it to the wound. It didn't take long before it was little more than a slight reddish mark on her fair skin, and she joined Glaurakos as he picked up a tome, reading the open page. With a raised brow he flipped through it.

"Her spell book," he said, "She was performing a ritual."

They glanced down to where the intricate etchings of a rune begun, but was left unfinished.

"Well, talk about timing," Lilah hummed quietly.

Her slender hand pulled the book downward so she could see, reading over the strange language. Both of them were well versed in magic, but Lilah had the most experience. Though each spell might differ slightly from caster to caster, who all added their own flairs, she recognized the basis.

"A portal?" she mused, tilting her head and reading the pages quickly. "Odd," she paused, looking down at the half-etched shape on the floor, examining it, then gazing back at the book once more.

Glaurakos slid his sword back into place in his scabbard. Slipping his muscular arm about her waist, he rested his hand on Lilah's hip, gently touching around her healed wound as he thumbed through pages.

"A powerful portal spell. More than just a permanent casting too..." she murmured, furrowing her brow in consideration. "As though she were trying to reach another plane. But not quite the same." This was big. It wasn't like anything she'd ever seen before, and Lilah felt her stomach flutter. The witch wasn't just some haphazard caster, flirting with magic. She had skills, talent beyond even Lilah's when it came to this portal spell.

Briefly glancing at Lilah, Glaurakos then turned his attention to the crates.

"There must be a fortune of reagents here alone," he said, his voice filled with quiet awe.

"We should look through them. See what she might have been planning for. If she was going to visit another realm, her supplies might tell us more," Lilah said, her voice tinged with curiosity. Glaurakos glanced up from the book but after giving it a moment's though, he continued flipping through.

"This is mine regardless," he continued, claiming the spell book for himself. "Mine was taken from me... Aha!" Glaurakos paused on a page, finding something.

He plucked some things out of the crates and turned to Lilah.

"Hold still," Glaurakos commanded. Quietly, he began to murmur a spell, his words a deep intonation as he moved around her, making myriad signs and gestures.

Lilah stayed put, looking confused as Glaurakos continued to walk around her.

She had no fear in her eyes. Privately, she mused that this was the closest she had ever felt to trusting someone.

After a few moments, Lilah's outfit began to glow, the black spell's damage undone until it was as good as new.

"I missed that spell," Glaurakos grinned, snapping the spell book shut.

"So it's a spell to mend clothing, is that it?" she grinned widely, stepping closer to him, "Seems pretty tame for someone like you."

Lilah pressed a hand to his chest.

"A simple but useful ritual, my dear," Glaurakos smirked, shrugging his heavyset shoulders. Bringing his free hand back to her hip, he held her with it firmly, half-lidded eyes gazing down upon her.

"Now then... we must find out what this wizard wanted with such a bizarre portal. Don't you agree?" he asked.

"If someone so... rich wanted to go there, I don't see why we wouldn't, at the very least, want to see where she was headed. Besides," she said, plucking through the witch's possessions, noting a few things of value, "I think we hit the jackpot. Wherever she was going must be a step up."

Grinning smugly, he glanced up from his book to watch her, still flicking through the pages.

"Check her things. She must have been carrying something of value."

He searched for something in particular, trying not to be intrigued by the contents so much as to prolong his search.

She nodded, fingering a few remnants before stuffing them into an inside pocket of her cloak, leaving the most expensive items — those required for the portal — out and available. She hummed softly, finding a small crystal, oddly shaped with a dark speck inside. She placed it down again, turning to look at Glaurakos.

"Why do you think she wanted to go to a different plane?" Lilah asked.

"I couldn't say. Perhaps to funnel in an army of fiends, perhaps to take a vacation, who's to say?" Glaurakos shrugged, continuing his search through the book. He moved over and sat down, crossing his legs beneath him before the ritual circle.

"Aha," he intoned with a raspy voice, "Here. We can find out what she was after with *this*..." he grinned. "Help me."

She sat cross-legged, the milky colour of her thighs a stark contrast to the black of her fur-lined cloak.

Glaurakos laid the book out on the floor. Between the pair's supplies and what the witch had left over, they were able to analyze the beginnings of the gateway in what proved to be an hour-long ritual. Willow's Ire was arranged just so, powdered wyvern talons used to doodle out such and such profane emblem, ancient hymns echoed at just the right angle.

CHAPTER 13

It was tedious, and their success was subtle in its completion. The other side of the portal came into sight so quietly that they almost didn't realize the gate had been opened. Glaurakos' eyes were alight with curiosity as they gazed through to a world frozen in time.

Mountains and towns stretched before them, with images of wealth and treasure laid out, the inhabitants all frozen.

"How... interesting. She wanted to go there?" he asked, licking his lips with his pointed tongue he slowly breathed. "Ahhh, of course..."

Lilah blinked her hazy green eyes, looking at her companion with quiet interest. "Of course what?"

Narrowing his gaze he peered at the image of the portal's destination.

"Don't you see? Those on the other side are stuck in time — no, slowed," he corrected himself. Everything was still moving, it was just at a much different speed. "She wished to go there to take what she wished, or dominate it." Turning to look at Lilah, he continued, "Don't you see? We could control such a place with ease."

How far they'd come in so little time. From escaping from slavers and robbing a farm house to stumbling upon a treasure trove of magic and wealth. It made them both eager for even more.

"We'd be moving at our typical speed?" she asked curiously, her fingers drawing slow circles around the tops of her boots, watching the people with interest. She smiled a twisted grin, "There's a spell we could use to bring a bubble of our own reality with us. It would make it very easy..."

"Brilliant." He slid his gaze from the half-breed over to the dead wizard, a wide grin forming on his face, revealing the peaks of two sharp teeth before he looks back to Lilah. "This," he waved back at the crates, "will be nothing compared to what awaits us. No wonder she had expelled all these riches to get there. Oh how brilliant." His was brightened with a greedy hunger.

"So, Glaurakos... Do we complete the ritual?" Lilah paused her searching, looking to her lover curiously.

"Good question." Glaurakos looked into the scryed world, not seeing anything that would warn him off, and the way she gripped his thigh spoke to her enthusiasm. Her excitement.

"What's keeping us here is a better question," she continued. They'd lost everything, even before the slavers had gotten to them, and they had no real destination.

A sly smile spread his lips and he nodded. "Then what are we waiting for?"

"We'll gather what we can and then prepare?"

"Take everything of value from her corpse," he gestured to the dead wizard, "while I stack these crates before the door, in case some undead wanders by to interrupt us. The ritual will take another couple of hours by the looks of it." He flashed a grin behind at her as he lifted one crate, excitement in his red eyes as he began to stack them at the door.

She quickly set to her task, finding the wizard to have multiple enchanted objects. Two rings, a necklace, a broach, and a staff found their way into the possession of the deceptively innocent looking Lilah, her long black hair curling around her shoulders and chest as she moved. She discarded the wizard's scarred robe, not much caring for the design, but found a few scrolls of value, as well as a wand, secreted next to the witch's person. She smiled brightly at her treasures.

Finishing with the door he returned back to the circle, glancing to Lilah as set up the room.

"I trust she proved fruitful, yes?" he asked, plucking out ritual regents and arranging them, preparing for the incantations and the long process ahead.

"She had a few nice things," Lilah smiled.

Giving no objections to her claiming the wizard's objects, he set into the ritual. The two of them began the long process in concert. They chanted and went about the complex and obfuscating process with constant reference to the spell book.

By the end, Glaurakos' voice was hoarse from the process, the shimmering portal before them filling him with relief. He slipped the spell book into his satchel and grinned at Lilah.

She stared at the portal, entranced by the process and the prospects of what lay beyond. She stood gracefully beside him, offering her hand, "At the same time?"

He extended his hand and wrapped his claws around her palm. Taking hold, he nodded. They leapt through the portal, their legs raising and passing through simultaneously.

When they finally came through, they found themselves in a green, grassy clearing. Above and around them on most sides was the edifice of a tower, still in near pristine condition, except for a strange tilt. It looked like it may have been in use but a day ago, but it was half-buried in the ground.

Stepping out, the world around them seemed still, the blades of grass not moving, the mountains around them snow-capped and imposing.

"How... lovely," Glaurakos said lightly.

The angelic woman smiled, unfazed by the change of scenery. Lilah was simply pleased to be in a new place, with new clothes and new trinkets and new promises of untold wealth and power. She spun around to look in all directions.

Gradually, as the two reveled in the new world they found, a light tickling breeze began to graze their cheeks. It picked up, until finally the blades of grass begin to sway in the air. The effect rippled outward from the center of the portal. It was as though time itself was being righted back to its normal flow.

His brow furrowing, Glaurakos cursed and turned back, but the portal was a bare figment. It was there, but not. It was a conduit from one side to the other, but not the other way around. Not yet, at least, he thought with some irritation.

As he turned to Lilah to ask about her regents, he heard a battle cry. He spun around and saw five figures approaching on the grassy hill, charging for them. They didn't seem to be bandits, but they didn't have time to study them further. A blinding light was put between them and their attackers, and Glaurakos and Lilah had to shield their eyes.

Their arrival in the new realm was inauspicious to say the least. Caught unaware, they opted to flee rather than stick around and find out what they faced.

CHAPTER 14

Lilah and Glaurakos soared through the snow-capped mountains until the harsh winds hampered their movement. They stopped at the first cave they found.

There seemed to be no end to the massive mountain range. Standing guard at the cave entrance, Glaurakos kept his red eyes on the largest peak in the range, an imposing monster of a mountain. "I see something circling around it," he said in his dry, raspy voice, the wind whipping his hood around. He knew very well what it was. His lineage was dragon, and he knew more than most what danger they brought with them.

Lilah was tired, her face pink from the exertion. Her cloak wrapped tightly around her as her eyes settled upon the target. She squinted with a frown, cursing under her breath.

"Dragon," she said quietly, a breathless whisper to the windy lands. She moved in closer to him, "We need to find somewhere we can hide and collect ourselves."

Bracing himself against the cave mouth with one hand, he held out the other arm to block her and keep her back as she crept close to him to get a better view. He gave her a firm but careful push back, looking at the winged-demon as it soared effortlessly around the snow-capped mountain. A chill went through him, but he brushed it aside before, finally, he receded into the cave with her.

"We won't be going anywhere now," he said. Dragons were some of the most dangerous creatures. Large and lethal, and filled with greed and ego, they were horrific foes. Being part dragon, Glaurakos knew that well.

He looked back at her as they moved away from the cave opening, the sound of the howling winds dying down slightly.

"You're too tired, and," he glanced back out at the entrance, "that thing would see us flying away."

He shook his head and turned around, placing one of his hands upon her shoulder as the familiar heat built between them. "We stay here and rest. At least until that thing up there settles down."

"What if it has a nest nearby? It may be protecting its young, looking for potential danger," Lilah said, concerned. She looked vulnerable and young staring up at him, "There's no guarantee this entire place isn't overwrought with more of the same."

He brought his hands to her shoulders and held her firmly, the gesture comforting and domineering as he stared down at her with a steely gaze.

"It's circling that peak. Any brood it has is likely there. And we saw this land through the divination — you and I — we could see many things and peoples. I'm certain there's some dragon-free civilization," he said, his voice a soft, low rasp. Leaning in close, his features softened, "We just need to wait it out and rest."

She nodded, embarrassed at her hysteria. She lowered her eyes bashfully as she breathed, "I almost forgot... Is there any guarantee, though, that what we saw is the present?" She paused to clear her head, "Of course it is. We'll find a town, and then find out what's going on."

She sidled up against him, her hand stroking his ribs. "I'm sorry, Glaurakos," she purred, "It's been a long day."

He watched her tenseness and fear melt away at his reassurance; he lowered a hand and wrapped it around her fur-dressed body. It encircled her waist, holding her close to him. Though he wouldn't dare admit it, he was touched by her show of affection enough to return it, pressing his chin to her head.

"It has. We've had tension, dizzying highs and shocking lows, all in the span of a few hours, Lilah," he said, raspy but reassuring as he holds her, his eyes heavily lidded, "We'll rest and return to the dizzying highs quickly enough, as soon as we make our way to a town. We'll have an easier time tomorrow. Perhaps set out just before dawn, we'll be able to make an escape."

He pulled his head back and kissed her forehead, "Sit with me, we've something to do to prepare to make sure we're not found." He turned around and kicked some of the icy rocks from the cave floor, clearing a spot for her to sit. He sat beside her.

Folding his legs he reached into his satchel, pulling out the newly acquired spell book and opening it in his lap. The breeze coming in licked the pages, but did not interfere.

"We'll create an illusory wall here," he gestured about midway into the cave opening, "that way if the beast investigates, it won't see us. Can't do it too far forward or we risk it noticing the cave's absence."

Lilah curved her lithe legs beneath her, frowning slightly as her limbs met the cold rock and lingering dirt. She looked at the book, closed her eyes and thought. She took a deep breath, shuffling to his side to read over his shoulder, the ritual far too complicated for her to remember in full.

Together the pair cast the spell, offering up the required reagents and making the long series of hand gestures and chants. Finally, a perfect illusion of the cave wall was formed a few feet in front of them, hiding them from the gaze of passers-by. Closing the book he put it back in his satchel before laying out a thick, itchy, wool blanket for her.

"Rest here," He said, shifting onto his knees to face her as he laid out the blanket. "We'll be safe with that wall up. It's unlikely anyone would pay it mind as is." He looked at her, his face twisting into a reassuring smile for her sake. His elven features looked more handsome, she thought, than when he wore his usual smug grin.

She moved onto the blanket, stripping off her cloak with a soft shrug of her shoulders. Quickly, she kicked off her fur boots, leaving her in her corset and her skirt. Shivering, she said, "It's very cold here." The request was implicit.

Reaching over his back he pulled his sword slowly from its sheath, laying it carefully out on the cave floor within easy reach. He shifted over beside her, still in his leathers as he placed an arm around her form, resting back on one elbow.

"We'll huddle for warmth through the night," he said softly in a raspy voice. His red eyes flickered over her face as they pressed to each other in the still, cold cave.

Lilah smiled as she curled into him, her hand lingering atop his hip, tapping there for a moment before reaching down, trailing over his pelvis.

"Are you capable of quiet?" she mumbled softly, her voice tinted with lust, "Or should I silence you?"

The feel of her hand, those softly spoken words of hers, they all brought a wry smile to his face. He stirred beneath her touch, his heated body responding to her as his hand stroked over her spine to her lower back.

"It's uncanny the number of times you seem to pluck from my mind my very thoughts," he said, leaning in, pressing his soft lips to her neck and kissing, suckling lightly, letting his hot flesh explore her slender form. "We must be cautious... watchful and quiet."

"Then you watch," she murmured back, lowering her body, kissing down his chest, unwrapping him from his leathers with nimble and swift fingers. She moved so quickly he barely had time to resist as her tongue trailed down the centre of his torso. Reaching his belt she unfastened it, "Be watchful. And quiet."

Brows furrowing at first, his red eyes widened as he watched her. Lilah's movements were so agile and fluid he seemed entranced for a while, but knowing the seriousness of their predicament he forced his gaze away at last, looking to the tunnel entrance with furtive glances back at her. Bringing his hand up from her back, around her wings, he let his fingers move through her raven dark hair, clawing only lightly, grazing as he shifted upon the bedroll beneath them, allowing her to undo his belt.

She pried open his pants with a slow, careful motion, reaching inside to unveil her prize. Large and dark against her pale, white hand, his member throbbed against her palm, the phallus hot to the touch. She sniffed him lightly, catching the scent of her earlier defilement, licking the residual smell from him with a sultry look in her eyes.

Glaurakos' soft lips parted at the feel of her tongue at his member. He'd sigh in pleasure if he weren't struggling to be so quiet. Instead his hand tightened in her hair, and then loosened again, lightly massaging her scalp as his manhood throbbed hotly in her grasp. The preternatural warmth of his draconic heritage mixed with the lurid heat of his desire for her, caused it to fill and pulse larger in her dainty hand.

Quickly the head was engulfed in her wet mouth, her saliva coating him amply as she drooled down the length of his cock. Her adept hand coaxed the fluid down, covering his shaft and making a light sheen in the dim light. Her hand stroked the base of his member, wetly passing over it as her tongue probed under the foreskin, swirling there for a moment before retreating and repeating the motion.

Glaurakos struggled to stay quiet; the angelic face suckling upon his cock was such a sheer delight. Her skill with it is so spectacular his throat trembled. Swallowing his urge to moan, he stroked her head and hair fondly, his breath forming a thick condensation in the air. She buried her face into his musky loins, the rich aroma of male member strong in her delicate nostrils.

He gave her hair a slight tug, glancing at her appreciatively, watching her work him so expertly.

She remained relentless, never pausing to look up at him. She barely responded to his gesture of affection but for the slow movement below him as her lips sought to meet her hand. She pulled the foreskin away from the helm, exposing the sensitive area to first her tongue, then her mouth, then her throat as her eyes watered. She held herself there, her tongue swishing back and forth.

A shudder passed through him and he could not help but let his gaze falter from the cave entrance a moment, his vision blurring as she pushed him to the back of her throat. He was thick and full in her mouth, his cock large even for his size. The bulbous tip leaked his precum into her throat as his heavy pair of orange-dusted balls began to tighten beneath the ministrations of her hand and mouth. Grinding his teeth he felt the tingle in his loins, the little fire that signaled his release fast approaching.

She didn't falter, even for a second. Her breath choked off, her hand lowered between his thighs and came to press lightly upward against his sac. She slowly pulled it from his body as her tongue worked furiously in a back-and-forth wiggle. Tears formed in the corner of her eyes, but they went unheeded, the hot phallus filling her mouth and her throat to capacity. Her teeth grazed him ever so lightly, just enough to send an electric pulse up his spine.

His powerful body shook, his second hand joining the first at the back of her head as his breathing became audible despite his best attempts. The gentle tug of his balls prolonged his release a moment more for her skillful use of his manhood. Finally his breath cut off and he pressed her delicate face into his groin, unloading his thick jets of semen into her throat from the tip of his fiery hot shaft. Nearly done, he released her from his grasp to slump his arms back.

Her eyes widened and as she's released, she desperately struggled to swallow. Her throat was enlarged from the head hitting at it and it felt awkward and raw, though her pleased look didn't give away her discomfort. She lapped at his cock, cleaning the loose saliva and cum, letting the thin layer of spittle evaporate into the air.

Spurting the last bit of his release onto her pouty lips, he reached out and stroked her hair fondly once more. His chest rose and fell heavily as he smiled, relaxed, with heavily lidded eyes. His red fingers curved around her slender ear, fondling it carefully as he admired her features in quiet, nothing but the whistle of the chill wind outside and their breathing filling the silence.

She took a few moments to continue lavishing his cock with her tongued affection before she slowly backed off. She placed his cock back into his pants and slowly buttoned him back up, buckling his belt and leaving him much the way she found him, but for his lack of a shirt. She shimmied up next to him, her breath smelling strongly of his masculine virility.

His eyes twinkled fondly as he watched her dote on him so. As she joined him at his side, he twisted to put one arm in under and around her. His bare, red and golden flesh pressed to her heatedly, holding her firmly with a certain growing affection, despite his better judgment.

She was a clever manipulator, a lovely seducer, he thought, yet he consciously chose to bask in the affections she gave rather than question them, placing a kiss upon her cheek and the corner of her lips.

She spooned into him, holding his firm, toned body against her tightly. She allowed herself to seem diminutive and vulnerable once more, kissing his cheek in return. She slowly moved to his jawline with gentle nips of her sharp teeth, licking at him intermittently.

"No sign of danger," she mumbled hotly into his ear.

Her soft words sent a shiver down his spine, his muscular arms responding to the tenderness of her motions by squeezing her more firmly. Nodding slowly he let his eyes nearly shut, though he kept his red gaze down toward the door as he nuzzled her ear in return. His orange-golden hair tickled her delicate face.

"None, my Lilah," he said, the words tumbling out. His stomach knotted at the familiar address he gave her, as if he stumbled embarrassingly for her to see.

She paused, her breath holding for what would be only an actual couple of seconds, though it was palpable. Her eyes fluttered shut, and she continued to stroke along his back softly, enjoying every bump and ripple of his flesh, massaging out a minor kink between his shoulder blades.

"We'll need to take turns with the watch," she said.

"No" he rasped softly, "rest and recuperate. I'll keep watch." Before she could object, he said, "I can take the cold travel better than you can. It's not so important I rest as you."

He kissed her beneath her ear.

Her ear twitched, her eyes fluttering shut, even as she tries to protest with muffled words of how she doesn't mind. She stroked along his spine gently, ruminating for a moment.

"Where will we head next, Glaurakos?" she asked, her voice tired but sexy.

The chill of the cave didn't bother Glaurakos. He offered his heat to her, his head atop hers, tilting down to keep his eyes on the entrance. His voice sounded hoarse with his own post-coital state, "We'll continue the way we were going. Get away from that dragon's peak as soon as we can, try to get a glimpse of what lies beyond the mountains in sight so we can plan better."

"Would be nice to be gone from the tundra," she said with a shiver, even though his heat comforted her. "I'd like to be able to warm up. I feel like I have a chill right through my bones." She kissed his chest again, "Where do you think we are?"

Holding her in his arms, he found the slender, cold woman stirred some part of him, something deeper than his loins. A protective desire surfaced from that male part of him she so skillfully brought out.

"I have no idea, Lilah. But we will find a town near here and get what we need to return home. Then," he kissed her neck, eyes still glued to the entrance through the illusionary wall, "we'll find something of value to return with before making our way back, even richer for the trouble."

There was a pause. "And if I haven't a home to return to?" She inhaled, her words heavily laced with implication and hope, her body nervously curling into him more readily, willing him away from rejection.

The subtle curl of her body only amplified her portrayed impression of delicate weakness. He knew it to be a lie, he thought. She was a powerful, cunning woman in her own right, but none of that stopped the emotions. Truthfully, he rather liked it; it was new and thrilling.

"Then," he began, pausing as his words came out slowly, hands rubbing along her body to add friction to the heat he gave her, "You will come with me indefinitely. Without end."

She thrummed her fingers against his back, content with his words. She inhaled deeply, breathing in his scent and luxuriating in it, enjoying his company and his offer greatly. She pressed herself against him, then slowly rolled to her other side, pushing her backside in, hair pooling over his arm.

"Where's your home? Tell me about it," she urged.

He resettled upon her as he watched the cave entrance, his mouth at her ear to whisper, "I have no home left. Not anymore. I set out because it was destroyed, and those I shared it with are intolerable. They are unpredictable. Unreliable. They sabotaged themselves with their chaotic nature. I couldn't take it anymore, so I struck out alone."

"Then we're both alone," she murmured, "Starting all over, fresh, isn't it? No one to miss us or search for us, no one to even notice we've disappeared."

Nestling his chin into the crook of her neck, his golden-orange hair spilling around her, careful of her wings, he held her comfortingly.

"We are stranded together, at least. A much better fate than what might have awaited us had you been hauled back to Sho'ar alone and I took off by myself," he muttered.

"Do you think that wizard knew anything about this place?" she asked.

"She had to have known something we didn't. As to what, I can't say. Then again... Perhaps she stumbled upon it as blindly as we," he mused.

"I guess she left no clue in her spell book?" Lilah's body gave way to its exhaustion, her voice quieting.

Nuzzling against her neck he gave her a soft kiss, hearing her exhaustion. "I have yet to have the time to read through it all and check. Perhaps in the morrow, Lilah."

"Thank you for saving me," she murmured appreciatively.

He lay still against her, watching the cave entrance with a diligent stare.

"I'm glad I did," he responded genuinely.

"I thought for sure you'd just leave. I was resigned to that," she fluttered her wings softly, her body melting against his, allowing her to stretch out a little and still have warmth.

"I gave you my word," he said, stroking his hands over her wrist and stomach, "And made an ally in the process. It worked out well, don't you think? Something my former peers never understood."

"Words are only that," she said, wilting with fatigue.

"Perhaps. But mine to you carry some value at least, no?" hearing her exhaustion, he softened his voice to a whisper.

"They do now. I didn't know they would then," she admitted.

"Yes. Rest now, Lilah... I will watch over you," he trailed off, voice growing softer, "... safe."

CHAPTER 15

As the hours wore on and Lilah had rested for some time, Glaurakos finally broke from her, carefully sliding his arm out from under her to glance out the cave entrance.

Carefully he gazed out at the imposing peak where he had first seen the dragon. He didn't see it, so he made his way back to Lilah's side. He rested his heated hand against her forearm and quietly watched her, afraid to wake her just yet.

He slid next to her and placed his mouth near her ear, whispering, "It looks safe now."

"Morning," she said, her voice sleep-addled and coarse. She turned to hold him lovingly.

Glaurakos glanced to her hand so familiarly placed; the warm little tingle of feeling gave him a moment's pause. He was almost suspicious of her, he thought, but the sensation passed quickly. He reached his free hand to his satchel nearby, pulling it close to him. "Did you rest well?" he asked in a hoarse voice, his usual gruffness softened with concern.

"M'fine," she replied groggily, her dark lashes fluttering before they opened to the dim light. She pushed herself up.

"You're so warm," she cooed, seeming absolutely smitten with the revelation. And why shouldn't she, being where they were.

Her words, the way she spoke of his warmth, stirred something in him and he brought his hand to her cheek. He stroked her smooth, pale skin with the fleshy part of his thumb and looked down at her, his expression slow to be tugged at by a wry grin.

"I'm loathe to start the day without having you," he said, his voice more hoarse than usual after a full night without rest, "but our current predicament makes it unwise. It shall have to wait until after we make our getaway."

"I know," she said hesitantly, her pout mimicking his disappointment as her eyes fluttered. "Maybe there's a town nearby. With an inn. And then," she said with a slow, seductive twirl of her tongue around her parted lips, "We'll make up for time lost."

He grinned and rubbed her cheek and jawline more vigorously, giving a dry chuckle. "I don't need an inn, woman. Just you and a little less danger than a dragon poses."

"She's gone?" Lilah asked.

"She's gone, no sight of her since last night." He tugged the satchel open, "Come, and eat first before we set out. Making a getaway on an empty stomach will do us no good."

Though he rooted through the satchel for the food, his eyes peered back at her, slyly watching her seductive actions.

Lilah fixed her askew clothing, aware that Glaurakos watched her. She prolonged the adjustment, all the while seeming oblivious to his stare. She moved towards her own bag and brought out a large, round brush, patting it against her hand before bringing the soft bristles to her hair. Another gift from the bilked man back in town, no doubt, Glaurakos thought.

Still topless, Glaurakos' muscular chest was on display. He seemed unbothered by the chill of the cave, thanks to his draconic nature. He pulled out of the sack a jar of preserved dried fruit, something not easily obtained, and handed it to her. Reaching in again he took out a loaf of bread, breaking some off as he casually watched her.

"We have enough supplies to wander a long while, if need be. And I believe I saw a ritual in the spell book to conjure as much as we need on top of that. Our reagents should last us through months if it comes to that," he said, his rasping voice full of confidence and assuredness as he handed her the piece of bread.

She accepted the bread and began to chew it thoughtfully. She looked down at him, moving in and placing a light hand upon his shoulder.

"I have enough trust in that," she said, taking another bite, "Regardless, I'd rather us find somewhere a bit more habitable. Perhaps settle somewhere, a base of operations."

Crouched down still, his shoulders wide as she rested her hand upon them, he glanced to her delicate fingers before finding some dried meat for himself. Procuring a sausage he nodded to her, "Yes. Of course, my dear. We'll make that our first priority, absolutely. Then once we have, we can begin making plans and moves for what comes after. We'll start gathering reagents for the portal spell; it's just a matter of finding out where they're to be had," he said reassuringly, not allowing himself to sound troubled for her sake.

He pointed to the jar of dried fruits he handed to her, "Go ahead. I got those for you, they should help keep you spry on the trip."

She smiled down at the fruit, her cheeks flushing a pleasant pink. She looked touched at the thoughtfulness he showed. She gnawed on the rest of her bread, finishing it before drawing out a piece of fruit, sucking the sugar from it, her expression one of mixed pleasure and thoughtfulness.

"We won't be safe here, will we?" she asked, having pulled the fruit from her mouth only long enough to speak before putting it back in. She looked childlike, her eyes wide upon him.

Glaurakos puts his arm in around her waist, pulling her closer to him. It was a sort of powerful, commanding gesture intended to be reassuring, no doubt, Lilah thought.

"There are many unknowns. But together little should pose a threat to you and I," he said.

She swooped into him, her body finding his nicely. He gave her a confident smile before tearing off some more bread and meat, eating it quickly.

For a moment, her willpower faltered, her hands beginning to wander over his body. She stopped quickly, however, not liking the feel of rejection, no matter how genuine the reasoning. His chest swelled out at her wandering hands. He was perched on the edge of being sucked in by her charms despite himself when she pulled away.

She sucked the rest of the sugared fruit into her mouth, licking her sweetened lips free of its lingering juice.

"Which way will we head?" she asked.

Glaurakos exhaled slowly, picking up his chest armour and strapping it on.

"I figured we would continue to head as we were, southwest. We will round this mountain then see if we can make out anything beyond. Perhaps the clouds will have moved on to give us some view of the land ahead."

His armour fixed on, he stepped up behind her, his hand moving to her hip — though his palm firmly lands upon the swell of her pert ass — and he leaned forward, brushing her hair aside to kiss her neck, savouring the moment.

She paused, her breath held deep in her chest as she luxuriated in the feeling of his lips against her skin, once more lost in a haze of bliss and pleasure. She struggled to keep her mind focused on things other than the bulky Fae-Demon pressed against her. The way his golden flesh must look against her pale skin. The heat he caused as he entered her, something unreal in the manner than only a demon could be. Her lips plumped as she sucked her lower one in, letting it pop out, doing all she can to just resist the urge...

His lips finally left her flesh, and he uttered to her that familiar word, none of its authority lost in his hoarse rasp.

"Come." He tugged at her hip, "You can wear my cloak over yours to help keep you warm in flight." He plucked up the satchel, tying it shut and pulling it over his shoulder. He sheathed his sword on his back once more before handing her the cloak.

He smiled wryly, exuding confidence, "Basking in each other's bodies will be our reward for making a timely escape."

She nodded, pouting. She could not resist him, he thought, and would only have done so by his direct command. She pulled her cloak around her tightly, tying it around her stomach before pulling his cloak over top. She seemed a lot thicker with such bulk around her, though it only served to make her look like a haughty winter princess. Her cheeks flushed with the arousal of his teasing kiss and promising words, and she nodded, with no argument, relinquishing leadership, as usual.

His possessions secure, he eyed her appraisingly, nodding approval at her thick apparel.

"Good. Let's head out. Be on the ready though, dragons are notoriously cunning," he warned.

Allowing his gaze to linger upon her wantonly, he stepped around her and moved through the illusionary wall to the front of the cave. Peering out carefully, he kept his free hand out, palm open in warning for her to stay back.

No signs of a dragon outside the cave. He checked likely perches where one might be waiting still, but still, nothing. Finally he gestured at her to follow as his thick, leather wings twitched free from his body and began to flap. Moving forward, he dove off the cave mouth and took to the air, swerving southwest around the mountain. He looked back to be sure the dragon wasn't pursuing him.

Lilah moved swiftly, following Glaurakos. Her body was hidden entirely under the two cloaks, and her hair spilled out around the cowl as she pulled it tighter still around her. Her keen eyes glanced worriedly around her.

Satisfied with his companion's safety, Glaurakos turned his attention forward. Rounding the snow-capped mountain, he grumbled at the cloud cover hampering his attempts to scout their direction. With heavy flaps of his wings he came to a halt suddenly. A break in the clouds ahead allowed him to see green land in the distance. He beat his wings on the frigid air, waiting for Lilah to come close so he can point it out.

"Look!" he called, "It's not so far off after all."

She looked toward the green, her eyes hungry for heat and the warmth of her companion in some sunny, grassy place. She moved ahead, but faltered and waited for him to go first, trailing close behind, smiling enthusiastically.

He lunged forward, matching her energy, his wings beating harder as he pushed on ahead to lead the way once more. Seemingly unperturbed by the cold, he flapped his wings harder, pushing ahead to try and get out of the mountains for his partner's sake.

CHAPTER 16

Lilah and Glaurakos' trip was dragging on into hours. Communication was impossible with the high winds, devouring their words and casting them adrift.

Moving downward for some time they passed through the clouds and found themselves edging lower, the cliffs becoming big and craggy, with many sheer rock faces and apparent caves.

"Can you keep going, or should we find a place to rest?" Glaurakos called back to her, stopping again to converse.

"Let's just get through!" she shouted back, her face reddened with cold. "I'd rather rest somewhere with sun!" She beat her wings harder as she pushed herself forward to the sliver of green ahead, fatigued, but driven by pure enthusiasm.

Glaurakos carried on, concerned, his leather wings beating on the wind he pushed forward, the pair pressing on downward to the grassy edge of the hill bottoms below. Finally, after another hour, they passed the snow line, green practically beneath their feet when he called out, "Look!"

In the distance, a path headed into the horizon.

"A roadway!" He grinned excitedly, in spite of himself. Civilization surely couldn't be more than a day or so away.

She fluttered in the air, losing her tempo as she gaped at the road, her usually smooth movements coming to an awkward pause before she regained her composure and pressed on in her descent.

"We'll set up camp outside tonight?" she shouted, "We'll have to find some tree cover, especially with the road so near. Bandits may have camps set up to hijack them!"

"No!" he said, shaking his head. They descended, intent on reaching grassy ground. "We'll use a ritual to create a shelter, and then you can cloak it with invisibility. It should last us until tomorrow, so we can set out again."

"Alright!" she shouted back through the wind, "I was just worried they may have casters that might detect the magical interference," she explained. "Though if you feel we'll be safe...." she trails off.

Nodding to her he continued without another word until he fluttered to a halt, landing near a few trees. His chest heaved from the long expedition, and he reached to his spell book, pulling it out and looking to her.

"Let's work the ritual quickly. You look exhausted," he said, concerned, before peering around the horizon. The sky was a pinkish hue as sunset approached. Glaurakos scanned for any sign of bandits or predators. He saw none; the road was still some distance off and the land too close to the snowy peaks for much habitation.

Her knees nearly gave out as she landed, wobbling with exhaustion and the numbness that clung to the depths of her limbs. Even with the heat of the two cloaks, she had pushed herself more than she should have. She looked relieved as she toppled on the grass with a bit of a trip and a start, though she quickly recovered.

"Yes," she said, quickly moving to his side, hugging to him, hungering for his warmth.

Seeing her stumble Glaurakos dashed to her side, but her quick rebound rebuffed him and he placed his arm around her, and she leaned on powerful limb like a tree as he carefully lowered them both down to kneel upon the grass.

He wasted no time in beginning the ritual without her, a small spherical dome materializing over several minutes of incantations and gestures.

Finally she joined him, and they both cast in unison until they are shielded by the opaque surface. Inside, the two of them were able to gaze out. Kissing her temple he urged her, "The spell, quickly, so we can relax."

As she cast the spell he pulled his large blade from his back and laid it at a safe distance, still breathing a bit heavily from days of exertion. After a few moments of casting, Lilah crumpled into a graceful, exhausted mess. Her hands reached for him eagerly, urging him to join her upon the grass.

He slid to his elbow and pressed his heated chest down upon hers. The time spent performing the ritual allowed his natural heat to exude once more, and he met her puffy, peached lips with a kiss.

She pressed back, sighing against his bronzed mouth. Relief washed through her at the insistence of his warm embrace. She pulled him to her, her breathing becoming shallower from his weight.

His heated, deeply hued lips moved to hers, the kiss dragging on long as he let his hand slide down her side, across the subtle sway of her slender form, over her hip and to her thigh. He carefully pulled her layers of clothing away. With a low, hoarse groan he moved his weary muscles, pushing himself atop her before he removed her cloaks, his own body still fully clothed.

Her head tilted backward, her body arching, still holding the chill of the cold. Her flesh was numb and bumpy to his touch. As he presses his heat to her, her skin melted beneath his touch. She parted her legs beneath him, hungry for his desire, his pleasure, having waited far too long for it. It was their reward for the long trip, after all.

Grunting, he felt her pale, cold flesh beneath her clothes. He rose up, unbuckling his armour and peeling it away. With a swift urgency, he stripped down to bare flesh, removing greaves and chest armour, pressing himself back to her. The full heat of his draconic form smoldered against her cool skin as he sank between her legs. His thickness rested on her groin as he kissed her face, his long, golden-orange hair spilling down and tickling her neck and cheeks. Spurred on by lust, he helped her along, warming her.

Lilah was ready for him, with no pretence at foreplay. Her nether lips exuded her own natural heat, the subtle scent playing into the dome's air as it began to steam and fog from their panted breath. She whimpered in her want, legs wrapping around him as he joined with her, her mouth seeking his at every possible turn.

Grinding his hips, he slid his thick, darkly hued cock down along her wet slit, pushing forward, pressing his bulging crown to her entrance and forcing its girth into her. He groaned loudly, shedding all restraint in the long awaited fulfillment of their coupling. He forgot his weariness as he hilted into her, his molten shaft and pair of balls resting full within and against her with deep pleasure. He pulled back, not waiting to start the undulating of his strong body, the thrust of his member into her cunt coming on immediately.

Her legs coaxed him inward, her pelvis thrust toward him as she accepted the thick shaft deep within her confines. She clenched him tightly as she shivered with the ebbing cold. She clawed along his back with desire, moaning soft utterances of pleasure, marked with encouraging compliments about his expansive size and his hungry desires. She took him in deep, her back arching as she reveled in his heated pleasure.

Her fawning words urged him on, his hips colliding with her faster and more firmly at her encouragement. Groaning heatedly he bent down, kissing her cheek and lips as he supported himself on one arm. His back arched as his free hand slid from her thigh, helping her leg wrap about him. He fondled her breasts, squeezing them as he bucked and moaned. Through his groans and pants, he gave his own hoarse, rasping words, names and remarks that might be considered insulting to most women. For her, they were words of affection. Her tight cunt around him, her beautiful flesh, the luscious sway of her body and the way she milked him so.

"Such an angel of lust," he groaned, pleasured words, his climax fast brewing within her tight canal.

She reacted with warmth and caring, caught up in the steamed passion of the moment. Lilah awaited their tryst. She was pleased and full, reveling in the sensation of his thickness sliding in and out of her ever faster, her muscles growing taut around him as she urged him to his own pleasure. Getting her own pleasure by so controlling his, she sought to further enrapture him, her hips sinking into the dirt with the pressure of his thrusts.

He was all lust and pleasure. Seeking her flesh, her sensual, seductive self. He wanted to seek out more and more of the endless joy and pleasure she granted. His mind a fog, his worries melted away in the sensation of slick, tight cunt wrapped around thick, hard cock. He grunted, his thrusts coming in hard and erratic. His member swelled as the smoldering fire of his climax boiled within his loins, eager to burst out. In the midst of a garbled, moaning expression of how exquisite she felt around him, it did. He spilled himself into her thoughtlessly, his face contorted, brows furrowing as he bucked erratically, pumping her full of his seed, the throes of his lust come to fruition. He grasped at her breast through it, clenching the pert mound as he rode her to the last of his spurts.

She looked startled, feeling the orgasm writhe through him. She had forgotten something that was altogether important. She paused, though quickly she clung about him. She held him to her as the last of his seed is spent, her hair and face mashed against his chest as she panted lightly. Her own pleasure still eluded her, though she was unperturbed by it. Instead she stroked his back, cooing at him about just how wonderful he felt.

Even after he was spent, the whole of his load spilled within her, he kept a slow, languorous pace of thrusts into her, his member retaining its hardness almost fully. He seemed disappointed such blissful union would end so soon, and groaned softly with each new languishing thrust. He tilted his head down, kissing her lips, moistly amplified as he rubbed the edge of his thumb around her breast and areola.

She curled upward into him, encouraging his tender strokes, his slow thrusts, willing him to say close to her, her arms and legs wrapping around him desirously, her body seeking to remain with his. Her breathing slowed as his movements did, her own slight writhing coming almost to a halt as she lay awash in his pleasure.

"You are a fabulous lover," she purred honestly.

Glaurakos raised his hand from her breast, cupping her cheek as he wordlessly kissed her mouth, their two pairs of lips a bit puffier and redder. The motions of his hips don't cease, though they become a slow rub, his pubic region grinding to her slick clit as he spoke quietly to her in return, his own hoarse voice no less genuine.

"As are you. I can scarcely manage to keep my hands from you for more than an hour, and only in dire circumstances," he growled.

Her heart fluttered at his confession, her face warmed to another pleasant blush as she shifted to curl into him in a spooning position, wanting to feel the warmth of him against her backside. She knew he would need his rest more than anything before their invisible shelter dissipated.

The twisting of their bodies came with some effort, being so tightly pressed together and refusing to relent, but eventually they found themselves coiled upon the grass, back to front, his thick, muscular arms wrapped about her firmly. With his intense weariness, and the wash of post-coital tiring adding to it, his drift to unconsciousness approached quickly, unbidden but irrefutable as he held her tightly.

It took her a bit longer for her to meet him in sleep, her eyes watchfully looking outside as she fretted. Her heart pounded more quickly as she gnawed upon her lower lip, her hands trembling as she held onto him.

CHAPTER 17

She stirred with the early break of dawn, the dome steamed with their heated breath through the night, her body lying under his heavy, sleeping arm. She slowly wriggled away, trying not to disturb him. Her hair was tussled from a lack of sleep and she removed her brush from the bag, pulling it through her raven locks. She smiled as she watched him, though there was a hint of worry on her face. Contented that she looked beautiful once more, she put her brush away and lightly touched his arm, her fingers stroking along the golden flesh reverently.

He stubbornly remained at the very cusp of consciousness, only dimly aware of what was going on. Her fingers on his arm, though, brought him around gradually, and his eyes flickered open. He looked before him, found nothing there, and turned to look at her. Groggy and tired still, but unwilling to show it, he blinked his eyes then moved a hand to rub the sleep from them before looking to her.

"Is it late?" he asked, rolling onto his back slowly, his vision still.

"The sun is just rising. Do you need more sleep, master of the skies?" she gave a coy, slight smile that touched her eyes only briefly, the worry from the evening before still lingering within her, though she did what she could to avoid exposing her weakness to him.

Blinking his red eyes he then shook his head and smiled, obviously still weary, but not willing to admit so to her.

"No." He brought a hand to her cheek, carefully stroking it with the edge of his thumb, "Did you rest well?" He pushed upward to sit, raising one knee up, the other to the side as he peered at her, his vision finally clearing as he gazed at her pretty features closely.

"It was a calm night," she judged. She reached a hand toward his cheek, holding it there as she gazed upon him, smiling, "We should ready ourselves for travel, if you're well rested," she pushed her lips towards his, hesitating for only a moment in the split second before they meet.

Noting the brief hesitation and the faint signs of worry, he kissed her then furrowed his brow, pulling back. His hand still upon her cheek he asked in a low, rasping whisper, "What troubles you?" His clawed fingers carefully stroked her raven hair as he eyes her face, trying to discern what troubled her.

Her eyes flickered halfway closed, trying to block him out, her eyes moving upward in a small motion of a smile, her breath pulled in.

"I just need to get to a town to purchase some provisions I forgot," she smiled at him, "The man in Twin Stars hadn't access to certain magical ingredients I needed, is all." She pushed her lips back to his, trying to silence him as her tongue probed his mouth.

Silenced, he looked upon her curiously. Their lips met in a kiss, her tongue probing his mouth, the moment went on long and languorously as they enjoyed the press of flesh. Glaurakos tugged Lilah in close, his intentions obvious, as he lay there still bare, his heat rising.

She bristled slightly, pushing him backward as she slowly began kissing his throat, hurriedly hissing down over his stomach, her own intents more obvious still as she struggled from him, her hands seeking the warmed muscle, stroking it, first with her hands, then with her lips, as eager as ever to please him.

At first, her push struck him as off and he was about to resist and take over, but the press of her lips down his powerful form soothed the beast within. He stroked his fingers over her hair and down her back, appreciating the fine form of her body in great detail as he rested back upon one palm. The fullness of her lips pressed to his stiff, morning-hardened shaft, evoking a grunt and a groan. It took a while, but the sweet tug of her expert mouth pulled from him his desire and lust in the end with a spasm and jerk, his hand gripping her hair tightly.

She smiled up at him, gracious for the lack of his struggle, smacking her lips indulgently as she slowly pulled herself back up.

"We should get there sooner rather than later, my handsome Fey, for I mightn't have such strong resolve later." She stood slowly, looking down at him before he stood with her.

Her strange words coaxed a raised brow from him, and instead of rising, he reached over to grab his satchel, pulling it close and reaching in to pull out some food. "Who said you had to show some resolve in the first place?" He asked a bit gruffly, pulling out some bread, dried meat and fruit, "We should eat first, regardless. It will be a long journey, no doubt."

She nodded, avoiding the first question for a brief pause, "Well, once we get to the town, we needn't show any restraint for a week, should we choose. Out here we need to be cautious. We can't break to fuck every few minutes, after all," she smiled, moving toward the food and sitting with him, her legs curled under her, accepting the food graciously, "Thank you."

Glaurakos began to eat, his legs crossed as he inspected her oddly. Despite the fond times had so far, his mind interpreted her cagey responses poorly, and doubts crept in as he chewed the bread and sausage.

"You could barely contain yourself the other day, I practically had to drag you from the cave," he remarked.

She blushed and tugged at her bread, her eyes seeking his, a silent wish for him to understand without having to be explicit about it.

"I didn't think of it until now," she paused, "last night," she corrected herself, looking to see if he'd catch on.

His brow rose even further as he lowered the sausage to his lap, looking about ready to get angry or upset, his thick leathery wings twitching behind him as his mouth opened. He paused however, head down a bit as he looked over at her.

"What are you getting at?" he asked, not so dense as he appeared.

She lowered her head for a moment before meeting his eyes once more, not putting any more food to her mouth. She stared at him, not wanting to have this conversation, and being completely unsure of what to say.

"In my bag that the slavers took, it had several protective provisions..." she trailed off, taking a deep breath before continuing, "They were set to wear out. The ones I had already cast upon myself. They last some time, but..." she trails off once more, looking at him before finally blurting out, "I can't be with child out here."

His stare lasted long, his look suspicious. But when she reached the last of her words, the expression melted quite quickly. His eyes softened and he looked away.

"Right," he said, turning his gaze back to her, letting his red eyes move down over her form before nodding, "Of course, I'm s--" he nodded to her again, not finishing the word as he reached a hand out to her slender shoulder.

He gripped her there firmly, the hold reassuring, "I should have thought of it myself sooner, I just assumed." He brought his free hand to his lap, taking another bite of food.

"My... people," he said, hesitating to use the word, "were always consumed with producing more offspring. We never took precautions. Never." He peered back to her, hunching forward a bit as he chewed.

Her shoulders sloped with the weight of her admittance, shame burning at her face at the depths of her disappointment in herself with having to deliver such terrible news, before raising her eyes to him brightly.

"So you'll understand my enthusiasm for getting to town as quickly as possible?" she asked slowly, crawling over to him and pressing against him in his lap, "My desperation for it?"

Shifting his food aside to rest on his satchel, making room for her atop his lap, he nodded as he chewed, swallowing the last of his meal. He wrapped an arm about her, then the other, holding her quite firm and warmly, a wry, mild smile on his face.

"I do," he said gruffly. Leaning in to kiss her neck and cheek, he took a moment to pause and inhale her feminine scent, so enhanced by the long, uninterrupted travel and mingled with their rutting, "You could have told me sooner, and I would have maybe... yanked it out, I guess." He kissed her again, his hands stroking her pale flesh tenderly, that deep tan golden hue of his contrasting so to hers.

"I forgot," she smiled, shivering at his kiss, "and I so badly wanted," she continued, her voice laced with the obvious twinge of her desire, slowly moving to look at him once more, her green eyes filled with fire. "I want to feel you in me for as long as you permit," she cooed, seeking to ease his worries further, entrusting him with the truth, "I am enraptured in your touch," she stroked along his neck, following it with her nails, "And sometimes a girl cannot contain herself in the heat of the moment, and that's why it's important to plan before those times hit. But since we didn't..." she trails off, taking in a gulp of air, "It becomes a complicated mess."

His brow raised, he watched her intently as she spoke to him, trailing her fingers along his neck. He licked his reddish lips with his pointed tongue, her words titillating him despite himself, even so soon after she supped at his loins.

The way she expressed her lack of control in her desire for him provoked his own desires in turn. Leaning forward, his strong, heated arms holding her firmly as he kissed and suckles at her neck briefly before speaking in a whispered, gruff voice, "I understand."

"It would be irresponsible," she muttered, even between her moans and her obvious yearning, not enjoying the idea of going unfulfilled before their travel. She ground against him subconsciously, nodding in agreement, "It would be very irresponsible," she repeated, "and we hadn't much clue about where we are, and if something were to happen… the child may be something other than…" she looked at him with her tempting green eyes, "ideal."

Her subconscious grinding worked upon him regardless of intent, his manhood stirring beneath her lithe frame. His chest heaving with his heavier breath, he rasped deeply, whispering to her ear, his voice growing coarse, "Very irresponsible, my dear. Now is not the time for such… frivolities, you're right." His muscles tensed and bulged around her as he leaned in, kissing her neck and up toward her cheek and lips. "It would make keeping you safe harder." Something about the way he said it implied that he couldn't abandon her, even then.

Lilah understood, and a violent shiver ran through her body, causing her to cling to him more desperately. She had to struggle with herself, to put any distance between the two of them, her eyes lidded and heavy as they gazed at him, wondering if he thought the same as she, but not daring to ask.

His lips played along her soft, ivory flesh, rough hands doing the same down below, toying with her svelte form with a growing passion that broiled like his own body heat. His teeth nipped lightly at her ear; as his own heart pounded with excitement, lust tempting him little less than her. Manipulating her in his lap to face away from him, he leaned his head over her shoulder, his hands fondling her breasts and sides as he muttered hoarsely into her ear.

"Trust me," he sighed, before pushing her forward. He rose to his own knees, pressing his heated, stiff member to her slit, that honeyed entrance ready to accept him as he positioned himself behind her, no explanation as to what she was asked to trust him on, whether to spare her the trouble of pregnancy or to trust him in his ability to take care of her in case of it.

She gasped as her lithe form was so easily manhandled and, though she didn't struggle, she tensed as she was pushed forward, her smooth body exposed to him fully, her bare toes digging into the dirt as he found her slick, her lips even glossier than usual, more swollen and obvious as he pushed inside her. She cringed as her body leaned forward, the position lending him ability to plunge against her uterus painfully as her ass remained upward toward him, a quiet gasp on her lips.

Hearing no objection he sank into her, his own member more stiffly swollen, he throbbed down inside her cunt, filling it fully. He groaned as he positioned his shoulders wide and began to pull back. The tug of her tight cunt caused him to moan lewdly with its firm grip until he plunged back in again, replacing it with a grunt. The motions continued, punctuated by an ever increasingly louder slap of wet flesh as he gripped her hips and pummeled into her slit faster and harder. Surely he meant to pull out.

She whimpered slightly, as though she wanted nothing more than to protest until, with a swift movement of her hips, he hit the delicate patch inside her, causing her eyes to roll back in her head and forget she ever wanted it to end, slumping forward further into the ground, lost in that feeling of pleasure as she struggled to push back towards him, maintaining her position to allow him to pummel him.

Her total acquiescence to him, whatever his intent, only drove him on further. Whatever his original plans, his mind was clouded with a lust-fogged haze the further it went on. He rammed himself into her with increasing intensity and speed, his balls striking against her as he grunted and moaned, lost in the moment with her as it went on longer than he had even realized. Claws very lightly pricked at the flesh of her ass as he panted and moaned, striking at her sensitive depths for so long in their mingling, the sensations becoming a hedonistic blur.

She kicked her legs in a slight protest at the speed, as they walked the line between pleasure and pain. The steam filled the dome more readily, the beads of condensation dripping in areas, streaming down the sides as she panted louder, squeals of pleasure and excitement exhaling from her throat, mingling with the cursed mutters of her desire.

The intense fucking went on long, his shaft tingling and burning with desire, though he would not stop until the woman before him, pinned by his strength and the lust she held for him, quaked beneath racking pleasure time and again. His gold and red hued body was coated in a thin sheen of perspiration as he sought to bring her to joy again and again, his own pleasure in the act so intense, he almost didn't notice the slow rising crescendo of his own release approaching. He breathed a bit sharply as the rutting slaps grew more erratic, his hold on her steely and unflinching, no room for escape given.

She was so hazy with pleasure that she didn't notice the change in tempo until too late, her body startling violently and trying to cry out, the words only become mingled with the haze of profanities she had shouted before, her body slick with her roiling bouts of pleasure, her hair once more tussled and knotted with the force of her head rubbing against the ground as she tried to steady herself.

His powerful hands held her locked in place. Her slender body was unable to break free from his hold as he gave rasping shushes to quiet her struggles, seeming fully intending to go through with it to the end. His lewd moans only grew louder and more intense, his head swivelling back as he tingled with the fire of sensation. He shuddered and Lilah tensed up before, with a swift motion, he moved her body in time with a thrust so that he slipped from her completely. It wasn't a moment too soon as the bulging crown of his cock edged up along the cleft of her ass cheeks and let loose its torrent of pearly white seed, jetting across her supple rear and back as he finished himself against her, grinding into her flesh fully till the flood stopped.

The rush of emotions that filled her in those seconds of time were all hot, passion and fear and anger, combining into an awesome force and building within her until they were blown free of her with the swift and timely movements, causing her to exhale her baited breath, shock running through her violently, her body still quaking from her pleasure as she struggled to compose herself, feeling far too unguarded.

Breathing heavily, the heat of the moment robbing him of much of his senses, he looked down at the splatter of his seed upon her pale flesh, some even staining her lovely wings. He hooked his arm in around her waist and pulled her in close to him, heedless of the combined mess they made as he embraces her warmly, quite unapologetically like a true lover. Pulling the hair from her neck he kissed her there, letting his lips and tongue do some silent communication as she rested on his lap.

She caught her breath there, pausing as she struggled back to his arms, her hair a strewn mess as she slowly began to pant anew at his heated mouth pressing upon her so passionately, her whimpers of delight coming to him loud and clear as she exposed her neck to him, the thrill of what had just transpired causing her heart to thump in her chest loudly.

Despite the heavy breathing, the rise and fall of his broad muscular chest against her back, and the sheen of sweat that coated him, he handled her powerfully and completely. His two biceps swelled against her as he held her firmly. The kissing and suckling of her neck went on long, likely too long, marking her there before he finally pulled away to pant into her ear.

"It was so tempting, lover," he stated without thinking, the words so coarse and casual.

Her eyes fluttered at his bold statement, graced with the familiar crowning word that served to send a shiver through her.

"Ooh," she muttered lightly, pleasure lacing every syllable, "Yes it was," she cooed, reaching to stroke his face.

His eyes shut and his chin angles up as her hand touches him. He allows her to stroke at his face as he held her with such complete possessiveness, as if he had gone through with it. Not even allowing himself to be embarrassed for his bold choice of words, he gave a low, growling sort of noise as he held her.

"Mm, see? Your trust is rewarded again," It was a silly statement, he thought, but his high spirits would not be dampened.

She smiled, laughter finding and tickling her throat at her pleasure in his words, her arms encircling his as he held her so tightly, a bright flash of her pink tongue along her peachy lips, "If not rewarded," she paused, "you certainly haven't punished me. You had the power I didn't," she cooed, once more building him up with all the honesty she could, "You showed strength where I showed desire."

Giving a deep, coarse chuckle, he squeezed her in his thickly muscled arms, pressing his mouth and face to her ivory neck, kissing and suckling there before responding, teasing with his sharp teeth, "Perhaps I might not be so level headed next time. Let's hope the next town is not too far off, no?" He kept a firm hold on her, enjoying the feel of the delicate looking woman so fully embraced and under his power, his voice a bit deeper, raspier as he whispered, "And maybe save such thrills for another time, when we're not so far flung."

Her breath caught deep within her lungs and the promise of more, of later, of longer passions in the future. She wriggled slightly, never feeling as fully sated as she wished, and even less so now as she sat atop his powerful lap, pulled so close to him, the scent of their sex so thick in the heavy air. She whimpered as she let her head drop, encouraging his suckling, even as he broke the barrier and bruised her light flesh, she only urged him on with a soft, girlish moan of pleasure,

"You'll stay with me?" she asked softly, putting the power of the relationship in his hands.

"No," he replied quickly to her words, his powerful body, such a blended mix of the exquisite and the terrible, clung to her as his hoarse, rumbling words come out, "You'll stay with me, from now on. And that's how it shall be." His voice tapered off into a light growl worrying her neck with his lips, moving up from the poorly used flesh so bruised and marred to lick and suckle at her earlobe, feeling quite territorial over her despite any doubts so naturally put in him by his nature and upbringing.

"And what if I don't want to stay," she purred, the sound coming out with a growl of seduction, of yearning to be claimed and held, her wriggling in his lap giving away the true intents of her question, even if she weren't willing to explain it herself. It would be easy for him to see that she wasn't planning on getting up unless it was necessary, her body content to writhe there, already begging for more.

They had fucked twice already in so short a time, but the damnable seductress was working at him again, and the way she spoke, she moved, it managed to stir his loins — if only a little — again, deepening his breaths, heart thumping heavily in his golden hued, red-flecked chest. He squeezed his thick arms around her body, pressing her into his musculature tightly as he repeated himself gruffly in her ear, "I said... you will stay with me from now on." His final word a commanding, possessive punctuation on his claim of her, "Understood?"

Her heart fluttered with a brief pitter-patter of fear marked with pleasure, her face contorted into one of excitement, the rush of danger, leaving her craving more.

"It's been a while since I've been with someone who thought he could tell me what to do," she mused lustfully, moving back against him, her wings caught between their bodies.

Glaurakos lifted a hand up, the clawed, reddish digits stroking along her cheek with slow motions, some rough skin scraping against her lightly as he gave a low grunt. Their bodies pressed so tightly, his own wings pushed out behind him as his tongue dabbled along her earlobe.

His low, growling voice murmured, "I'm telling you what will happen. Fight it all you like," he grinned a bit smugly, only hampered slightly by the nagging thought that told him she's not to be had by any single man, "but I claim you."

Her breath caught at his brazen words, her body melted with desire for him, her shoulders sloped back into him, her wings pulled to the side to allow her flesh to graze against his, so soft and creamy against his own.

"I'd like to see you try," she cooed in earnest, the heat of lust clouding her brain, the words streaming out overtop of themselves as she let the pleasure of the moment completely work her over.

At her challenge, his upper lip twitched, his elven features contorting ferally as he pushed her forward, pressing her back to her knees upon the ground as he moved over her slender body. He knew it was a game inside. He knew she even initiated the game, and though he didn't fully understand if she did it to manipulate him or please herself, he played it all the same, because a part of him did want to regardless, of his own selfish motives. He kept one arm around her firmly as the other moved behind her wings, taking hold of her dark, raven hair firmly as his puffy, reddened member swelled again, the shaft almost sore from their constant fucking, but it didn't perturb him at all.

"I'll take you however I see fit, my pretty little angel," he snarled, tugging back on her hair.

A rush of excitement flowed through her, the implicit threat of the demon straddling her only serving to egg her on with desire, her body crying out to be taken, violated, the pressure growing too much too quickly as her passion overtook her. She wanted for him, craved him, and all the terrible and wonderful things she thought he could do. She squealed with the tug of her hair, unable to hide her moaning, her lower body immediately finding his.

"You couldn't!" she cried, completely incapable of stopping herself, or arguing with her desire, of falling prey to logic and planning. She was lost in this hazed world of desire.

Hearing her refutation, he tugged back on her hair once more, pulling her head back and moved his other arm, holding her waist in his clawed hand as he shifted his hips and prodded his searing hot flesh to her slit once more. Despite the straining sensation in his member, he speared her more savagely than he ever had before, harder than when he took her body as payment for favour, harder than any time since. He took her like an animal, callously and without any regard for her delicate form.

It was a stark contrast from the tenderness of earlier, but that only made it sweeter for both of them. He pulled back her hair painfully, nearly enough to tear it from her beautiful head as he pounded into her, the striking of their sex-dampened flesh a dull thud. His leather wings twitched, causing a fanning breeze that could not dissipate the extreme heat of their joined bodies even a little.

She cried out with pain and pleasure, though it was quite clear to him how much she enjoyed the rough strikes. Even as she screamed, her hips still bucked against him violently, trying to slump downward and get away. Though she was trapped in his grasp, her motions meaningless and only for their mutual pleasure, both all too aware of the game they play. Her silken flesh was bruised around the neck, a purplish hue of leftover affection, her cunt was sticky, mixing with the heady scented remnants of her own pleasure.

The game they played grew less conscious in his mind as he took her more and more savagely, his bestial side taking over as he let her goading, her seduction, drive him. The sweet grip of her cum stained cunt around him soothed his straining cock, her wetness like a cleansing wash over his searing rod as he fucked her savagely. He suddenly let go of her hair only to shove her face down, cheek mashed into the grass as he moved over her, battering her very depths as he swatted her with a cracking slap. Grunting and groaning wildly, he seemed to be on the verge of release, but it was the exertion and intensity of the moment, his third taking of her in the hours since awakening. His brow tickled with a trail of sweat as he tried to shrug it away in his rough ride.

She cried out after being so brutally shoved, her eyes widening at the slap as her cunt pulsed around him, suddenly wondering if she were the only one playing. Her body, however, only delighted further in the idea, the heat of the implicit threats in his actions, the threats of what he may do and the consequences of that filling her. The idea of her slender body filling and swelling with child, his child, rounding out her curves, growing her breasts with the fill of nourishing milk, the swelling of her cunt, was all too much to bear. Her legs kicked in protest as she cried out in real fear, her cheek slamming into the grass with each thrust as her cunt throbbed with her ecstasy, her pleasured nub pulsing with desire.

Ignoring her cries and flailing, he was only spurred on in taking her. Savagely riding and hammering into her lithe form, he slid his hand down from her waist and grabbed her breast firmly, squeezing and twisting the pert little swell of flesh as he too found himself wondering at her form and what he might do to it. His balls slapped against her heavily, his breathing ragged and coarse, coming on hard and fast as he felt his own pleasure a smoldering burn within his loins. She had aroused and seduced him so often, it stung to fuck her yet again, but he still showed no outward signs of wearying or disinterest in her. Whether game or no, he seemed both outwardly and inwardly intent upon demonstrating he WOULD keep and hold her, that his lustful taking was no mere bluster.

She was putty in his hands. She made no outward display at casting any spells, even to ease her pain, which may give away the comfort she felt with him, but her physical behaviours were nothing short of desperate and passionate fear, mixed together as her chest heaved into his hand, hitting at him roughly as her face mashed into the ground. She writhed there, pleasure stripping her insides and leaving her smoldering to his touch, her pale skin a variance of flushed hues of reds and purples where his mouth had sucked on her flesh. She cried out in a shriek of anguished joy, the warm gush of fluid overtaking him as she shivered and collapsed as hard as he'd let her.

The flood of juices around his searing member made him arch his own neck back and cry out, like some barbarian claiming a ravaged war trophy of a wench. With another savage strike of his hand upon her pert ass, he left the ivory mound red, stinging, with the harsh strike of his palm. Crying out loudly, his hoarse voice barked his pleasure and command at her, words of commanding possession bubbling from his lips, sounding almost angrily committed to making her his as he pummeled her cunt. His own release was slow building, so soon after his previous climaxes it was almost painful to feel the burn of pleasure tear through his puffed and engorged flesh. Release approached, budding and building within him at such an agonizingly slow pace as their bodies crashed together in quick succession, over and over.

Her words were nothing more than a blubbering mess of post pleasure-nonsense, her body twitched with each grab and slap, sparked with a sensitivity that she hadn't felt in quite some time. Such was the powerful orgasm that racked at her body, honeyed lips drawing him in with their slickness, his balls slapping against her and coating themselves in her juice, only making the thrusts to send an extra spark through her. She whined and begged for him to stop, knowing he wasn't going to listen, her mind vaguely curious of what he might do should pleasure strike him once more.

Her words to stop were nothing more than syrupy fuck-talk that didn't register in his mind as anything to even consider pausing over. Taking her, he fucked her ceaselessly, their rutting extending on well beyond the rise of the sun. His long building orgasm burned in him like a searing hot poker working its way through his own cock, until finally the fruits of his savaging began to bloom. His upper body seemed to shudder, shoulders spasmed almost violently as they buckled forth, hands moving to her ass as his head drooped down. His muscular body went tense, so sweaty and glistening as his climax took him again.

The sensible, responsible man who managed to reign in his lust for their greater good was no longer present, his hands holding her firmly in place as he bucked wildly, his release going on long and firmly depositing itself down into her cunt, splattering itself against her upturned cervix as he crooned out a long, undulating series of groans and moans. He managed amidst the cacophony of noises to utter a firm claim of her as his own, but it's so hoarse and croaks as to be almost lost amidst the sea of sounds.

She gasped as she felt the final thrusts, knowing full well what they signified and shouting out a panicked word of "Stop!" But she knew the futility of her actions. She gasped into the ground, struggling away from him and not succeeding, her face scratched from being fucked into the grass for so long, her cunt swollen and useless, puffy and looking painful to the touch, seared as it was with his preternatural heat. Nothing could stop him from cumming in her, and the mood shifted.

She flailed beneath him, whimpering as her mind slowly returned to its logical place, leaving her to wonder just what she had done.

Wearied from the long fuck sessions of the morning, he pressed down upon her with much of his weight, huffing with heavy breaths as she sank further onto the grass. Finally, still lodged firmly within her, he moved forward, tiredly slumping himself onto her back, his sweaty chest pressing to feathers and the trail of her spine in between. The wash of his heated breath over her neck and ear, he could hear her whimpering so close. His mind had been full of doubts, and part of him nagged at the stupidity, and how he might've taken the game too far, the lust-addled part of him that told him it was necessary to dominate and claim her now silent. He shushed her lightly between heavy breaths, one hand stroking her raven hair, the other over her chest and stomach, lingering over the lower section of it.

"Shhhh, shhh. It's okay," he hoarsely croaked. "You're mine. I'll take care of you."

With a light hum of concerned murmuring, she shrank against him at his coddling, concern overwhelming her as she took tiny snippets of breath, working the air into her lungs as she soothed herself in his grasp, her head knocking backwards as she began to gasp for panicked air.

Sweaty and exhausted, Glaurakos panted atop her, his muscular, large build pressing down upon her slim back as he moved in, his horns getting caught in her raven hair as he kissed her neck and cheek. He seemed stiff and weary, the life drained from him for the moment after the rapturous act. Hearing her panicked gasps he twisted to the side, relieving the pressure upon her as he slid them both onto their elbows and arms.

Though she still struggled for breath, she didn't shy from him, curling up against him eagerly, as though relying on him for protection. Her eyes were wide and borderline manic, her flesh still in several manners of discolour after their passionate lovemaking, but still she sought his body to wrap around her, keeping out the thoughts of the potential what-ifs and the possible consequences of their passion.

Having toppled his bulky frame to his side, it pleased him to see her seek him out, his fear that he had gone too far assuaged by her act. He placed his thick forearm around her body, crossing over her chest and breasts as he powerfully held her close, his lips seeking out and finding her slender, elven ear once more as he kissed it, supremely soft in comparison to the wild passion of moments before. Murmuring quietly there he assured her, mumbled phrases of comfort and fondness in his hoarse, rasping voice, the words barely intelligible.

Though her lower lip trembled, her body was soothed, relaxation slowly overcoming her, though it took a while for her normal breathing to return. Her slick form pressed to his, her fears finally satiated. She murmured quietly, "We haven't long before the dome is visible."

Peering up at the steaming dome, he nodded slightly, his own golden-orange hair and horn rustling against her raven black strands.

"Passion did conquer us in the end," he said coarsely, shifting, as though to get up, but only making it part way before relenting. Propped up another few inches he squeezed her body to him and kissed her cheek fondly, his other hand moving to her shoulder beneath her head.

"Lust has devoured the morning whole," he mused.

"That happens sometimes," she mused, struggling to smile at him, her hands rolling over her stomach, feeling damp flesh, her dark hair mussed once more, even after she had so recently ran the brush through it.

"We'll need to do that talking thing at some point if this is to continue," she said softly, embarrassed that she had to say them aloud and hating the way they tasted in her mouth.

His red eyes followed her hands on their trail down to her stomach, his own then leaving her chest to join it, resting clawed digits over her fingers carefully as he hears her words.

"We can talk all you like," he responded before kissing her shoulder, his palm grazing over her soft lower stomach, "but my words stand, regardless. Seeing you in such a state would not lessen my commitment to keeping you safe, on the contrary." He took a deep breath, his chest rising with the action, "Enough of my fae self exists to cause the contrary, I assure you." His powerful hand rubbed at her shoulder and neck as he rose up and sat behind her back. "All the same, we should hope the next town is close and well stocked."

She shivered with the loss of his heat, the back of her body flushed from his warmth. She made no motion to move as he left her side, instead holding her spot and staring out the dome. Brief moments flutter by as she replayed his words to her mind.

"There are other things to consider..." she trailed off, finally turning to look at him with pitiful eyes, wide with fear. She was in a world she didn't know, with nothing to her name, and he was the only solid thing there keeping her sane. And she knew it'd go to hell, just like everything else she'd been involved with. The question was one of time, she thought.

Still close to her as he sat, his hands lingering upon her, he met her gaze after her words, studying her face. After a moment of thought he seemed to interpret her meaning, his golden brows contorting in a furrow before relaxing again. Sliding his hand from her shoulder he brushed his knuckles to her cheek and jawline down to her chin before nodding.

"Such as?" he asked softly.

She smiled at him, a tender and delicate look that gave him the impression that she was but a mere child, coy and afraid of having to give bad news, or ruin a happy day. She lowered her head to his hand, letting her long hair drape over his red flesh, her large eyes hidden from view, "Perhaps when we find a town you may take me to dinner?" she asked with a tilt of her head, "and we can discuss?"

It was such a civil thing, and she wondered at how much she hoped he'd say yes.

They were demons. They weren't made for softness or for dinner dates. They were made to rut and fuck everything up, to start wars and leave the cities in ruins.

So when her fingers ran over his hand, dancing along his skin so affectionately, he had to stop and ponder. For so long, he'd been on his own. Never trusting another, especially not one of his kind. Yet she hadn't betrayed him. She'd stuck with him through so much, and he stroked her flesh more gently.

Staring down at her girlish look, his lips then crooked up in the corners in a wry smirk, hiding the more contemplative feelings he had.

"Yes. Very well. Though I doubt we shall find anything too fancy in this area, assuming they even welcome us into town at all," he blurted before he could watch himself, his expression deflating before he pushed a smile back to his lips, "Yes, we shall do that."

"Why wouldn't they?" she asked fearfully. There was a silence before she suggested, "Or we could go on a picnic. Something a human would do for fun."

Glaurakos leaned over and kissed her side, near her stomach, "As you wish. But," he paused, lifting his head to look to her from the corner of his view, "if it's intended as some act to blunt news I don't wish to hear, you should know that it's pointless and silly. I will take it as well now as ever." He stroked his hand over her stomach lightly.

"It's not that," she said after some pause, "but more a concern that the conversation may last longer than this dome will," she looked at him and gave a pleasant smile, trying to allay his fears, her own body slow to move but still quite a bit more rested than he, if not a bit bruised.

Seeing her stir he slid his hand in beneath her waist, between the grass and her body, helping her rise.

"But of course," he said reassuringly, leaning in and kissing her shoulder, "whatever you wish. The going shall be easier from here on out, I hope, regardless."

"Without the cold, I'll travel better, at the very least," she smiled softly, her eyes downcast as she let him move her as though she were a doll, "I'd just feel more comfortable if we had a place to stay... But by the end of this Cycle, things will be better."

His two powerful hands stroke over her side and arm, holding her fondly as he kissed her shoulder and neck again softly, "One way or another, they shall be, my dear. Of that I have little doubt. But put your mind to rest," he said soothingly, pushing himself up to his feet then holding out his hands to her, "whatever happens you have protection and care in me."

She nodded as she followed his standing motion, looking so frail this morning, especially against his sweaty, bulky form. She slowly removed the brush and began working it through her hair.

"So we'll head to the road, then?" she asked.

Bending over, albeit more slowly than usual, he began to pluck up his armour and clothes, pulling them on, snapping studded leather pieces into place over his body.

"No," he shook his head; "we'll keep the road in sight, but avoid it until we near the city. Flying too close to it will only invite trouble, and isn't something I'd care to do unless in an emergency."

"We can travel just as well on or off it, after all, so why chance? He shrugged his shoulders in reply.

She nodded, embarrassed by her own lack of foresight. This was probably why slavers caught her, she thought. She really should learn from her mistakes. She fluttered her wings, smoothing out the crumpled ones with care, still standing in the nude before him.

"Which direction will we take?" she asked.

Bending over to snap his greaves into place he looked up at her, her nude form causing him to pause in his dressing a moment. Breaking the delay, he finished with the leather and rose up, looking down to her.

"Due south, parallel to the road but far enough away to hopefully not be seen from it," he smiled reassuringly at her, picking up his sword and sliding it into place upon his back, his leather wings beating in the air before pulling in around him as usual. "Do not worry, it won't put us any further from our goal, or take us any longer this way."

She nodded, taking a deep breath before she finally moved to grab her discarded clothes, hesitating to pull them on and, this time, putting her boots in the bag, leaving her feet bare and curved, "I'm not worried," she said lyrically, "They will accept us."

Hefting their satchel over his shoulders, he nodded to her sternly as he gave one last check over his gear.

"If not us, then you at least," he smiled to her encouragingly, reaching out and grazing her cheek with the backs of his knuckles lightly. "You can conjure up some spells and charm for the task, no doubt."

"Yes," she said softly, taking a breath, "I have options available for us if we come to trouble, but I don't have the reagents I need and I'd rather not have to. We will cross that bridge when we come to it, I suppose..."

Nodding to her he paused a moment, eyeing her ethereal beauty before turning abruptly and stepping out of the dome. He peered around, his leathery wings twitching and flapping with a loud noise like thick pieces of canvas being pushed by the wind before turning toward the invisible dome and waiting for Lilah.

"Let us hope the first town we come to has all we need. If not, we should be able to find out about any others in the region that will."

She nodded, her wings fluttering as she took off, meeting him in the air, smiling reassuringly, "They'll have what we require, I'm sure of it."

CHAPTER 18

Having been flying for some time, the sun was low as they neared the city. Light shone off the structures ahead in brilliant hues, the buildings making a stunning sight in the distance. Glaurakos looked to Lilah, then back at the city ahead, stunned silence overtaking him before he gestured onward; they had scryed the city from a distance, and made out its denizens, but to see it up close was another thing.

Swooping in together they landed near the road, Glaurakos' leathery wings folding in around him as he made the rest of their way in on foot, his hood tugged up around his horns. Steadily they approached the gateway as planned. A tall elemental – a humanoid form shimmering with wind — approached with a halberd in hand.

"Halt!" she commanded, her metal armour imposing, "What's your business in Shimmer City?"

Glaurakos, his head tucked down, allowed Lilah her to speak. The avian took a tentative step forwards, bowing in a regal manner and keeping her head lowered as she spoke, "We seek supplies. We have been camping for many days and find ourselves wanting for more comfortable rooms to stay in. We seek to eat a well cooked meal," she raised her eyes, though not her body, seeking out the elemental's gaze. "We will cause no trouble."

The tall, heavily armoured guard spoke a bit glumly, as if she had heard such things a million times before, "Do you have gold with which to purchase such services? We don't let in penniless beggars to harass the citizenry." The guard looked blankly at the pair, used to turning away many a refugee for their poverty.

Glaurakos shifted in irritation, looking to Lilah to gauge her reaction.

'What we cannot afford, we have the means to barter for," she said with another embarrassed bow, mostly for show of submission to the other woman, "And there will be no harassment involved. If we are unable to strike a deal, then we will return to the forest and bother you no more. But I believe we have many items of value that your citizens will be interested to purchase."

The guard sized the pair up, her lips parted and looked as if about to demand show of proof for such means of bartering. After a brief appraisal, she noticed the winged woman's staff and the man's sword, deeming them acceptable enough proof that they were adventurers with things to trade. She stepped back and held her halberd to the side.

"Go on ahead. But be warned, if your coin runs out or you become a nuisance, you will be expelled from the town."

Glaurakos waited no longer, stepping beside Lilah and placing his strong hand upon her shoulder as he led them both into the city.

Beyond the front gates they found a large street leading through the core of town, buildings of coloured glass and bronze providing a beautiful vista. Despite the guards at the gates, the streets were bustling with activity, vendors ahead hocking wares every which way. He looked to her and nodded, "It seems this place shall have what we need," he said in a rasping whisper.

"Yes, let's hope. Though," she added, "I wish we had more reassurance that we'll be leaving this place with what we need, or at least the extra gems for what else we'll require. I'd have to barter with a lot of men to get that many rare items," she returned quietly, barely above a breath.

Peering at her from the corner of his view he glanced around curiously before looking back at her.

"We have spoils still left from our encounter with the witch; we could part with a few things to get much of what we wish. As for the bulk of the reagents we need..." he took a deep breath, "Such a price will be beyond bartering and trade, I'm afraid. If this place has them, then we'll have to find... other methods, to procure them."

Glaurakos peered at her. "For now let's just concern ourselves with accommodations, food, recuperating- the basics," he resolved.

Lilah looked troubled, a mixture of eagerness and apprehension clouding her vision.

"I'd like that," she said simply, not altogether too fond of the idea of having to fight to get what she wants. It was more useful to charm such things from people.

She looked around the bustling city slowly, trying to find direction. She pointed at a building not far from them with a bed carved into the ornate glass sign.

"I guess that'd be an inn," she suggested.

He squinted at the direction she pointed, "Yes. Did you wish to head in and rest first? Go get that dinner you wanted, or just head straight off to get our supplies?" He turned back and looked to her, rather than charging off and dictating the course of events as he usually did.

"We'll need supplies before we do either of those things," she pointed out, looking at him with unbridled honesty in her green eyes, though she flickered them away shyly, unable to endure his scrutiny.

His gaze unchanging, he squeezed her shoulder.

"Very well. Go get your things, I will investigate the town and we'll meet back at the inn." He slowly slid his hand from her shoulder, reaching to his belt and tugging out an amulet, holding it out to her, "Here. Sell this for coin." He looked to her, adding pointedly, "Do not trade your services for anything until after you have sorted everything out."

Lilah's long, slender fingers clasped the amulet, looking down on it.

"It's not special, is it?" she asked nervously, apprehensive about the idea of being alone in a strange city.

Glancing down at the amulet he looked back at her.

"Not too special to be spared selling off for our benefit. It's worth a fair bit; barter well for it," his face broke into a smile, confident in her to extract its best price.

She leaned in, then, laying her mouth on top of his in a furtive series of kisses, as though she feared she'd never see him again. When she pulled away, her lips were laced with a frown.

"You'll get us a room?" she asked meekly.

Her kisses took him by surprise, but he pressed in and met them all the same, enjoying the moist, fleshy contact of their mouths before breaking off. Nodding to her he said, "I shall. Did you wish to rest then once you're done, or go eat somewhere? Or have the food brought to our room, I suppose."

"I don't care, surprise me," she said, giving him one more look before bouncing off into the city, as though lingering with him there would only make it harder. They had, after all, spent the last couple of weeks together non-stop. It would be strange to strike out alone again, and though a part of her relished the freedom, she had come to enjoy his presence, she realized.

Watching Lilah bound away, he savoured the sight. He had always been independent. Even back in the long, magical imprisonment when he lived with his kin, he had avoided entanglements with the others.

It was odd that Glaurakos felt a twinge of regret at parting from Lilah. He worried she might not return to their appointed meeting spot, though the worry was pushed aside by practicality. Besides, if it was so, he'd rather find out now than later.

She glanced back at him, over his fiendish good looks, thinking of the way he spoke to her. Was it just a ploy? To lure her in and betray her.

He was far from the most persuasive or charming talker, so he was probably oblivious to the game he was playing with her. The way he was leading her on.

As she vanished into the crowd, he made his way towards the inn, preparing to gather intelligence about the new area and prepare them a room. Though as they parted ways, it was hard not to think back on the many times he was betrayed, by creatures too venomously wicked to even know their own interests lay in being faithful.

In the face of that, he was amazed he could trust her at all. Yet part of him yearned to trust another. The same part of him that caused so much trouble in times past.

CHAPTER 19

After a few hours, Glaurakos heard a knock at the door of the room he'd acquired. Opening it, he saw Lilah. She paused there, a small satchel of goods clinking together as she waited, her fingers fidgeting nervously.

Opening the door to the room, great sword in hand, the towering fae-demon peered out, glancing to her then up and down the halls before ushering her in. The room was not big, but the bed was sizeable. Glaurakos guided her in, a hand on her shoulder

"It went well, I trust," Glaurakos posited, securing the door after her.

"Yes," she said softly, "Though I must mix the ingredients. It was, of course, a rather specialized order, and they haven't many of *me* floating around," she added with a pause and a small smile, turning to look at him, "Did you find anything?"

He smirked and reached out to take her satchel, carefully laying it upon a table.

"Then I hope you have all you need," he said simply. He placed his great sword back in a scabbard by the satchel, giving her a brief appraisal.

"I told them to send up the meal I ordered after you arrived, it should be here shortly. Unless you've changed your mind and wish to go out now," he suggested.

She smiled and blushed. "Eating in is fine. I should..." she paused as she looked to the satchel, "I should mix this sooner rather than later, though," she worried her lower lip into her mouth, saucer eyes up at him, wide with implication.

Watching her indecision and anxiousness, his wry smile softened. He reached out to touch her face.

"That would be the wisest thing to do," he agreed, though his rasping voice betrayed some reluctance to admit it, or even a desire to ignore the wisdom of their words.

"We'll see how things go once we're off here," she promised, her voice dropping lower, her look sincere, though she quickly flusters at it and moves towards the basin, turning on the cold water and letting it run a few minutes before splashing it upon her face and chest with a tiny cry of surprise.

He chuckled and leaned down to place a kiss upon her shoulder as he plucked up his sword, pulling it with him as he recedes to the bed, seating himself with a groan of the mattress upon its edge. Pulling it from its scabbard, he began to clean and oil the weapon quietly, though his eyes were drawn to Lilah.

"How long does that work take you?" he asked casually.

"Longer than you'll care to wait, so better I take it sooner rather than later," she said, seeking out the satchel and plucking it up, opening it and unveiling a strong smell of sweet flowers and something spiced like cinnamon. She moved to the floor, and set up a makeshift alchemy area, complete with a stand to place the vial on which would be ignited underneath, causing the mixture to melt and boil. Her hands were steady as she crafted the potion, having made the same brew a few times over the years. She paused and looked up at him, "A week and a half."

Glaurakos arched a brow while continuing to sharpen his blade.

"To make it? Or for it to start working?" he asked.

There was a knock on the door. Glaurakos carried his weapon with him as he opened it, the sheepish serving boy stood there, carrying a tray. Glaurakos took the tray from him. Without another word, he shut the door and laid the tray out on the table, a lid covering the food, keeping it warm. Glaurakos sat back down, resuming his work of slowly honing his blade.

"To start working, for certain. It will take the rest of the evening for it to cure, though, and grow to its proper potency," she said with a pause. "If I hadn't let the dosage lapse, there wouldn't be a period of wait at all, but..." she trails off, gnawing at her lips hungrily but wanting to finish setting the potion. She lit a flame underneath the level, the scent of rich spices wafted through the air before she dropped in a tiny droplet of a liquid, causing steam to rise and the concoction to bubble slightly before settling itself, an eerie purple glow to the mix. She sets it aside and stood, looking at him.

His head tilted as he listened, his gaze passed from her to the concoction curiously.

"We shall have to do our best to control ourselves in the meantime," he responded. Seeing her stand he put his whetstone aside and sheathed his sword. Gesturing to some doors on the far wall, he moved over and opened them, revealing a look out onto the streets, and more than that, a small balcony; nothing impressive, but with two seats and a table to eat at. "I saw this while looking about outside, and asked for the room specifically." He smiled back at her then moved to the food.

"Hungry?" he asked.

She smiled, obviously touched and pleased with the extra little space and she nodded eagerly, moving out the door and spreading her wings, knocking into the table slightly.

"Ooh," she blushed, grinning back at him, tossing her hair over her shoulder, "This is beautiful! It's perfect!"

Bringing the tray of food out, he laid it on the table. The balcony was tiny, barely able to fit the table, chairs and them, and the view was nothing spectacular, an alley between the inn and the city wall, but with a bit of a view out over the fields beyond. He pulled out the chair for her, then pulled the lid from the food, some steam rose as he laid the dome lid aside. Before them was an assortment of steamed vegetables, clams, fruit and other rare meat intended for him. Beside it was a decanter of wine and two glasses.

"Take what you like, of course," he said.

She smiled, her fingers hovering over the choice fruit. Lilah plucked it up, pressing it to her lips, making an exaggerated sigh of delight as the sugary sweetness hit her tongue, her eyes closing in pleasure.

"Mmm," she mumbled, her eyelids fluttering at him, her dark lashes hiding her gaze. She pulled the fruit away with a smile, "This tastes as good as home," she mused.

Glaurakos sat across from her, his forearms resting against the edge of the table. "Word is, this is the most prosperous trade city on the island. And so much comes here that can't be had elsewhere. Enjoy it, my dear. It's been some time since we saw any sort of civilization."

He turned his attention to his food, plucking up a piece of meat and biting it.

"It feels strange, doesn't it?" she asked, looking at him sincerely as she finished the first fruit and picking a new one, "I mean, we could settle here and be no worse off, but something about this all seems so strange. I don't know how to describe it, but not being able to get home makes me want to get home all the more..."

"I would be very much willing to explore this place further, but not until I'm sure of a way out of here for us both." He laughed, looking up at her. "By all accounts," he said a bit glumly, "this place is stranded. Everyone's stranded here, unable to get back to where they came from. This is the better part of the island, elsewhere there are many other issues, hordes of desperate refugees and banditry. They keep those types out of here to maintain the prosperity of the city. Take in wealth through trade, but keep out the needy." He shrugged his shoulders, his long golden-orange hair hanging down around him, "Could be good for us, at least. its bronze walls doubtlessly hoard great wealth and rarities."

"I just feel like something is off. Maybe it's what we saw before we came... time not moving properly. What if we changed something? Or what if that's just how time looks here to people not within its barriers?" she ruminated, spearing a steamed vegetable and popping it into her mouth as she stared into the alleyway, "I don't like the feeling of not having a choice."

He peered out over the grassy fields before looking back at her.

"Neither do I. But look," he pointed out over the fields, "When we came through we saw time shift out from the portal. So we're no longer slowed, I am sure of that. The permanent gateway helped time flow through here to put it back on course. Until then," he shrugged his heavyset shoulders, "the island must've been adrift between planes, cut off from time itself."

She frowned, thinking it over, "And if it wasn't just us catching up with the slowed time? Perhaps now we're affected by the time. If we're slowed, we might live here for a dozen years and come back to find nothing changed back in Sho'ar... or wherever..."

Lilah considered their predicament, "I suppose it wouldn't matter. Not like we have anything to return to in that regard anyways, and I imagine we'd still age."

He shook his head as he looked down, biting into another piece of meat, "No. We saw time here moving slowly. If we were slowed, then when we do finally make it back, so much time will have passed that an age would be gone from when we left."

Glaurakos' red eyes darted away then back again, taking on a reassuring gaze at last, "But don't worry about that. I'm certain that's not how it is. Time changed in an outwards spiral from the gateway, if it had been us changing everything would've seemed to shift to normal all at once."

She nodded thoughtfully, "Right."

Lilah sighed, chewing on another vegetable.

"Do you feel trapped?" she asked, "When I was taken by those slavers, I thought my life was over. I know what they do to slave girls, and I'd be a husk by the time I'd ever escape. I thought it was over," she frowned, lowering her eyes, "I know that's a terrible way of thinking about it."

Hearing her admission he lifted his head and gazed across to her, brows furrowing, one raised above the other.

"Fortunately we came together then. Such a fate would be a terrible waste for us both," he rasped, "It is worth the loss of all those items and reagents if it saved you to be by my side. Trapped? No. We'll get off here one way or another. It's just a matter of time."

"I never did get to travel as much as I liked," she admitted, looking at him, "I will stay and stay happily if you can promise me something."

"Go on," he said suspiciously after a short pause, taking his time with tearing some meat away from the bone and chewing slowly.

She allowed him to stew a bit, against her better judgement, simply because she enjoyed him looking so serious.

"I will stay and stay happily," she repeated, "if we can treat it like a vacation. A honeymoon or something fantastic. And the pieces we're after are just trinkets that we are seeking, for a game of finder's-seekers."

"That's your big thing?" he asked, "What you made such a big deal about needing time to discuss?" After a silence, he cleared his throat and looked over at her, his golden brow arched curiously. He stared a moment before breaking into a chuckle.

"Oh, no, that wasn't the big deal thing. The big deal thing was that you have to be able to accept certain things about me that aren't likely to change. You seem fine with them now, but honeymoon periods do end and suddenly you may not find my aptitudes so amusing," she blurted, unapologetically, "But I do think it will be more enjoyable to view this as a vacation."

"I assume..." he began, crossing his arms, "you refer to your nature as a half-breed, Fae-Angel? All of that?" He poured two glasses of wine for them, lifting one for himself and drinking, "You worry I'll get jealous or try to keep you from... cavorting?"

"Bartering. We call it bartering," she said lowly, "We as in me, anyway," she paused, biting on her lower lip, "It has been a problem in the past. And sometimes you look at me as though I may fly off if you don't keep me chained," she said slowly, her eyes raising to meet his, forcing herself to hold them, "Our kind do not make terrific wives or mothers or partners."

"I understand your fears," Glaurakos replied, popping a piece of fruit in his mouth and chewing, "But know that I've spent the entirety of my life among our kind. Half-breeds with an immortal's fickle nature. We didn't know commitment or trust. Partnerships dissolved quickly. It was the demon blood in them, left them unpredictable." But Glaurakos had always thought himself an outlier. As someone better than that. Someone that wasn't so chaotic.

He washed the fruit down with some wine before wiping the back of his hand across his mouth.

"I hated that about them. But..." he continued, "you're a different sort. If I eye you strangely it's only because I'm used to everyone behaving like a self-destructive loon. But I should think that my intentions obviously do not include chaining you, though if you intend to take off on me I'd rather it sooner than later." Laying down his glass he shrugged his shoulders. "As for the rest," he flicked a hand dismissively, "nothing you've done or indicated so far troubles me. I have come to expect far worse of our kind."

She watched him as he spoke, forgetting about the food momentarily as her green eyes remain chained to his. She noted his hand as it lifted the wine to his lips, the movement of it across his mouth, his casual demeanour.

"I have spent my life among those within Sho'ar. It was a city of great magic, but run by full-blood mortals. Very rarely have I come across... one of us. I dare say I don't hold their mannerisms, though I couldn't be certain, for there's so few to compare myself to." She lowered her eyes demurely, "I enjoy your company, Glaurakos. I would not have lingered with you if I didn't."

Nodding slowly to her he leaned forward onto the edge of the table, a hand moving beneath it to rest upon her knee as he looked across at her with his preternaturally red eyes, "I understand that. You have paid any debts to me in full, our relationship is purely a barter in the beginning, and what I gave to you, you returned to me in agreement. I do not assume you've stuck with me out of any feeling of obligation or necessity. After reaching Twin Stars you could've managed well on your own, after all."

She returned her eyes to her food and slowly reached for her own glass of wine, stirring it a moment as she stretched her knee towards him, encouraging his hand upon her flesh.

"The first thing a woman must do on a honeymoon is find something to wear that makes her attractive to her companion. Something sultry," she suggested in a low, seductive tone.

Glaurakos' lips parted, showing a sharp-toothed grin, his hand responding by squeezing and rubbing at her leg, up and down from her calf to her lower thigh.

"Something sultry? How could I refuse that?" he asked.

She smiled devilishly at him, "I would hope you wouldn't," she cooed. "We could go for a walk this evening, see what the night life is like here..."

Beneath the table, his powerful hand rubbed and groped her, moving up her thigh, close to her loins as he spoke lowly.

"We shall do that then," he said, his tongue grazing his reddish lips, "this shall be a trying week, my sweet. Quite a honeymoon indeed."

She smiled with a girlish blush, her eyes fluttering away from him in the most modest manner she could possibly muster, her hair falling to her face as she sets aside her glass.

"Ah, a trying week it will be," she frowned, licking her lips and glancing at him, "and altogether risky."

Her girlish response makes him grin widely, his hand continuing its path beneath the table.

"I have no reason to want to produce children right now, but lust and nature do take their courses upon us both, my dear. And should we fail again, or it's already too late," he raised his brows, watching her intently, "how will you respond?"

"I suppose we'll know when the time comes," she said slowly, the pink hue of her blush trailing down over her neck. She reached to her glass once more, taking a long sip as her legs parted for him, encouraging his wandering hand.

The parting of her legs does not go unnoticed and his hand slipped further in, moving up beneath her skirt toward her loins, his knuckles grazing her sex.

"I suppose we will," he said gruffly. Peering out over the balcony briefly he added, "At least now if it comes to that, we know there's civilization to take you to and be kept in relative safety." His words grown slow and emphatic, "No wandering the wilds with a swollen belly, fearing each shadow in a bush."

Lilah's pale pink skirt rode above her hips as she slowly moved one of her legs upward, placing her bare foot lightly against his package.

"If you make this honeymoon too good, my dear friend, I may never wish to leave. And then what will you do?" she asked with a pout.

Feeling her bare foot press to the large swell of his groin, he lowered his other hand beneath the table, this one cupping along the underside of her thigh there, not hindering or preventing her actions, just feeling her leg, encouraging. His other hand grazed along her sex, feeling the labia and teasing the sensitive nub hidden inside.

"The lives of our kind are long indeed, my dear. I am in no terrible rush for anything that would cause me to behave hastily or foolishly. Anything, that is, but you." His final words punctuated with a squeeze of her thigh and a firm press of his hand.

Her head tilted backwards, a soft sigh of pleasure exhaling from her plush lips as his fingers find her silken lips, soft and sweet against his hand, the slickness there allowing his digit to slip and explore readily. She rolled her head before she rights herself, taking a long sip of her wine before placing it down atop the table, her foot flexing and running up the length of his member slowly, hindered only by that layer of tight leather clinging to him.

"What were your mates like before?" she asked.

Her slender, bare foot found his package stiff and large, the shape of his member so pronounced it was traceable even through the leather of his armour. His own finger nudged apart her damp folds, pressing between them as he buried his index finger's knuckle inside her, circling her sensitive clit.

"Ravenous," he growled, "Often violent. Deceptive bitches, but utterly transparent to me. Amusing, but they grew tiresome. All the same, all utterly without long-term worth. Like something spicy you eat once, but thereafter its effect is lost on you, a tolerance built to it. But beautiful, quite beautiful. And you?"

She whimpers as his knuckle presses into her, her mind momentarily clouded by lust, but eventually she regains enough of herself to respond, her face burning hot, as though she truly was an angel, so confused and frightened by such fragrant descriptions of sex and sexuality.

"Trysts are the best way to explain it," she gasped, "Eventually they always wanted more than I could offer. They wanted me to be more than what I could be to one man or one woman," she twisted at his continued movements. "But there are many avenues for me to travel, so I was never without for very long. Not with the size of Sho'ar being the size it is."

With his knuckle encircling her clit he raised his thumb, sinking it into her sodden cunt in time with the finger, a low growling noise coming from him as he eyed her light clothes, marvelled at the feather wings.

"I couldn't imagine you going long without, no," he agreed, "You must draw eyes wherever you tread." His hand massaged her thigh, encouraging its rub upon him, "To think I thought you a pure angel when I first laid eyes upon you." He grinned wryly across at her, "How devious," he breathed, "how exquisitely sexual you are."

She shudders with his skilled ministrations, the press of her foot becoming more powerful as it glided along his clad member, the sun leaving a lingering heat to everything, even as it dipped below the horizon, the shadows gently playing upon her face as fires were lit within the town.

"I can be many things," she cooed softly, her hips rocking in time with his movements. "A good many of things," she opened her eyes to look at the broad figure across from her, the shadows making him look harder and more sinister, which only served to arouse her further, tiny cries of restraint fighting against her lips.

Giving a low, long groan, he pressed his thumb into her more deeply.

"Of that I have no doubt," he said. With his hand upon her thigh he turned her, rising up from his chair and moving closer, keeping her foot upon his groin as he leaned down to her. His deviously grinning lips, enshadowed by the fading light, press to hers in a passionate kiss. Tasting those peachy lips, he groaned, his thumb sinking into her past the knuckle.

She moaned against his mouth freely, frightened no longer of being heard as her cries were muffled against him, her arms fluttering around his thick neck and holding onto him tightly, dragging him in closer as her foot readjusted, knocking at the table with a clatter of food and utensils. Her soft top proved a hindrance to her as she tugged it open the corseted front, peeling it back and exposing her petite breasts to the air.

Hearing the tug of her clothes, his hand left her thigh and bangs against the table to add to the clatter as he reached for her chest, feeling her small, pert breasts, groping them exuberantly, squeezing and kneading her flesh. So taken with her form, he plucked his hand from her cunt and slid it beneath her ass, plucking her light frame from the chair and backing into the room through the door. He turned around then and dumped her upon the bed, standing tall as he undressed, prying open buckles and clasps.

Lilah removed her corset entirely and revealing her full alabaster flesh to him, her areolas the lightest shade of pink, the nubs hard, her breath quickening. She spread her legs, letting her bare feet dangle over the side of the bed as she watched him

"There are risk-free ways," she breathed deeply.

Glaurakos' chest armour came loose as he let it drop to the side.

"Speak quickly," he said, baring his broad, muscular chest. He tugged his arm guards, and worked his belt.

Lilah flipped over, feet hooked into the side of the bed, legs spread at the knees, back arched, her hair flicking over her bare shoulder. Reaching one hand across her back, she caressed her backside. Slowly, though quick enough to not keep him waiting, two fingers delved into her depths, retreating with a thick, sticky coating following her as she trailed it up that final inch, re-enacting the motion with her deep brown hole, pressing those same two fingers in and, though she groaned, she shows considerable resilience.

Glaurakos tugged his belt abruptly and his leg guards dropped away, revealing the large bulge in his thin undergarments. He tugged the ratty brown garment away, revealing his thickly throbbing organ entirely as he slid out of his boots.

"Such a woman," he mused. Stepping up onto the bed behind her he watched those fingers of hers delve into that tight hole, seeing the brown ring pucker about her slick digits as his hands find her slender waist. "You could tempt the devil itself with your offerings."

She shuddered with his touch, or perhaps because of her own, and whimpered softly at the sight of his cock. Rethinking her position for just a second before letting her fingers continue their work, a slow third digit is added, stretching herself before him, her head dropping down between her shoulders. She took a deep breath and exhaled, licking her lips before suckling her lower lip in to silence her wanton moans.

Watching as that third finger widened the gap of her hole, he decided himself to wait no longer. One hand leaves her hips to grasp his shaft, lifting the member to nudge it against the pucker of her hole right beside her three digits, the fat tip nudging and trying to press its way into her hole with them, slick from his own precum. He paused, thinking better of it, then lowering his shaft and dipping it into her tight, honey slick cunt, sinking to her very depths and coating himself in her nectar with a moan of his own.

She gasped at the unexpected press of his member inside her, collapsing forward briefly with the heightened sensation, the backs of her fingers pressing against the descent of his cock, her toes curling as a slight gust of warmth spilled out around his shaft, dripping downward against his sac. Her head flicked back, hair spilling over her spine and waist. She panted and briefly considered removing her fingers from her tightened bud, but she enjoyed the sensation too much to do so.

The pleasure of her reaction, the sweet cling of her honeyed slit about his girth. He gripped her hips and pulled back, sliding his length nearly out of her before pushing back again, giving a few slow pumps of his cock into her cunt, intending to only wet his shaft but finding the pleasure so irresistible it's hard to tear away, the added pressure of her fingers deep in her ass not helping him. With some heavy breathing he looked down to her before sliding his length out of her fully, seeming like the act itself took a tremendous amount of willpower to pull off.

She whined as her slick cavern emptied of his heat, her body instinctively seeking after it, her hips thrusting toward him in protest. She panted, slowly removing her fingers from her dark hole, encouraging him to fill her there, offering it to him, her clean fingers pressing at her clit angrily as she wiggled before him.

Her thrusting made him grit his teeth, the gape of her slickened asshole tempting him as well. At any other time the new offering of her asshole would be an easy choice for the dragon-blood, but his dark nature did urge him to do what was wrong all the more. It took some effort to guide his bulging crown up to her brown ring and press to it, grunting as he pushed inside her forcibly with a squeeze of her waist and hips.

His heat was less noticeable within the tightened ring and yet, at the same time, it was more acute as well, and she began to squirm. Quickly she reminded herself to relax and her wings fluttered to cool herself off as she moaned and rubbed her clit more frantically, begging herself to not fail the massive member as it speared her.

The broad demon-spawn let loose a throaty, rasping groan of such deep satisfaction, her tight canal gripped his length so firmly. So completely.

It took so much more of his strength to plunge that organ into her resistant ass, even with the preparations she had made, but strength was one thing Glaurakos has no shortage of. Grasping her pert ass cheeks and slender hips, he held her tight as her wings fluttered, battering him with little feathery gusts of air.

The strange sensations of cool against searing, hot inhuman flesh were pleasant, but all he felt was the tight tug of her anal canal as he began to push and pull against the resistance. Forcing his sizable girth into her again and again, his heavy sac swayed with an increasing tempo, beginning to batter her slender digits as they rub.

"Fuck," she whimpered, her entire body trembling against him. It was a glorious sensation to be giving her such pleasure. Such pain.

It made him feel powerful and whole, and her feet kicked at his sides as she writhed.

"Fuck."

It became her mantra, repeated over and over, spurring her through the intensity of the moment.

Her words of pain and exultant joy like a drumbeat ushered him on faster, harder. The slap of his balls against her fingers grew louder, the sweet nectar of her quim coated her digits and adding to the music.

With great effort he was able to match the overpowering tempo with which he had ravished her cunt, instead hammering her poor, abused asshole. Again and again he struck deep, hard, his fingers curling into her flesh, pricking her fair skin as he gruffly panted and groaned.

She was taken to another plane, a realm outside her own, as her mind hazed over. It was bliss, pure and simple, and her moans were animalistic. She wanted this, wanted him, yet her body fought against his intrusion, grasping him so tightly in the dark recesses of her body.

The intensity of the moment was nearly overwhelming, and Glaurakos arched his spine, feeling the fiery brewing in his loins, driving him onward to the inevitable fruition of his climax. He was like a beast unleashed, hammering into her seemingly fragile and porcelain body, his low grunts, growls and groans filling the air as he pummeled her.

"Fuck!" she repeated, louder this time as her back arched and her head jerked back. A scream of pleasure split the air as her body shuddered around him, a flood of warm fluid soaking down over his sac as she jams him in further. Her ecstasy manages to dull her pain, enough for her to take him in deeper than ever.

All Glaurakos could take he took, and then some, he impaled himself into her a final time, digging the full length of his impressive cock into her ass he felt the electric current shoot up his length. The explosion of creamy seed that shot forth into her a seemingly endless torrent, wave after wave cresting, ebbing then spurting forth again until it slowly began to taper off and his loins emptied themselves inside her dark hole.

Lilah whimpered as she gasped for air, her wings fluttering as if she wished to flee but simply lacked the energy or the willpower.

The intense grind and slap of flesh at an end, Glaurakos leaned over Lilah's sweat glistening form so rudely pushed down into the bed. Breathing heavily he let his hands move over her body, feeling out her back and shoulders as he lay lodged inside her, the exuberant fucking at an end, the winged woman battered and exhausted.

In a hoarse, panting voice he said, "You had so pleased me elsewise I had all but forgotten of such pleasures." He bent forward and kissed the back of her neck then, a lazy grin grazing his face.

She lay pinned forward, all but completely exhausted, her body spent and unwilling to even twitch any longer. She struggled out a word, but all that came was a breath of air, a low, exhausted moan from deep within her throat as she struggled to breathe, pitched forward as she was.

With a low growling groan he lifted himself up, his broad, well-sculpted chest on display as he slid from her sweat-slick skin, falling from her gaped pucker. Resting back on his ass, he raised his knees up in the air and stroked over her form as he reclined.

"It's always so intense, huh?" he asked.

She managed another garbled grunt of a word, her eyes flickering at the sudden emptiness of her bottom, allowing herself to topple over to the side as she panted, looking quite pleased. Her face still red and laced with perspiration, her body shivering as its sheen hits the air with her movements.

Watching her topple to her side, he reached over, shifting to rest against her, his heated fiendish form pressing to hers once more as his hand stroked along her collarbone and up to her neck, his lips kissing upon her cheek,

"Our inability to talk for long without needing to fuck could become a problem eventually," he chuckled.

With a coarse, hard swallow, Lilah finally speaks.

"You started it," laughed, spooning back into him lazily, her hair sticking to her neck under his lips, her body still trembling just slightly at the change in temperature, "but you're right."

His glowing red eyes narrowed, nearly closing as he smiled smugly, an arm draped across her stomach. Giving a dry chuckle he kissed her jaw line muttering lowly, "Couldn't help myself. And now I fear I've worn you out for that walk about town you wanted." His coarse palm stroked over her smooth, pale flesh with great admiration.

She groaned just thinking of moving her limbs, though the thought of a new, sexy outfit flitters through her mind. Finally, her body became more enthusiastic at the prospect of moving.

"You can't wear out an angel, you only calm her down for a while," she purred.

He looked at her incredulously.

"Oh? And what of that other half? Did I wear her down?" He leaned in and bit her ear with his sharp teeth, his tongue flicking it a bit before finally letting it snap back, free.

"You maybe, MAYBE tuckered her out," she bit her lower lip, trying to suppress her smile. Tilting her head towards him as he bit, she groaned in pain.

"You do pose quite a challenge though," he murmured.

"If anyone could wear me down, though, it'd be you, Master Glaurakos," she smiled at him, returning his look.

He looked at her quizzically.

"Master, is it?" he said, stroking her stomach, admiring her form, "You do make me wish to try though. Such a tempting morsel you make," he grinned.

"Have we enough for a small token of sensual clothing, oh husband of my home?" she said quietly, the edge of laughter following her words.

"Husband now? From master to husband? Is that a demotion or a promotion?" he growled, his sharp claws raked over her stomach, careful not to cut or mark her. Breaking into a slight smirk he stroked down to her thighs, "Yes, I do believe we can scrounge up enough for you. I am a prisoner to your lustful form, I suppose."

"Well this is our honeymoon, Master Husband of mine," she purred. The post-sex silliness was infectious. She curled onto her back, looking upwards at him, "I can barter tomorrow. CAREFULLY. If we need anything. You know."

Shaking his head slowly, he reached down, curling his clawed fingers about her calf and lifting her leg up, bending it at the knee as he leans in to kiss her there at the knee.

"No need. We have enough to do us well for a while. Once you're... set again, however, we can begin to recoup." He smirked to her playfully.

She closed her eyes and enjoyed the feel of his lips upon her calves, shivering slightly before forcing herself to stand, straightening her belt of a skirt to cover over her ass and her heated cunt, taking a deep breath.

"Are you ready?" she asked, though she was still topless.

Glaurakos moved to the edge of the bed and stood, towering over her.

"Very well. And if you truly wish it, you may go barter. But," he paused, the delay amplifying his words, "only if you are truly very careful." He sized her near-nude form up and down slowly, "I'd rather not spend my time caring for and protecting a woman pregnant with another's child."

"You're the only one to make me press the limits," she protested, pressing a hand to his chest. Her eyes widened and her lips pouted. "I am usually very cautious with that," she rubbed his chest lightly, "It's not my fault you drive me to the brink of insanity."

"It is hard to imagine you any other way than when you are with me. Very well, just know I won't be pleased if it goes badly. I trust that suffices between us." He kissed her forehead.

"I didn't really see any place that sold what I was looking for, but I didn't get to look much and, who knows, maybe there's different evening vendors." Lilah laced her corset top back up with nimble fingers.

Watching her step away, he bent down to scoop up his armour, clasping it into place, piece by piece over his muscular form.

"By now many places are no doubt closed. But hopefully finer shops will have displays still up in windows at least," he attached his sword to his back as usual, the scabbard in place as he moved to her, "I don't wish to settle for this."

"I don't want anything too fancy," she purred, looking upward at the roof, "Just something half there and half not, maybe? Do you have something in mind?"

"Fashion is not one of the things I excel at, my sweet," he said, ushering her toward the door, "And whatever the price, we shall just get whatever tickles your fancy best."

"Well, I'll just have to try on everything. And see what you like best. How does that sound?" She smiled, her pink skirt tight across her thighs, her corseted top allowing her small breasts to be pushed up fuller, her feet still bare.

"That sounds perfect," he whispered.

CHAPTER 20

Moving through the hallway after locking the room's door, Glaurakos and Lilah made their way down the stairs and through the inn's main door into the streets outside. It was a cloudless, moonlit night and the streets were shining even in the dark, the coloured glass and metal reflecting the light beautifully. With one hand at the back of her shoulder Glaurakos guided Lilah protectively toward the main boulevard where some vendors still operated for the benefit of the diverse crowds, and people still shopped, though far fewer than earlier in the day.

She looked at the stores with a passing gaze, really not finding much of interest, though the pair drew many glances. They didn't exactly blend into the crowd despite the exotic mix of races. With her tight fitting outfit, it wasn't a strange sight for Glaurakos to catch people staring at her, mixtures of lust and false outrage on their faces. Lilah slowed as she spotted a clothing store.

Giving cautionary looks to some of the gawkers, Glaurakos strode alongside her, a towering half-dragon, warding off anyone too adventurous. He gazed to the leather store, a wry smirk crossing his face as he nodded, leading her to it.

"Very well," he said, opening the door. Inside, the shopkeeper seemed to be closing the store.

Lilah smiled at the shop keep, waving frantically.

"You don't mind if we look around?" she said loudly, a girlish giggle not far from her lips as she bore her cleavage.

The shop keep, a human in a town of elemental and mixed species, was balding and stocky, his gaze transfixed upon her as she teasingly traced her assets. With a mumbled response and a nod he waved her to the display items, turning his head back down but secretly taking glimpses up regardless. Glaurakos noted the little human's look with some dry humour of his own before turning and watching his companion flit through the merchandise.

His eyes followed her hand as he nodded his acceptance as she bounded further in, tugging at a shelf of leather bracelets and clothes and thumbing through them.

"I don't see anything," she complained lightly, moving further into the store, some silken and satin items in with the leather. She pulled out a frilly white dress, partially see through and held it to her chest, looking at Glaurakos curiously.

"What do you think of this?" she asked flirtatiously. The straps were off the shoulder and larger frills flounced at the bottom, the material clingy and tight.

"That could be it," he remarked casually, glancing at her face, "But at this point I might be amazed by you in anything new." His hand brushed the material lightly.

"Oh, you're bored of my outfit?" she said with a mock pout, quickly becoming distracted by something soft and silken, a matching bra top with a sleek, see through skirt, both a soft pink colour, nearing nude. Black lace ran up the sides of the skirt and the front of the bra cups.

"What about this?" she asked.

"That's not what I meant," he complained as she distracted herself with new items. Looking to the new scandalous items he glanced at the stocky shop keep then back, "I had no idea they'd carry such a thing."

He lifted the skirt up in his hand curiously, "I'd say it's so you as to be almost uncanny, my dear," his deep, husky voice held an element of genuine surprise.

"Well I suppose they need some variety. All leather, all the time," she paused, "Well, some things are just better to be girly and pink when hogtied, I suppose," she looked over at the shopkeeper.

"Is that why you have this?" she raised her voice, shaking the outfit as he stared back at her. He laughed, and she smiled at him — good enough, she supposed — and looked to Glaurakos.

"Is it *too* me?" she asked in earnest.

"I hardly think such a thing could be possible," he said, gesturing to the garment, "It will need to be fitted, no doubt. I don't say many share your stunning measurements, no?" he grinned smugly, as though complimenting her elevated himself.

"Can you tailor this to me?" she shouted at the shop keep, ensuring that he heard her.

He looks down at the garment in her hand and, with a lowly grunt he said, "It'll be extra."

"Can I try it on?" Lilah asked, frowning and looking to Glaurakos, then back at the shop keep.

"There's change rooms in back," he paused, his beady eyes narrowing.

She smiled and, with a quick hop-step and a bounce she fluttered behind the black curtain.

"I will bring you some specifications tomorrow. Can you handle that?" Glaurakos asked, eyeing some armour he fancied.

"For a price, of course," the balding man said, looking up at the Fae-Demon, giving a longer than appropriate stare before finally looking back down at his work.

Lilah pranced back out in the little outfit. The diamond shaped slits in the bra under the lace were next to invisible Lilah's nipples protruded against the tight, flexible fabric. The bra fit rather comfortably, in fact. The skirt, however, she clung to at her waist.

"The skirt is too big!" she proclaimed and with a demonstration she let it drop. The smooth material fell to the ground, leaving her sex bare. "Can you fix it for me?"

Glaurakos' eyes widened at the new outfit. He stared wordlessly even as she let the skirt drop, glancing to the flustered shop keep as his rounded face turned blood red and flustered. Blinking he began to stammer something all but incomprehensible, he seemed to be trying to mount a defense based on the quality and value of his workmanship. Glaurakos arched a brow in some surprise at his stubbornness before looking back to his near-bare partner.

She stared for a few moments before bending down and pulling up the skirt again, holding it at her waist.

"Come on, if I don't want to buy it, it's not like anyone else will. I got it all wet," Lilah pouted with feigned disappointment.

"Fine! Fine! But you pay now, pick it up tomorrow." The shop keep twisted his head down, though his eyes never left her. His face grew almost impossibly red before giving a quick nod and barking out the words, He looked away back to his work, though the motions of his fingers were simply pretending to go about the duty.

She smiled triumphantly at Glaurakos, clearly pleased. She wasn't even really trying, she thought. She skipped happily back to the changing room and quickly pulled off the new outfit, positively glowing with her enthusiasm.

Glaurakos stepped to the shop keep's desk, a slight smirk tugging at his lips despite his best efforts as he reached to a pouch at his waist and pulled out some coins, stacking them upon the counter. Without a word the tall dragon-blood stared down the shop keep as he waited for the man to accept his payment. The balding human managed to muster a defiant stare back.

"And quarter more in tip if she's pleased with the work on the morrow," Glaurakos said gruffly.

The shop keep, glancing to the stack and picking it up, counted it and nodded in agreement, "Come back tomorrow then. It'll be ready."

Lilah held the bra and the skirt in her hands as she pranced back out, putting the noticeably damp skirt down and exclaiming, "I'm keeping the top. It doesn't need altered."

She smiled seductively at the shop keep and he avoided her gaze all together. She smiled at Glaurakos, completely unfazed.

"Ready?" she asked.

Nodding to her sternly he doesn't so much as pay the shop keep a second glance as he moved to the door and opened it for her, ushering her out into the street with a firm, guiding hand upon her slender shoulder.

"Well done," he remarked, looking at her from the corner of his view, "and the outfit is quite lovely too."

"I thought so!" she said with a smile, looking quite a bit more relaxed and comfortable than she had since she was first kidnapped. Glaurakos noticed she seemed at home in the big city. She smiled and hummed to herself, reaching downward to clasp his hand in hers.

"It's really nice here, you know. More welcoming to our kind than human cities back home."

Nodding to her he peered around, sizing up the rather orderly trade town until he felt her hand wrap around his. Peering down he watched her pale, slender fingers move across his coarse, red-flecked palm before he squeezed them in his grasp.

"It is surprisingly stable from what I've heard so far. They must guard the city tenaciously to keep it so, if half the stories of the rest of the land are true."

"Stories?" she asked with a touch of confusion, so enraptured had she been in this day and her spoils of it that she had forgotten just what he had been doing while she was shopping earlier.

Looking about with a calm collectedness and sense of purpose he nodded once more.

"Yes. Everyone seems new here. Or at least, none who claim to be here first seem to have much legitimacy. And so there are few places with much stability and order, as they're still adjusting after tumultuous chaos." He looked at her, "We're fortunate this is our first stop," a reassuring smile graced his fiendish lips.

She smiled, "Well, that's good. I wonder where they got all the stuff to trade. I guess they had it on them when the traveled through? How did everyone else get here?"

Shaking his head slowly he peered back around, her tiny hand still in his large palm.

"I didn't find out much solid information yet on that. Though it seemed people came here in various ways. I heard mention of the War of Binding, but that was so long ago." Smiling again he continued, "As for what they trade, yes this town is apparently one of the few to make it through whole, or mostly so. They had more to start with than others, and being on the river they leveraged their position to become a hub. Their craftspeople produce much of what's used on the island elsewhere, I believe."

"Huh", she uttered, looking around at the copper buildings and the people, her steps slowing as she dipped deeper into her thought, "The entire town comes here? How is that even possible?"

Slow to reduce his speed he looked back at her, thinking. With a shake of his head, eyes upon her, he said, "I have no idea. It's a mystery to me too. A local claimed that they just woke up here one morning, but he said it a bit glibly, so perhaps he was just being a smart ass."

"That's likely," she nodded with a small shiver as she moved back toward him, her arms and body wrapping around him as she looked up at him. "You are quite the devil," she admitted honestly, quite taken aback by him. She smiled and tugged him close, breathing in his post-sex scent.

"Oh? What makes you say that? Besides the obvious, I mean," he said, a thick arm moving around her, holding her close.

"Oh, I'm sorry," she said with a pause, "I *was* just stating the obvious." She grinned and fluttered her eyelashes at him, "Let's go back to our room."

Chuckling hoarsely he nodded to her, his thick arm tugging her forward.

"Come," he ordered in that familiar tone, leading the way.

CHAPTER 21

Moving in through the doors of the tavern, Glaurakos struck an imposing figure, broad shoulders blocking out much of the frame. Heading inside he looked around the busy tavern at the many patrons. The diverse crowd drank and engaged in vibrant discussion. Finding his target amidst the crowds easily, he kept his hood up as he made his way toward the angelic figure, a standout in any group.

Two males seemed to be rather smitten with her, gazing at her beautiful face with tankards in hand, listening to her lovely voice, though none of this stopped the large half-dragon from stepping up behind her, placing his hand on the swell of her ass.

His coarse digits moved along the edge of her skimpy skirt and beyond, feeling the pert flesh beneath as he looked down and to the side at her, ignoring the men entirely, leaving them looking awkward and out of place.

Her eyes fluttered shut briefly, letting her mouth dip in a bit of a moan. Her outfit was, as usual, strategically placed. A belt of a skirt hid her nethers, a light, transparent pink top drawn over her hard nipples and small chest, pertly pressing out the fabric. She smiled at the two men, daring them to fight for her, contest for her affections, but instead their heads dipped low and they went to seek easier prey for the evening.

Though always a tall, brooding figure, Glaurakos had a certain air about him this evening. His ruddy lips parted displaying hints of two fang-like teeth as he looked down upon her through his narrowed, red gaze. Though powerful, coarse digits pressed under her skirt quite blatantly, without hesitation or shame as he felt out her cheeks, prying and nudging into the cleft of the bottom, seeking to meet her heat with his. Leaning in, he breathed hotly upon her cheek and neck, his voice rasping and low as he murmured to her, "Such meek boys to keep you company while I'm away. A pity."

She leaned back against him, her body his willing tool as she molded herself into his hand, helping his grasp with brief movements as her skirt rose up over her naked behind, exposing her porcelain ass to his golden finger as it probed her depths, finding the sweetness hidden within.

"Maybe I like variety," she purred back at him, though her face never turned towards him.

His fingers didn't stop, for they had found the heated reservoir of her womanhood, nudging and rubbing, his large hand cupping her backside in his palm as fingers moved shamelessly. Leaning in, his nose brushed against her cheek and ear, his voice came deeper and harsher than usual, his devilish nature evident in his words as he rasped into her ear, "You do. I know this. But regardless of what you like, you *need* something more. Someone like me." His hot breath became a hot touch, moist lips and tongue moving up along her neck to her ear as he licked and bit.

She barely realized she was still in public, her emotions quickly overcoming logic, despite the sounds of whooping and catcalls filling the air. She tried to keep in control, but as she began to rub back against him, her nether lips slickening eagerly over his touch, there was only she and he remaining in the room. She flipped her hair slightly off her shoulder, exposing her long, slender ear to his mouth, her body undulating in rhythm against him.

As his one hand worked at her nethers, sharp fingertip plunging between her slickened lips, two others roughly rubbed the labia about it. He reached around her with his other arm and turned her toward him. Their lewd display hardly went unnoticed. He rubbed his hand up her side, pushing her top along, the pink fabric rolling beneath his palm.

She barely heard him, and let his words slide out of her mind. Instead she lifted her leg, pressing her body against his wandering hands, letting out a low moan of anguish and pleasure as the sharp finger found its way inside her womanhood. She coaxed his mouth and tongue to explore her flesh, her pert breasts tilting expectantly towards him.

His impulse grew, his own breathing as heated as his flesh. His powerful arm coiled around her as he worked his finger into her slit, the moist flesh growing so slick that it made soft wet noises with each new plunge. His other hand groped at her chest, encircling and squeezing her breast as he suckled and kissed her neck. Relinquishing her breast he slapped his rough hand to her lifted thigh and squeezed it against him.

At his release of her breast and the quick smack of pain through her thigh, she let out a loud moan of pleasure.

"We're going to get kicked out," she purred, the words morphing back and forth from fear to a dare, enjoying the aspects of both as her nails raked against his flesh.

At that he snapped his eyes back open to gaze around. He saw burly bouncers muttering to each other and eyeing them.

"I'd let them try," he muttered in venomous rage, "But it would keep me from having you longer than I'd like to dispatch them." With a rough press of his lips to hers, he pulled back and snatched hold of her arm. Yanking her roughly he pulled her through the crowd, navigating them out into the cool night air, shoving bar patrons aside.

Her ass shown to all she passed, she quickly followed after him. As she reached the door, she took a cool gulp of air before her hands sought his stomach and chest, hurrying him on.

"Let's get home quickly," she purred, her fingers finding his nipple and giving it a quick nip.

Her fond, lavishing affections upon him as they moved elicited a rasping sound akin to a snarl. His intensely red-orange eyes locked upon her as he stopped suddenly at an alleyway outside their inn. Impatiently, his iron hot grip still on her, he pulled her into the dark recess, shoving her before him, pushing her against one of the bronze walls of the fantastical city. He was on her again, body to body, hands grabbing at her flesh, feeling her ivory skin with both an intensity of desire and attention to the detail of her form.

"I can't wait any longer. I won't," Glaurakos growled in her ear.

Lilah released a cry of pleasure, legs wrapping around him as she pushed herself up, pulling him between her legs, her pink skirt riding up further around her stomach and cinching in at her waist. Her hands found his head and suddenly she pulled his lips to hers, her tongue delving deeply into his, her own feminine heat meeting her feral fiendish state, a moan of pleasure traveling from her throat to his as she handed herself over to him willingly.

Her slender, waifish body was mashed between the firmness of the metal and the nearly equal hardness of his muscled flesh as he mercilessly pressed in against her. Their passionate kiss was met with intense desire, though its heat and bloomed to near violence and then beyond, Glaurakos' sharp teeth biting at her lower lip and pricking it. His hands moved over her body and pushed the thin slip of her top up, freeing her breasts as he pushed his hips between her legs further, his bulging groin grinding between them.

She was a flurry of fevered grinding, helping him lift her top, pulling the soft material between them for a moment before tossing it away to the side. The material fluttered down to the ground as her pale white skin mashed against his golden tinted flesh, the fiery heat between them growing with their lust and desire, her body pulsating with the need to feel him deep inside her, to fuck her until she couldn't think, couldn't walk.

With one hand slipping between her legs, he reached to his own pants, sharply clawed fingers manipulating the garment hurriedly as he tugged it apart, reaching in and unleashing his own ruddy manhood, the thickness throbbing and searing as it pressed her flesh. He burned with a need to have her that consumed reason. He pressed himself to her, angling his shaft up to pierce into her slick cunny, impaling her fully to the very hilt of his veiny member with one sharp, merciless thrust. With a loud groan at that entry that forced their lips apart, he pushed his mouth back to hers immediately, gripping her thigh and pert ass cheek, the other hand moving to her chest as he immediately began to pull and then push back, bouncing her with the motions.

Her head fell back, slamming against the wall before rebounding back to his lips, the sting deep in the back of her head as his shaft impaled her. She moaned lewdly into his mouth, her lips parting hungrily as her tongue sought his, rewarding him for his power and virility as her breasts were mercilessly grabbed, her pink nipples poking into his hand. Her movements were smooth as he slammed her between him and the wall, her cunt gushing around his cock in her delighted enthusiasm.

The initial sink into her honeyed depths was beyond compare, the refreshing moistness about him, the loving cling of her experienced nethers to his thick organ, it set a low thrum of a groan through his throat that continued on long after the first thrusts. He jarred her back, harder, faster, more and more filled with the need he felt in his loins. Their mouths met in another frenzied kiss; he sucked on her tongue, his desire urgent. He ground her against the hard metal painfully with each new loud crash that echoed in the dark alleyway.

Her legs clung to him, his urgent need rubbing off on her. She responded to his frenzied motions, rubbing his back, digging her nails in to his neck, encouraging him to fuck her, and fuck her hard, reckless, with abandon. To force her delicate body to yield to his bulk, to give him what he needed, to be what he desired most, her moans and cries coming out quick and loud, the sound echoing off the close buildings.

He increased the intensity of his strikes, hammering her tender quim with force. Each thrust was punctuated with a loud, low groan from the tight cling of her cunt about his cock, diving to her very depths and battering that deep barrier within.

"I want you," he growled. His sharp claws dug into her ass and thigh as he continued to be rougher still.

She breathed a sound of unadulterated delight, something primal and deep that came from within her own fiendish nature. Her slick cunt made schlicking sounds at each new thrust, burning red and throbbing angrily as she built her inevitable climax, finding her way through the fog of bliss and pleasure.

Revelling in her beautiful form, her delightful flesh that wrapped about him, he gazed upon her face in the throes of their rutting, and it charged his desire all the more. He growled with lust, releasing her pinkened breast, the abused little nipple that smarted from his savage manipulations, and grabbed for her neck. He choked her, his powerful hand seizing her tightly, his body growing furiously; the brutal thrusts striking as he tried to make her cry out from him — for him — despite the impediment.

Her pleasured smile faded as his hands found her throat. Even as her breath depleted, she never bothered to stray from her path of pleasure. Her body began to twitch involuntarily, her hands clawing at his arm in her desperation. Panicked pain pressed through her throat.

He held her there, her beautiful frame pounded and bounced cruelly by his thrusts, kept her choking and strained as he rutted her harder and carelessly until her struggle grew past the point of safety. Releasing her to gasp for breath he pressed back in and she scarcely had time for air to rush back into her lungs before their tongues melted together. He kissed her puffy, reddened lips, passionately loving, lustful and aggressive. His other hand pressed back her legs to bare her cunt to him more openly, so that his thrusts could strike harder.

Her lips suckled and mashed against his alternately, her own desperation only increasing as a sudden rush of pleasure coursed through her veins, flipping her stomach as it rose and dove, her head lolling back as she screamed his name into the night.

That crest that took her and brought his name to her lips claimed him, too. He was titillated and pleased at her cries, feeling his own barriers melt. All the sensations and desires that drove him coalesced as he pounded in with hard, long thrusts, burying his face against her neck and cheek as he let out a low, budding cry. She whimpered in response, creating a crescendo of pleasure that filled the air around him.

His searing hot shaft pulsed within her as he let loose his own release into the flood of hers, thick creamy white pulses of seed being thrown into the flood of honey. Without even realizing it he hoarsely rasped out her name as he bucked himself into her fully, pushing his cum up into her with erratic motions beyond the point where its flow stopped.

She shivered in absolute delight.

CHAPTER 22

That night was cloudy and dark, but Lilah and Glaurakos could still see. Perched on the dome-shaped roof of the wizards tower in the Shimmer City, their wings carried them up quietly in the night from their quick sojourn out of town. They had managed to tear themselves away from each other long enough to plan their next move and act upon it. A miracle in itself.

Glaurakos wore his newly crafted armour, a mix of black leather and dark reddish-black wizard robes he had scavenged from the mage of Sho'ar. It was a strange amalgam of materials that made him look more devilish, a high collar around his neck that pushed beneath his jaw. The shredded remnants of a robe hung around his waist, forming the loose flaps of a kilt about his leather-clad legs. He eyed the large glass windows beside him, and then peered back at his companion.

"It's enchanted with protective dweomers. We can remove them but the lock will remain. I've no skill with locks," he rasped to her. "If we have to bash our way through, we'll have to be prepared for a fight."

Lilah sat next to him, wearing a full black, fitted robe with long slits up the side, revealing her black boots underneath. She decided not to around in her typical, flimsy top and skirt, not when stealing the reagents they needed from a fellow wizard. She tied her hair back, her eyed following Glaurakos.

"There's a ritual," she said, frowning deeply. It was not the same sort of simple lock she had spell-cracked on the farm. "Unless the mage had the ritual written in your book, I don't remember it off hand."

Glaurakos pursed his lips, steeling his resolve, "There is one, but it will take a while, and we might be sighted out here in that time."

Peering around cautiously, he murmured, "I saw some familiar of the wizards patrolling around earlier, we haven't long and getting caught in the middle of a ritual would be bad." He reached a clawed, ruddy hand out to her in offering. "I'll break us through. Be on your guard," he rasped huskily, with a hint of concern, "I don't know how powerful this wizard really is."

"If they have what we're after," she said, hefting her staff, "I'd estimate at 'very.' Try to break in ... quietly," she purred, her voice low and seductive. She smiled at him and then turned once more to watch the way behind them.

Her ever-present veneer of seduction soothed and assured him against his worry. Giving her petite hand a squeeze he unsheathed his great sword, the blade piercing the protective dweomers and lodging between the two panes of glass. Taking a moment he tried to pry the window open, his muscles making short work of it. Hearing nothing in the silence, he stepped into the round-ceilinged workspace. Cautiously, he made his way to the shelves, rattling through items there, pocketing occasionally useful reagents in his search for what they were after: the means to get back through the gateway.

Glaurakos pried open a small box and found the figurine he needed. Suddenly, the wizard who was alerted to the break in ascended the stairs. The fiery-haired wizard, clad in a purple robe and irritated at being awoken, trained a spell on Glaurakos' back.

Lilah watched Glaurakos with swift eyes. Upon seeing the wizard, she let out a startled cry disguised as an animal's voice. Lilah began weaving a defensive spell to protect Glaurakos from the hit. She hoped to the Abyss that the elemental was using fire, just in case she didn't cast in time.

Twisting around at the warning cry from his companion, he turned in time to see the wizard finish her spell. The flames that tried to singe him did nothing against Lilah's ward. His sword still in hand, he swung it in a smooth arc, lightning moving like a whip to the wizard and tying an arm to her waist, tugging her across the room to him. Glaurakos whipped his sword at her again then, though she managed to deflect it with her own defensive enchantments. The wizard cast another spell of some sort that sent a shrill piercing cry out, awakening her sentries to defend the tower.

Lilah moaned, covering her ears from the shrill cry. She looked behind her and recklessly, moved into the room to protect her lover, immediately casting another spell, poisonous and corrosive.

"We haven't time for this! Get ready to leave!" Glaurakos exclaimed. He grabbed the wizard. With her robes in hand he glared, his fangs protruded out of his mouth as he casted his scrying spell. Vanishing from sight, he and his captive reappeared behind Lilah. Glaurakos gave the wizard a shove and the woman plummeted off the edge of the building.

Lilah looked disoriented.

"You have it?" she asked, looking around more alertly than before, barely noticing the cries of the woman.

"No!" he growled, watching the wizard descend quickly into the dark of the streets below. Turning around he moved back inside quickly. "I wasn't able to grab it in time."

The sound of something large moving up the steps reached their ears, and he snarled irritably, "I don't know if the wizard will be able to save herself in time," he grabbed the statuette and tucked it into his satchel, smirking at Lilah as he saw the source of the noise appear. It was a golem, large and made of brass, much like the rest of Shimmer City, moving purely through magical means towards the two intruders.

"Let's go!" Glaurakos shouted.

Lilah flew upward, meeting the wind with quick and easy grace. Her heart pounded, her breath caught in her throat. She looked back at Glaurakos more than once as she made her way toward what she hoped to be a safe spot.

Glaurakos pointed his great sword towards the approaching golem, an arc of fire shooting out and striking the thing. The fire's high temperature began to melt the brassy surface. Glaurakos' wings unfurled and he flew behind her several moments after securing her safe getaway.

"It's too dangerous to spend the night in the city! If she survived, the guards will be looking for us!" Glaurakos exclaimed.

"We can go to the forest! The one down the road from here that we spent the night!" Lilah replied. They had, of course, prepared for this chance and none of their personal belongings, as modest as they are, were left in the inn. Lilah had layered her clothing, and everything else was kept tucked in her bag. They hadn't done too much shopping, after all.

"It's a shame, not being able to blend in once in a while!" Lilah remarked.

Chuckling gruffly into the chill air he nods to her, his golden hair billowing in the wind a smile formed on his lips, he seems to enjoy the hectic violence, the obviousness of it is written all over his face.

"Indeed, my dear. With any luck we'll be back on our world in a couple of days," Glaurakos chuckled gruffly, his golden hair billowing in the wind. He enjoyed the hectic violence, he thought, and he was sure Lilah noticed. "We can rest in the forest or move on. The mountains aren't far from here and we may have a search party out after us soon," he said with a confident look.

Lilah's eyes scanned the darkness ahead of them, making out the trees and the mountains beyond them.

It took another few moments for her to speak, looking at him as her black hair whipped around her face, freeing itself from her bun, "What will you do when we get back?"

The corner of his lips curled, a wry grin forming at her question. He laughed singularly into the cold night air as the city grew further and further away.

"I had intended to ask you the same question upon this last leg of the journey," he replied. He was reluctant to answer her question or know her response. He went quiet as the forest grew close.

"We're here," he said, pointing toward the spot they hid their things. "Do you wish to break or push on and hope for a spot in the mountains?"

"We'll push ahead," she decided after a long pause. She looked forward pensively and kept flying toward the mountains.

"You should put on your fur coat. It will be chilly up there, and," he paused, "we'll have to fly around that dragon's mountain for safety. It will add more time to the journey." Glaurakos swooped down, plucking up the extra satchel of miscellaneous goods.

She frowned, pulling on her fur coat, wrapping it securely around her and letting her wings poke out the slits in the back. She looked with disdain towards the mountains, opening her mouth to speak before deciding against it and nodding in agreement, "Then we best hurry."

"Come," he beckoned softly, extending his hand, "We have much to discuss. Won't do us to land on the other side of that gateway without a clue in hell, will it?" He took her by the hand, and while she had a more thoughtful look in her eyes, he unfurled his wings and took to the air with a kick of his feet, the mountains their destination as they set back to flight, the snow caps growing in their sight.

Truthfully Lilah had no real idea what she could or would do once returning back, she thought. She was sure someone else had moved in and filled the void she had left in the drug business, and she wasn't looking forward to warring to get it back. But what more did she have to return to? She set her sights on the mountains and flew quickly toward them.

Ascending higher into the sky the clouds approached. The familiar chill of the mountains returned.

"If you worry about my controlling and using you to sire some offspring once we're free of here, you needn't be," Glaurakos finally broke the silence. It seemed a random concern, Lilah thought, all things considered. Some cold flakes of snow could be felt as they flew over the snowy reaches of the mountains.

Her milky skin blended into the cloudy sky as the white flakes pelted her face. For most of the journey she, too, was quiet. Approaching freedom had never tasted so burdened.

"I... never thought you would," she finally replied, looking at him, confused. She added, "Or could..." Golden specks glinted in her watery eyes.

"It was just something you worried about some time ago," he said, a wry smirk forming on his face. His long golden hair and blade-sorcerer's armour flapped around him as he continued, "I have no real rational desire to want to sire younglings, Lilah. I was moved in the heat of my passion for you. The thrill of the moment to show you my desires and how deep they went." His golden brow furrowed a bit, "You understand?"

She tried to resist looking back at him, glancing quickly before turning to face forward.

"I understand," she said, sucking her lower lip into her mouth for a moment before her eyes scan the horizon, planning their path in silent contemplation, "I don't know what I'll do," she finally admitted, pulling her fur coat tighter.

Watching her, the chew of her lip and quiet contemplation he peered ahead as the skies grew colder and harsher.

"I have a few ideas," he said weakly. They soared into the mountains, their long journey well under. "Once the gateway back is secured... there might be a sizable profit in coming back. Selling the location of the gateway to those here. A ticket back, to the highest bidder," he suggested.

Lilah mulled his suggestion. They'd need security, of course, because something like this wouldn't last long without being known. Aside from that they'd need, well, what exactly she asked herself?

Word of mouth would do it all for them. Once the rumours were started, and they could ask for whatever sum of money they wanted. It wasn't a bad idea, she thought.

"You'd stay?" she asked Glaurakos.

"No," He said, shaking his head and raising his brow briefly, "No, not stay. Just come back for a quick profit."

The mountain's peaks moved past them slowly, despite their adeptness at flying.

"We've been flying a while, and we've plenty of supplies, there's no need to push ourselves. If you need a rest, we can look for a cave for shelter, or a clearing to create our own magical one," Glaurakos said, licking his ruddy lips.

"We'll rest," she said, a bit more breathlessly than she'd like. She was tired, truthfully, and not altogether thrilled with having to leave the city. She would have been content with staying a bit longer, but his drive to get them home filled her with the purpose she lacked.

Glaurakos angled himself downward, moving closer to the peaks, seeking a suitable spot to land. With a jerk of his head he gestured, "There," and guided them in.

He found a sizable ledge before an opening in the rock face. Landing near the opening with care, the wind whipped him as he peered into the cave and spied a yeti. He held a hand out to stall Lilah as she fluttered above, and then vanished inside.

Before she could pursue him, sounds of fighting erupted from within the cave.

CHAPTER 23

Lilah landed quickly despite his warning, but Glaurakos had taken the creature by surprise. Blood was splattered upon the stone surface of the cave, and he emerged, triumphant, to toss the dismembered body of the yeti over the side of the cliff.

"Give me a moment, stand aside," Glaurakos grumbled, annoyed that she'd landed before he told her to. Vanishing back into the cave he conjured up a whirlwind, the currents causing a blast of air to vacate the snow and bloody rubble from the cave, along with the stench of the now-deceased yeti. Taking a moment to wipe his blade clean he moved back out, hand extended to her, palm up, "Come, we'll lay out the blankets and things. It'll make a good resting spot." His voice was warm and reassuring as he led her into their new abode, pulling the travel satchel out to extract their things.

He laid his satchel to the side and rolled out their beds for the night. He placed his precious sword within easy reach and crouched down, thick leather-encased limbs. He did have his handsomeness to compensate for his charm, Lilah thought, but it was likely only she could find his demon-tinted features handsome.

She allowed him silence, finding peace within it. She wasn't even sure she wanted to stay with him. She shook the thought from her head, reprimanding herself for being so juvenile. He was a male and he'd gotten what he wanted, but it didn't explain why he stayed after rescuing her. Perhaps then he had simply not had his fill, she thought. The past weeks had, surely, calmed his need. She looked up at him, admiring his stature. It was fun while it lasted, she consoled herself.

The silence had grown awkward, Glaurakos thought, and he looked at her. Sat cross-legged in his dark new outfit he looked like a demon lord.

"Come closer, I've heat enough to warm us both," he said softly, wrapping an arm around her form and pulling her close. Her lithe form rested against his chest and between his legs, wrapping his limbs about her fully, comfortingly.

She spooned into him trustingly, not put off by the weakness in voice. She rubbed her bare hands over his clothing in slow, exploratory movements, rubbing along the outline of his chest, warming herself against him. Where he was golden and fiery, she was pale and chill. Her head nestled up under his jawline, her soft hair rubbed against his flesh.

Even in her layers of clothes, the black stealthy gear, the fur coat, she seemed frail and tiny in his grasp, he thought. His arms quickly warmed to her, his natural heat building through his leather to her as he cradled her form.

"This time together has been enjoyable. I almost fear reopening the gateway and seeing what becomes of my angel-winged temptress when the cage swung open," he confessed finally.

Her eyelids had fluttered closed as she relaxed against him, enjoying the closeness of their bodies, the slow feel of her fingers exploring him. At his words she paused; her breath, her motions, her fingers. She pondered over its meaning for a brief few moments before letting in a wave of air.

"And what will happen to my fiendish devil?" she asked.

Rubbing his clawed hands over her arm and leg, his every breath was filled with the steam of hot meeting cold. He took his time answering, but his words were sure.

"If you wish to leave, you needn't sneak off or backstab me. I will share with you all the spoils of our expedition and let you go in peace, without the risk of trying to do one another in and suffering the backlash. I'll linger a while and likely do as I say should you go your own way. Recruit hired help to return and bargain the portal for more profit."

Both of them were locked in the same fears, struggled with the same desires. They'd been betrayed, hurt, and their tenderness for one another was a risk neither of them wanted to take. How could they trust another of their kind?

Their growing passion was only stoking those fears hotter.

Her lithe body bore signs of tension in her shoulder and neck, conflicting emotions rising within her. It had been a long time since she had been with anyone, even so long as she'd been with him. She, surprisingly enough, wasn't usually good in anything qualifying as a relationship, she thought. She took her time formulating her response.

"I don't want to backstab you, and I won't," she pondered calmly, licking her lips slightly. "You wouldn't wish that I leave?" she asked after a pause.

"No," he answered promptly, "But I fear it's in your nature to do so." He held her closely even as her face screwed up in protest. "Lest I planted a seed in you, I imagined you to be quick to go in search of other things. Newer experiences." He thought 'more powerful men' but he wouldn't say it; it'd be too low a blow to his own ego and sense of self-worth.

The tension in her shoulders slowly relaxed and she curled into him more warmly, her thick lashes covering her eyes from his gaze as she inhaled deeply.

"I haven't wanted to," she said finally.

"I'd prefer you'd stay with me. So that together we might hatch plans and find success. We do make an excellent pair, don't you think?" he said, his lips curling in a pleased, confident smile. His two rough hands grasped her more firmly, rubbing the chill from her limbs thoroughly as he cradled her to his body.

Her responses buoyed his hope, though his better senses told him to be more wary with the woman and her seductive ways.

She nodded, her movements slow, subtle and fluid, her black hair shimmering in the dark light as her eyes searched his eagerly, for some sign of truth or lie.

"Though we end up getting one another into trouble a fair bit," she added with a wry grin of her own, slightly calmed by his amorous rubbing and his gentle words, though she still feared his fickle nature. They were half-breeds and outcasts, after all, no matter how much better than their ilk they felt they were.

His own lips matched hers in that wry manner, meeting her grin at the memories of their careless exploits, the bubbled over lust that consumed them both recklessly time and again.

"Mm, indeed we do," he responded, leaning in and tilting his head at an angle to kiss her soft lips, his fiery hot pair pressing to hers, pointed tongue delving between them before they broke. "I won't make silly promises that we might not keep. But I want you to stay with me."

"I want to stay," she affirmed with breathy air against his heated mouth, her body pressed to him, eager to consummate what could be taken as reconciliation, at least in her mind. Not that it mattered, she thought. Whatever had happened, whatever had passed through them had filled her with a fiery passion that she pressed onto him, her hands wrapping around his neck, eagerly holding herself to him, daring him to take her.

His heated breath washed over her with each rise and fall of his chest, holding her tightly in his strongly muscled arms. Barely restrained passion resided within those limbs that held her, a light tremble in his lips.

"I'll make you want to stay a long time. I'll find a way," he murmured. Pressing in, his eyes shut and he met her lips once more, but with a greater fury, less restraint, his pointed tongue pushing into her mouth as he rubbed his hands across her upper body, feeling her through the coat. Seeming to grow impatient with it, he lifts his hands and pushes them inside the fur, wanting to feel her, twisting her form so that he could peel away the layers and get at the flesh beneath.

It was unfortunate the cold required her to dress in layers that night, she thought. The cloaks hindered his progress as he tore through to her body, her bare flesh, the smooth, porcelain skin so welcoming and accommodating to his heated passions, able to accept him in a way that mere mortals couldn't, finding him strong and beautiful, a force to be reckoned with. If there was anyone that would be able to keep her interests for a while, she thought, it would be him; he'd already proven that. Truthfully she hadn't spent so much time with a sole man since her father, and this was something different altogether.

Maybe it was the fact that he was more like she than most she'd met, or perhaps she was just drawn to the brilliant, handsome brute that had shown her such kindness at her lowest point. It didn't matter, but it added to her fury and her passionate kisses and feverish movements as she worked the leather away from his chest.

Rolling his shoulders back he bared his chest to her, helping her slip off his chest piece to show the powerful muscles beneath, the flesh a deep tan flecked with ruddy spots in certain areas, and all of it richly heated as if a fire burned just beneath the surface. His own hands pulled at her robe, tugging it up, pulling at the fabric so the slits at her sides press along her legs until finally it's all bunched at her waist. Sex and companionship for him had always been a distraction, he thought, a thing of play with partners unable to be trusted and likely not wanted back a second time regardless. But with her he found himself with a seemingly endless fountain of desire, and he pressed to her, wanting her flesh so very much.

"So many clothes," he rasped gruffly to her, amusement tingeing his irritation.

She moved against him with the same desires, the same motivations as he, desperately trying to reveal herself to him, and at the same time, to reveal more of him to her. One hand worked away his leather as another tugged at the strings of her tight robe, working it down and revealing more of her torso, her body cold, and yet at the same time, burning with fervor.

His ruddy muscles revealed, the heat of his body met the cold, and the fiendish warmth won over. Moving her lithe frame in his hands with ease, he shook his long golden hair free and twisted around, pressing her back to the thick blankets they had laid out upon the cave floor for them. Eager lips moved down to her neck, sucking amidst nips of his sharply fanged teeth, as his two clawed hands pull her top up and press his palm to her breasts, squeezing through her bra as he hovered over her.

She took all the nips and bites in stride, letting out little whimpers, but otherwise not acknowledging the pain, instead rubbing along his chest, over his shoulders, feeling him out and luxuriating in the feel of his strength, the heat from his body, his hovering motions, his nipping licks only seeking to stoke the fire in her loins, lighted by the lack of betrayal and rejection.

The long golden-orange strands of his hair fell down around her neck and shoulder, his dark horn grazing her cheek just barely as he went about suckling and nipping at her tender, ivory flesh. The strong thumbs of his hands pressed up in under the cup of her bra, forcing it over the rise of her firm, petite breasts, baring them to him and the rough strokes of his thumbs, grating over the sensitive pinkened nipples and areola as he ground the manhood trapped within his leather breeches to her loins with an instinctive rhythm.

She let out a soft gasp as her nipple hardened against his rubbing, the tiny pink nub pressing against him eagerly, even though the rough skin causes a momentary glance of pain. She ground against him to his own beat, her pelvic bone rubbing against the head of his cock slowly, carefully, and yet with an urgency that belied her enthusiasm to have him slip within her.

As he so often did, he left behind a mark of his frenzied suckling upon her neck as he raised his head, those intense red eyes gazing at her as his hands continued, not pausing for a moment. Shifting her robe away down over her legs, he then slid his hands back up in under her skirt, rolling the slight fabric up in the process as he hooks his finger into the undergarment beneath and tugged it aside, all the while gazing into her eyes with heated, heavy breaths.

Her green eyes matched his, her pinked lips parting as she panted into the new, steamy heat of the cave. She writhed and helped him free herself of the 'so many clothes' she wore, only too eager to be once more unpeeled, revealed to him, to solidify the understanding in their relationship and ease her mind at his sincerity. As her legs were freed, they ascended around his waist, drawing him close to her own natural heat.

His eyelids narrowed into thin, red slits. He leaned in, giving her a soft kiss that hardly fit the moment of their frenzied passion. His own relief at her assurances assuaged his worry, but he still wished to savour her, enjoy the odd seduction while it all lasted. One of his rough hands grabbed her by the hip tightly, another moving back to her chest to squeeze and maul at her pert breast as he jabbed his fiery red spear to her revealed cunt, ramming into her before forcibly sinking into its embrace. His groan at the entry came out as more of a growl than anything else, and his nostrils flared.

Her wings readjusted under her back as she shifted to kiss him, meeting his mouth with slow, delicate licks and kisses, enjoying the closeness as his cock struck her, impaling her in a slow, sweet manner, filling her wholly. She tugged him nearer still, her calves pressing against the bottom of his ass as she tempted him to delve deeper within her, her canal squeezing him tightly all the while.

Groaning deeply as he felt his thick girth spread open her channel and make way for him as he sank lower. He bit her lower lip, his digits sinking into her pale, slender body. All the while his own mind raced, not only with his lust and desire but with the many things he wished to say. But he thought better of it; the things on his mind were things he had no doubt he would find silly or embarrassing with a clearer head. Reaching her utmost depths he felt himself snugly pressed upon on all sides by her and he couldn't help but groan out some gruff words, unbidden.

"I'll keep things interesting with you," he promised before tugging his hips back and feeling the cling of her cunny lips upon his shaft pull in the opposite direction.

Her back arched to allow her pelvis to rub along the upper portion of his dick, putting an additional pleasurable rub of pressure on him. She loved this, she thought. The excitement, the adoration, the new feelings.

It wasn't just sex. It wasn't just doing what she was wont to do.

It was something new and different, and even though there were words for it, they were not words she'd lightly use.

All she knew was that she kept pulling him in deeper and deeper, her body succumbing to his powerful form.

The hoarse moan he let loose, so deeply sincere, as he slid his rough hands up and down her sides, grasping a breast, a hip, and lifting his ass before crashing them back down into her again with a firm thrust. Every sinewy muscle, so strong, so honed, used to piston his fiery cock into her moist cunt as they reconciled their situation.

He was so hungry for her; he wished to devour her with his intense, slow kisses. Suckling, biting and tugging at her lips as he pumped his shaft into her tightened quim. Reveling in the feel of her slick canal gripping every inch of his veiny girth so perfectly, like a tighter second skin.

Her fingers explored his golden mane, her plush lips pressing eagerly to his. She tasted sweet, her tongue playing with his as they rutted in the cool cave.

They were living like wild animals, flying and fucking everywhere they went and Lilah was surprised by how much she enjoyed the ravenousness of their conjoined play.

Glaurakos never felt more at home. More himself. The wilds, the beautiful temptress beneath him as his mate. Nothing had ever felt so right to him, not in all his long years. His mind went to places he dared not let it go before, all thanks to the dizzying high of her flesh. Her companionship.

He bucked into her harder, to both chase the feelings and thoughts away and to embrace them more fervently. To cling to her tighter with his two powerful hands, clasp that pert breast, her tight ass cheek, and pound down into her harder. Make her his with every new act of debauchery.

Perhaps it was their isolation. Maybe they both would have grown bored with one another back on their world, surrounded by temptation and adventure.

Here, the greatest things came from sticking together, and it was bringing them so close together.

Dangerously close.

Lilah kissed him harder, her wings angled awkwardly beneath her lithe body, her pussy teasing him with well-timed squeezes.

Her expert ministrations, how every movement of her body was so perfectly timed to usher pleasure and temptation, did not go unnoticed by the draconic brute. With a lusty roar of ecstasy, his dick swelled within her, throbbing so thickly, and he pounded harder, faster.

The passionate, slow kisses were lost amidst the tumultuous sea of hammering muscular flesh on lithe porcelain. He was a beast unchained, and instead of taming him she only urged him to be wilder. To be more of the animal that lived within as he teetered closer to that precipice of pleasure.

She coaxed out the best and the worst of him, of his nature, and accepted him wholly. Mind, body and soul.

And for one amazing, perfect moment when she looked at him with those seductive and lidded eyes, he saw the acceptance. The acknowledgement of what they meant to one another, of what they shared.

Her lips began to turn upward in a smile of pure adoration, when it was stolen away by a shudder and a moan. Her muscles contracted and released, her body arching as she toppled over the precipice.

Then him with her. Explosively abrupt, he pounded himself into her, each thrust punctuated with a virile flood of seed as he thrust harder with his climax. There was no gentle easing into that moment, nothing but the primal fury of mating, the lust he felt for her so deeply.

Such a shuddering roar came from him that he silenced it with her mouth in a passionate fit. She was his pleasure, his peace, his obsession. She turned him into the full, fiery beast he was always meant to become, and he felt the gratitude for that as he shuddered out the last of his cum in their primal embrace.

CHAPTER 24

Soaring among the snowy mountainsides upon his leathery wings, Glaurakos saw an odd series of structures in the distance. Gesturing back to his companion he swooped around, heading toward a rocky outcropping of wind-blasted stones. With a few heavy flaps of his wings he touched down upon his dark leather-booted feet. Lifting a hand to shield his eyes from the fading sunlight he curled his wings around his shoulders and scanned the structures in the distance, the odd spiral towers, their bizarrely designed steeples. The ancient monastery was peppered with tents and makeshift structures. His handsome face contorted in curious concern, unsure of the inhabitants there.

Lilah's reaction mimicked his concern, slowing to a stop on her delicate wings, letting herself linger in the air as she looked first at the structures, then at him, frowning in thought.

"Be careful," she warned slowly, giving voice to their collective fears. "Anyone or anything could live there. Bandits, maybe." She frowned and looked around at her surroundings, "It'd be a decent enough place to knock off any trading caravans or travelling merchants, for sure. Can you see anyone?

Shaking his head slowly, he finally lowered his hand, turning toward Lilah.

"I can't make out anything that clearly from this distance. However," he started, folding his thick arms over his broad chest, "I can see that it IS occupied, and apparently beyond capacity." He gestured toward the place over his shoulder before turning back to it, "Can you make it out? There are makeshift structures all around the area." His reddish glowing eyes slid back to her, watching for her response.

She squinted and cupped her forehead.

"That's what that is?" she slowly mused, pursing her lips, "Will we go in or go around?" She smiled encouragingly and flew toward him.

Her deference to him did not go unnoticed or unappreciated. She no doubt saw it as manipulating him to her own ends to build him up so, he thought, but he simply enjoyed the way she made him feel regardless.

"You could use a break from the long journey in the cold. And some fresh supplies wouldn't hurt either," he nodded, "We'll check it out — cautiously — and see if we can't purchase a bit of respite. But," he added, pausing briefly, "only after we inspect it close and carefully."

She looked toward the camp as he rendered his verdict, trying to get a better look at the place.

"If we get in close enough I could make myself look as one of them, perhaps, and walk among them. Get a sense for their purpose and disposition," she offered with a small smile, "If you'd so choose." Lilah moved to him, her hands on his chest as she watched the outlines of the tents flitter in the odd breeze.

"Very well. But I'll remain close. I don't wish you to be trapped alone should they see through your disguise," he said, taken in by her sultry voice and slyly worded recommendations. "We'll proceed on foot cautiously," he added protectively.

Lilah sank toward the ground, slowly and carefully so as not to alert any to her presence. As she gracefully touched her toes to the ground she stayed perched atop them. She walked toward the buildings. Moving toward green cover she tried to stay low, her ears perking alertly.

Glaurakos took cover in the rocky landscape as the pair slowly made their way nearer to the structures. When they were within reach, he held up a hand silently, ushering her to stop. Crouching behind a rock he turned to her and drew her in close, whispering to her with his rasping voice in her ear, "They have patrols set up around. But they're amateurs. These aren't bandits. Or if they are, they are lousy ones."

"So, then, what will we do?" she asked, looking to him for guidance, her smooth lips curling into a pleasant smirk, "Should I enter and try to get a better handle on them? We don't exactly look... friendly," she pointed out with a small frown. She could easily pass for a being of ultimate good, of course, angelic as she looked.

Pausing to consider her words, he peered over the rock again, taking sight of the few poorly armed and amateur guards.

"I see a human and what looks like a half-orc... ah, and a half-man," he noted, rubbing the golden skin at his chin. He pondered the situation a while before looking back to her. "They look ragged and unkempt. And the camp appears over crowded, no?" Licking his dark lips he hesitated.

Finally, Glaurakos concocted a plan.

"Here," he offered her one of their satchels, "make yourself look human and approach them casually. Say you've been out foraging for supplies and see how they react." He pulled his hood back up over his horns and golden-orange hair, "If they react well, you'll say your partner is in tow with more, then I'll come. If, however, they give you any hesitation or trouble..." he glances back over the rock, "I'll take them out quickly."

She nodded, taking the bag before moving to sit so that she could better concentrate on her spell, her eyes closing lightly and flittering as her hands and lips moved subtly. After a few moments, her visage changed to one of a strikingly gorgeous human woman, her clothes form-fitting but modest, her hair a light, butter-coloured blonde, pinned up, but messy. With pouty lips and wide, expressive eyes, she looked innocent and beguiling. The smile she gave her lover made her seem even more radiant, and she leaned in to kiss his cheek lightly.

The spell wouldn't last forever, of course. It was a great drain on her energy to create such an elaborate illusion, but it would do in a pinch.

"Be back soon," she whispered before hoisting the bag and walking cautiously toward the buildings.

Ever the obsessive spell caster, Glaurakos watched with intense fascination as his lover changed form before his eyes, taking on the likeness of a striking human woman.

Returning her kiss with his own, those heated lips lingered at her cheek a moment before he let her leave as he crouched at the reach. As she advanced, the scruffy guards, in tattered, worn clothing, mostly ill-suited to the cold climate, were slow to respond. A young human male with light brown hair and a thick, but poor quality fur coat and tattered breeches called out to her, holding up a spear.

"Halt!" He shouted. "No more refugees 'lowed in the camp! We're over full as is!"

Lilah raised her hands in surrender, her sack strapped to her back, her posture modest. She quickly looked over the guards, noting all weapons. She gave an apologetic smile to the human male that spoke to her, a look that most would find disarming, her voice coming out as coy, yet earnest.

"I understand your predicament," she said with a pause, a hint of sadness to it, "I have been foraging for days and would be willing to share my supplies in return for a place to rest. I have a friend, and he bears more. Should we be allowed a place to rest... I'd be ever so grateful," she eyed the human male, fluttering her lashes, a small, pleasant smirk rising to her lips.

The other two guards within range slowly made their way toward the pair as they talked. The others appearing as poorly trained and ill-prepared as the young man, except the half-orc looked on with a glower, seemingly ready to get angry. The young, brown-haired man however, susceptible to Lilah's charms paused a moment.

"You are foragin'... out THERE?" he responded, pointing to the cold wastes all around them. "And you just happened to run across us now?"

Glaurakos, hearing the conversation, tugged his hood down low and then began to walk slowly, as if weary and uncaring, lazily trudging with a slack gait.

She looked behind her, where he pointed, then back at him, smiling.

"So you'd understand why I'd like nothing more than a safe bed to rest upon, Mister, ah..." she paused.

"Aphim miss. Name's Aphim. And if you're in need of a bed, I'm guaranteed one for doin' sentry duty..." his dark eyes trail to the large male slowly approaching behind Lilah, "No room for him though, of course."

"My friend has been of great help in protecting me against threats," she added with a grateful, modest tone, glancing to the other two guards.

The half-orc snorted and turned away, disinterested, while the shortling half-dwarf called out, "Just tell her to share some of those supplies with *us* if she wants to try and get a spot inside!" The tiny woman's voice was shrill as she snickered at the notion of finding a place within to rest.

Lilah smiled, offering her hand, "A pleasure, Aphim. I'm Lily," she blushed a bit as he makes his offer, her eyes twinkling mischievously before she looked behind her to her lover, then back to Aphim.

She leaned in to whisper, her hand on his shoulder, pressing against him suggestively, "Are you sure you haven't room for the two of us? We have bedrolls and can stay on the floor if you wish. It'd still be better than being stuck in a damp cave," she pulled away and looked into his eyes, waiting to see if she'd have to offer more.

The young man was taller than he appeared at a distance, huddling in his coat, his hair long and thick about his ears. He tugged a thick mitten off one hand to take hers, leaning into her as she did to him. He was by no means the match of her half-breed lover, but he had a certain huskiness to his own voice, enhanced by the cold air he breathed in day and night.

"Well miss, that's a tall order. I'm afraid there's no room for that many in my bunk. But if you're willin' to offer somethin', I could see myself to making a sacrifice. 'Course I'd rather just offer up the spot to you to stay with me without any goods," he flashed a toothy smile to her as Glaurakos came to a halt a few meters behind, keeping a distance while she negotiated.

She smiled back at him, pleased with his response; he was clever and played games appropriately, at least. She was grateful for the distance that Glaurakos had given her. They both knew the extent of their bond just as well as their relationship with outsiders, but having grown up around more elves than devils she still concerned herself with the potential for jealousy. She thought back on his possessive grasp earlier with fondness, forcing herself to keep in character as she leaned back into the man.

"My companion can take in the sights of the post while you show me to the quarters. He'll give us ample time to get acquainted and then return to the room for slumber. What more," she said with a pause, peering directly at him, "would you require?"

The young sentry grinned widely, seeming quite pleased with her offer. So much so, he nearly blurted out that he'd accept. More clever than he appeared, however, he gestured towards the camp.

"We'll talk on the way. I'm sure ya foraged up somethin'." He slipped his arm around her shoulders as he turned, calling to the half-orc, "Keep an extra eye out for me, I'll be back in a bit." The orc snorted in annoyance, moving back to his position. The half-man merely rolling her eyes, took watch in her current position.

Lilah cast a fleeting glance to Glaurakos, smiling with a slender shrug of her shoulders, her eyes almost apologetic as she walked away with the human, uncertain whether he'd been granted passage or not. She imagined the orc and the half-man would be more bitter and willing to lash out, she thought, because of the double duty they were serving so the human could get some tail, but that wasn't for her to worry about. Instead, she looked up at the human with her rosy cheeks and innocent smile.

"There's berries, and some bread. Spring water," she added, thinking about what else might be in the bag. She avoided the things that they had gotten from town, "but that's not your interest, is it, Aphim?"

The young man led her back over the rocky terrain to the makeshift town nearby. The tall, elaborate buildings crowded with tents and numerous people crammed around fires. Holding her closely, arm still about her, he leaned in as he spoke, "Well... it's certainly not in competition with what else you've got to offer, Lily," he flashed a handsome smile to her, taking her through narrow corridors between buildings and tents, leading her towards one of the monastery's inner ring towers, "But I'll take some of the rest too," he added with a confident grin.

Meanwhile Glaurakos gave the pair a head start before he followed them in, the other sentries paying him no heed, considering him part of whatever deal was struck. He tailed the other pair until they stepped into one of the buildings, noting where she was before he made any further plans.

Meanwhile inside, Lilah blushed again, modest, letting Aphim feel in control, as though it almost embarrassed her to be striking such a deal but the sweet little schoolgirl in her just couldn't resist his charms. At least, that was the sense she tried to convey. She pressed against him as they walked, entwined in him as they took the stairs upward.

"How long have you been on guard here?" she asked.

Leading her through the chilly wood-and-stone structure, Aphim passed other numerous rooms, most curtained off and containing inhabitants crammed to tight spaces, rooms originally intended to house a single monk in prolonged solitary prayer.

"Months now. Close to a year, I guess," he said, passing the more makeshift shelters and reaching one, the same size and make, but with a door. Unhooking his arms from around her, he reached up to the top of the door, his fingers found clasp, which caused a click as the door swung open. Inside, true to his word, was a space big enough for no more than two people to sleep together, and his meager personal belongings took up much of that, though the look on his face and the status of the other inhabitants gave the clear impression he lived well comparatively.

As she had since she arrived, she took in everything with a quick glance, picking up all nuances and, though she didn't think she had cause to fear, seeking any potential threats. Calming herself with the idea that he was just a lonely guard, stuck in a shitty little town that was overcrowded and depressing, she moved into the room first, placing down her bag next to his things, then turns to look back at him, a seductive glint to her eyes, though her posture spoke of her manufactured nerves.

Pulling off his boots before he entered, Aphim bent down and tucked them in around the corner of his tiny room, in one of the few spots clear of his things or the bedroll he used. Stepping inside with her, he shut the thick mahogany door behind him and undid his fur coat before stepping in, wrapping his arms around her.

"So we got a deal then?" he asked quietly, the slim window above them letting in faint bits of light upon his features.

She looked up at him through her eyelashes, beguilingly, before she glanced away, pretending to be shy, "I've never really..." she paused, blustering at the words, "I mean, you ARE a looker," she paused again, and, as if just realizing what she said, her hands pop over her mouth and her eyes widen, her flush trailing through her body.

Aphim's grin widened as his hands moved over her own fur coat along her shoulder blades and back, feeling her through it.

"Good," he responded before leaning in, the hunger in his eyes betraying his restraint at having such a beauty as he leaned in to kiss her cheek, then lips, his excitement growing quickly.

Lilah yielded to him, playing the role of the shy and inexperienced human, maybe a little too simple for her own good, even as her hands slowly moved to his arms, her body trembling a bit as his lips meet her cheeks, then lips, stealing a gasp from her.

Her eyes closed as she pressed back against him slightly, her breathing heavy through her nose at the anticipation of what was to come. She almost cursed as she thought back on the potion she had taken to prevent pregnancy, though she quickly calculated that it had to have been enough time. Safe, she thought.

Feeling her press back to his lips, his excitement and bravery increased. Hands slid from her, prying at her coat until it fell to the floor, his own quick to drop after hers, revealing a lean but athletic build. He was dressed in worn faded-peach top and grey breeches. He kissed her lips hungrily, licking those pouty morsels as if it had been a long time since the man had gotten such a blessing as a beautiful woman to bed, and never one of her calibre. And it was indeed so, and the boy was bad at hiding it. His hands dove in to feel her body atop her clothes, his pants tented by his arousal.

Her clingy dress ended part way down her thighs; her boots ended at her knees. Even when dressed modestly, under the guise of a foraging woman, she couldn't help but bare a little thigh. Her body was curvier than she was used to, softer and with less tone, but pleasing, exquisite to explore. Feeling his excitement grow as she returned his affections, she let him guide her, following his lead as she explored his mouth with her tongue, her breath warm against his upper lip.

The young sentry was in a hurry, and guided her down to the bed roll to lay her out as his hands moved across her legs, feeling the bare thigh before curling in her skirt to tug it upward. This was no romantic fling, it was a barter, and he was going to get his part before he had to rush back to his duty.

He'd was pleasantly surprised to find that no underclothes hid her body from him, and though her knees bent inwards for a moment, hiding her slickened slit from his eyes, her scent rose to the air and she slowly let her legs fall lax, clothed from the waist up as she relaxed against the bedroll, looking up at him with a heated flush.

"Be gentle?" she pleaded softly, definitely more of a question than a request. Lilah figured she might as well get something for the bargain, after all.

Dropping to his knees between her legs, he paused and looked into her lovely — albeit mystically fake — eyes before nodding quickly after a pause and kissing her again. One of his hands moved to his waist, tugging down his worn breaches to reveal his shaft. Though nothing approaching her usual lover, he was sizable and girthy, and his swollen tip was already half exposed from his foreskin even before he sank between her thighs to prod it at her cunt. Finding her ready, he wasted no time, though tried to keep her request in mind, plunging nervously into her slick slit with care as he gave a low moan.

Lilah met his kiss, hungrily lingering against his mouth before resting back, staring at him with anticipation. She watched his face, his eyes, studying him before she suddenly felt hot flesh touching to her swollen mound, and her head tilting backwards. She couldn't help but to moan as he pressed into her tight entrance, her legs tilting her pelvis upwards to allow him a deep descent, her back arching at the same time.

The tightness of her surprised him, both from how long it had been since he had taken a woman, and from her other worldly body yet again astounding with another flawless feature. It took all his concentration and focus not to lose himself right then and there, but he quickly began to pull back then push in again, thrusting into her as he began to fuck her for the offer of trade. The handsome young man was all breathy moans, unrestrained as he rode atop her, her slick cunt gripping him as he let his hands feel over her body, squeezing a breast through her top.

As she felt his tense shudder of pleasure as he plunged into her, she let out another long, drawn out sigh of pleasure, inhaling deeply and, as he began to thrust.

"We have time," she said before adding, "if your libido is strong," she blushed and tilted further, feeling him plunge so readily into her slick cunt, reveling in the feeling, writhing beneath him. Sure, it wasn't Glaurakos... but she was sure he'd come to her out of jealousy and take her as soon as they had a moment. The thrill ran through her deeply, and only made the fling more exciting.

Hearing her words he lunged down, his panting mouth kissing her as he thrust wildly, clumsily. Where his motions lacked in finesse, they excelled in eagerness. He restrained himself somewhat, as per her request. He felt her slick cunt cling to his throbbing cock, coaxing him toward her. Suddenly, he shot his load into her with a loud gasping groan, pulling his lips from hers as he writhed and bucked atop her with each spurt of cum until he was finished, and merely laying atop her panting.

She was filled with warmth, emotional warmth, at bringing another to pleasure, having one use her so, trading her way to what she needed. It all filled with a strange type of pleasure and warmth, and her arms rose, holding him to her as his cum slowly leaked from her slit, the pearly beads descending toward the bedroll. She gasped for breath below him, licking her lips and moving to stroke along his jaw line.

Finished, he seems somehow pacified, and looked upon her as if he'd like to linger and remain held by her, and likely go again before long. After a brief kiss he responded in a whisper, "I have to get back to duty. Else I won't have a place to trade you for long," he gave a slight smirk before kissing her again, "Let's say... we meet for this again and all's even, huh?"

She nodded, sneaking in for a kiss after his words, her head tilting, her nose pressing to his. She pants beneath him, not able to do much else with him atop her, her hand traveling through his hair quickly, "How long may we stay?" she asked quietly, her voice still laced with her latent charm.

Slipping out of her cunt, he tugged his pants up over his still turgid cock, tying them shut as best he can over the bulge while smiling down at her. Standing up he pulled his coat back on in a hurry, "As long as you'd like to keep paying 'rent'," he replied, winking to her as he slipped on his boots, preparing to leave.

Lilah sits up, dribbling his cum down along towards the bed, nodding in agreement at the arrangement,

"You're too kind, Aphim," she stroked his ego with a smile, gnawing on her lower lip for a moment,

"I'm sure I'll see you again soon," she moved up to her knees, lowering her dress around her thighs modestly.

Her house warming party having left, she took the time to look around more carefully at the small room; it really didn't take her much time, however, and she quickly cleaned herself of the other man's spent seed. She was unsure of her footing with Glaurakos as is, and didn't want to upset him. It was just work. For him. She hoped he wouldn't be upset. She was stuck in the human woman's form, at least for the time being, uncertain when the human male may poke in and how he might respond to an angelic figure laying within. She mused for a few more moments before slowly settling down to rest her mind.

CHAPTER 25

Having followed the pair to the tower, Glaurakos was going on about his business of skulking through the monastery, doing his usual listening and observation. These adventures of his were always solitary, quiet affairs. He hung close to the shadows and kept out of sight of crowded refugees as best he could. He left his lover to her business with full confidence she could handle the situation should it turn bad, the male appeared nothing impressive by all of his reckoning. All the same, he didn't tarry over long, and returned before she was left waiting alone too long.

Scanning the aisles, and the numerous little chambers that served as bedrooms he counted down until he found the one the pair had disappeared into. Cautiously he pressed his pointed elven ear to the thick wooden door, listening for sound. Hearing none, he rapped his knuckles in a brief knock upon it, waiting.

Her eyes opened slowly at the knock, as though coming from a deep sleep. She slipped to her feet, still wearing the steel blue dress and brown boots, her coat hanging on some of Aphim's things. She opened the door slowly, peaking out with a warm smile on her face for whomever may have knocked. Seeing her lover there, though, the look turned genuine, and she ushered him in to the tiny room.

"Ah, there you are. I was wondering when you'd come," she chimed.

With his back straight, he peered in as she cracks open the door. Then with her greeting he brought his hand up, placing it within and helping push open the door further, inspecting the tiny room with an obvious amount of disdain, going so far as to even let his upper lip tremble with an urge to curl.

"This is what you paid for?" he asked angrily, shutting the door behind him as the large, hulking dragon-blood seemed to make the room far more crowded than it had been when Aphim had occupied it with her. "This whole place is packed to the brim with the refugees here."

She frowned at his words, taking it as a slight chastisement, feeling defensive for a moment, "It's likely the best the town has to offer. If you'd rather me sleep in the caves while you watch over for me, I'm sure I wouldn't have to pay over much for that," she states rather sullenly, her lower lip drawn into a pout as she looked up at him, finding him so much taller than her in her new human form, "I'd like to see you find better in this place."

His thick boots carelessly tread upon the bedroll and items, soiling them with the traces of snow and mud he tracked in. She frowned at the mud and snow, knowing she'd soon be sleeping there and caring not to mimic the living quarters of the outdoors any further than she had to.

The large half-breed noted her response, and read more into it still. More than she was likely to feel. She, he thought, had traded an act of carnality for the place and took offense to her sacrifice being diminished by him. A pang of remorse hit him, and he perceived himself more than a little brutish then, his brows lowered and expression softening. Reaching out, he took hold of her by the elbow, then swept his other arm in around her waist, finding her form more full than he was accustomed to after their long sojourn together, ever in her natural form. Tugging her in against him he looked down upon her before lunging in and kissing her lips excitedly before breaking off to murmur in his deep, gravelly voice, "Our arrangement is beyond need of payment now."

As he drew her into him, she found herself less concerned for the snow, the brief flurry of the passionate embrace sweeping her up and calming her down, her lips meeting his eagerly, stood up on tip toes as always, though it still didn't bring her to an appropriate height, "We can stay as long as I," she paused, "pay rent."

Still holding her firmly at the arm and around her waist, he stroked his hands over her form, his apology had been the silent type, given in gesture and not words it would embarrass him to say. "But of course," he said in a rumbling voice, a slight edge of distaste to his words. "We won't be around long, regardless. I wished only to give you a respite from the cold winds and travel a while. And in the meantime, I'll see if I can't find you something better to rest in. Of my own means." He gave her a slight smile then.

She nodded, relaxing against him and fluttering her eyes closed, "I doubt we'll be able to get many supplies here, from what I saw. But perhaps they'll know of nearer places that might serve our needs." She frowned as she worried vaguely over how long they'd be in this place, having run from the only town they've come across with anything even remotely suitable to her tastes. She had pushed the agonizing aside while they were in the wilds, but it crashed into her now that they were relatively safe.

His large hand stroked the center of her back, his heated grasp soothingly touching upon her as he leaned down and gave a brief but moist kiss to her full lips again.

"I've some ideas. But you're right, we won't find much here. And whatever we do get will come at a high cost, because they cling to what little they have tenaciously." His glowing orange-red eyes sized up her face slowly, fully, taking in her now foreign features, from the blonde hair on down, "There seems to be at least one powerful gang that runs, or at least lords over, much of the enclave here. They'll be first upon my list for dealings."

Her eyes followed his with an intense flare.

"I see," she said, licking her lower lip, worrying on it in her thought, "That makes sense, I suppose. I'd be loath to lose anything we have as well."

She trailed her fingers down over his arms, feeling his unnatural heat and instinctively moving toward it. "At least we don't need to worry about any dragons," but one, she thought. "And you can rest, finally."

Presumptively, perhaps, he often took on a protective, possessive demeanor with her. His look, the way he gazed at and held her, often seemed so very territorial, so very jealously male, she thought. Though it rarely seemed to bubble over beyond that, as he did not attempt to restrict or control her — much anyhow. Releasing her arm he brought his hand up, brushing his sharp fingers over her cheek affectionately, seemingly touched by her concern, though he wouldn't let it show upon his stony, masculine exterior.

"Yes," he grated, his usually gravelly voice all the more hoarse from his lack of a good night's sleep in so long, "But don't worry about what we have. I don't plan to trade away our things."

She looked toward the bedroll with a frown, drawing in her lower lip and once more looking up to him, "Should we, perhaps," she looked back at him, her lower lip glossy from their kisses and her repeated worrying over her mouth. "You should relax. You've earned it many times over for keeping your eyes on me as I slept," she said, then suggested, "I could massage you."

His eyelids drooped, from weariness and increasing desire.

"I'd like that," he said in his low tenor, "And you'll curl up with me to sleep after." It wasn't a question. Shifting his head and neck, he reaches up and pulls back his hood, shaking free his thick head of lustrous golden-orange hair, refusing to let his weariness show as best he could while lowering down to the bed roll, pulling her with him as he sank to his knees.

She melted down with him, her hands moving around his neck. When at last his body met the rather uncomfortable bedroll, adequately cleaned of her payment arrangement's messy after effects, she moved behind him and, with slow, tender fingers, began to prod at his muscles. She sought to relieve his surface tension, her fingers eagerly rubbing along his neck and the tops of his shoulders under his clothing.

Eyes shutting at her touch, his head dipped forward a little, giving a low groan that turned into a growl as she rubbed his heated flesh. Reaching his own hands to his chest, he undid some clasps, the dark leather immediately loosening, ready to be removed.

"What's this tower of yours like?" he asked, his gruff voice betraying his curiosity to know more about her and where she came from.

Her hands paused their removal of his tunic for only a moment as his question passed his lips, her head tilting to the side. She closes her eyes, resuming her gentle ministrations on his flesh.

"Rather splendid. Along a tall cliff side, partially built into the natural side of the rocks. Fabulous number of hidden rooms, libraries. You'd be happy," she said, silently wondering what might have come of Sho'ar, of her home. Her facial expression fell and she had to avert her eyes. Had it been lost in her absence? Her hand touched over the top of his gently, stroking him with a tenderness she rarely expressed. Her city wasn't what it once was, but being stuck on another plane... all she wanted to do was go home. With her new companion.

His flesh was tough with the thick muscle beneath his orange and often ruddy flecked skin, but he seemed to respond well to her ministrations, groaning lowly with her rubbing. Nodding ever so slightly to her words, he replied, "Indeed. And what shall we do once there, hrrmmh? Do you have plans already made that our alliance might help bring to fruition, is that it?" His husky voice was filled only with curiosity and appreciation as she works his body with her skillful hands.

"I'm open to suggestions," she said finally after digging out a tight knot at the base of his neck, "Any plans I did have would need to be modified after so long away."

Reaching a hand up, he grasped for one of her slender wrists, taking hold of it as he then twists his upper body to stare up at her from beneath. The gesture came slowly, wearily, those glowing eyes of his peering up at her as he twisted around onto his elbows and lower back. With a slow lick of his reddish lips he hoarsely continued, "I am always full of plans. But I can't say much until I know what it is I have to work with. What it is your home offers us, both in and of itself and with its location." His other hand moved to her leg, sliding up her thigh, rolling her skirt a bit upwards.

She looked at him as he moved her, eyes drawn to his tongue before flickering back to his eyes, her breath coming in rapid beats as her voice lowered, "I don't know the situation in Sho'ar," she started slowly, her eyes moving between his and his hand along her thigh, the skin creamy but darker than her usual tone, the leg fleshier and more womanly, "It's hard to say what the situation would be there, I hate to say," she admitted with a worried frown.

The sharp points of his claws traced up her creamy flesh, leaving indented trails along her skin as he slowly hiked up her skirt, rolling it to her hip before releasing her hand again. His own broad, muscular chest heaving slow and rhythmically as he gazed up at her with lidded eyes that contained a strong desire for her. "I've no doubt of our combined abilities to exploit any situation, Lilah." His heavy voice was full of conviction, confidence. He touched her with a certain amount of kindness, though, rather than power. As if he were trying to reassure her.

She smiled, nodding and tilting her head downwards for a moment, "I just fear I don't have enough to go on for plans until we get back. But, if nothing else, my tower will provide you with anything you could want for luxuries. It's... large. Spacious. My father was wealthy and left it all to me," she said softly, as though ashamed, her body moving towards his with a small, crooked smile.

His other hand slid up her thigh, moving her tight little skirt up to her hip. He then trailed both palms back down before hoisting her a little, tugging her so she sat atop his groin while he pressed up against her.

"Luxuries are nice. Though you suit me just fine for my luxurious requirements, Lily." He said with a smirk, grinding himself suggestively up against her in his weary state. "It should make a fine center of power for our burgeoning plans, I imagine."

One hand flittered to his chest while she balanced herself against the wall as he positioned her above him. She looked down upon him seriously. She hated feeling soft, but being raised around the avian angels of Sho'ar, as wicked as they were to one another, had imparted some sweetness there. She had mourned the death of her father, but it had to have been done. She consoled herself with that. That and the fact that he knew it was coming. He had to have.

She smiled down at her devilish lover, wondering what might happen to her should he ever become cross with her. She couldn't wait to get off the island; at least then she wouldn't feel so afraid.

She rubbed his chest playfully, "Then you'll love the tower," she said.

One of his hands moved back up her thigh then across to her ass, cupping a cheek and lifting her. She hadn't taken his hint, or perhaps she just wished to force him to take the hand in starting their tryst even now, regardless, he reached between them with his other, unbuckling his pants and freeing his thick, heated shaft. He, of course, knew she had just a while ago fucked that simpering human, but it didn't seem to bother him as he rests her back down atop his now bare member.

"Love's a strong word," he said simply, letting a hand roam up her body, feeling her chest through her top. Truthfully he did feel strongly for her, and his constant resistance to that seemed to do little to stop it. "With my help you'll re-establish yourself quicker than you think, and from there... we expand."

She often enjoyed putting the power in his hands and tonight was no exception, moving gracefully atop him as though part of some dance as he unsheathed his member, settling her slickened slit atop him, still wet from the quick fucking not so long ago, her heat paling in comparison to him. She ground, lightly, teasingly, as she looked down at him, a studious pause to her face.

"There's nothing that you won't adore in the tower. Spell books beyond your reckoning. Ancient tomes. A massive..." she paused, "alchemy lab," she said, licking her lips as she leaned forward, her slit positioned against his head, "I think you'll love it."

With a long, appreciative groan, he nodded, wearily angling his hips to nudge his tip to her slit, though lacking in his usual finesse and control. He leaned up and licked her pouty lips before he answered, "I'm beginning to believe you," he replied, adding huskily, "And what will that make us then, hrrmmh?" He regretted the words before he had even finished saying them. He didn't truly understand their relationship, and feared such questioning or delving would only succeed in either alienating her or opening him to being manipulated by her all the more.

She stared at him as she slowly pushed back, her hand aiding her in the impaling of herself upon his thick cock, the slickness of her cunt rapidly heating as it met his unnatural warmth, her eyes rolling back just slightly as she does so, letting out a small sigh of satisfaction, both hands upon his chest. "What would you like it to make us?" she asked softly, kindly, her human body beginning to slowly pump up and down his shaft.

His own eyes rolled back the same as hers, a low rumbling growl coming up from his chest as she sank down around his shaft, then began to slowly ride upon his thick, hot cock. Hands dug into her thicker flesh, grasping her thigh and breast, claws curling into her top to tug it down and expose one of her mounds of flesh. Her response was probably the most calculated and cunning. Oh, how she played upon his weaknesses so effectively, he thought; she was a masterful charmer, and even then, in his weary state, he could only admire that aspect of her.

Licking his lips and sharp fangs, he was slow to respond, mulling over his response as best he could. "Partners," he concluded on.

She maintained her speed, careful to allow him as quick of release as possible so he might find some rest. Her cunt tightened around him with a strong grasp, her juices allowing easy movement, a silken ride. She smiled as her back arched, exposing her larger breasts to him, the globes bouncing with each masterful pummel downwards. She smiled at his sly answer, her eyes lidded as they examined him. It was, really, the best she could hope for, she imagined. She felt he would, at least, honour any agreements they made. Or, at least, she hoped.

He watched, through narrow slits, as her large, heavy breast bounced and slapped against her chest with her motions atop his shaft before grasping at it, clutching and squeezing the ripe mound as his other hand gripped her hip, encouraging her motions with a squeeze. His lips were parted, breathing heavily as her expert body rode him, eliciting such pleasure, and though they hadn't given their fucking a rest upon the long, harsh journey, he knew she would get what she wished from him before long. He always had a nagging feeling that she was playing him like a puppet, and that any long-term agreement would see him being her willing pawn. But there he was, willing pawn, and he justified it even now upon the premise that even if it were true, he could reverse his fortunes later.

Grunting beneath her, he croaked, "And what would you like it to make us?" mirroring her question back at her.

She smiled, a look of lust tinted pleasure and happiness that reached her eyes as she looked down upon him, holding her rhythm before slowly picking up the pace, her leg muscles tensing before dropping down, feeling his thick cock slam into her tender inner wall, a quick bolt of pain-induced ecstasy trailing through her. Her light curls bounced as she continued to ride him, her voice seeded with lust.

"There are no words for it," she said, a mysterious hint to her voice, teasing and seductive.

The abandonment with which she rode him, the teasing and skillful way she responded, all succeeded in awakening the last of his energy reserves. With a sound like a snarl, he rose up and clutched his arms around her, plunging in and kissing her ravenously before flipping them both over and resting her ass and back to the hard floor. His powerful body woke from its weary rest, and he rutted into her with fierce excitement. When finally their lips broke, he groaned out his words, "Dammit, I--" his voice became strained, his sentence broken either by the moment or by restraint not to embarrass himself or give too much away, but he pounded into her roughly and felt his loins tingle with satisfaction.

She delighted in having him take control once more, to have brought him to the brink and forced him to take action, even as the bedroll scratched her sensitive flesh, she revelled in the feeling of him pounding into her, a flurry of sensations traversing her body, her head fogging over as her mouth mashed against his hungrily. As his words were cut off she stared at him through lidded eyes, curiosity pushing aside her pleasurable sensations for a brief moment as her hands trailed along his neck and in through his thick hair.

"You?" she asked.

So roughly he pounded into her, in such quick succession, the noise of their fucking echoed loudly in their tiny room, and made a ruckus that bothered and alerted nearly all on the same floor as them. He could feel his cock tingle and swell within her, his release impending as he took no pause in fucking her, his muscles tensing as he struck at her expertly, his body perfectly poised over her to display his amazing physique, the tracing of his abs and pecs bulging with the strain as he hammered into her. He responded to her with some delay, drawing the final moments of their fucking out as long as he could manage, her cunt clinging to him.

His words came out slowly, "I will have you, again and again... for a very long time." It wasn't likely what he was going to say, but it sufficed, he thought.

She softened back into the bedroll, eased, her hips tilting upwards towards him.

"Cum in me, lover," she demanded, her eyes beckoning him, her body teasing him to the point of no return, urging him to delve so deeply within her, unbothered by the noise they were making. "And again and again," she added, her breathing coming out in rapid pants, her eyes wondering over his displayed body and enjoying the contrast of their two tones of flesh striking at one another.

Her request aided in his timely arrival, eyes shutting as he huffed, thrusting into her as his body shivered and pulsed with his oncoming release. Arching his head back, he let out a deep, loud moan and cry as he gave long, hard spasming jerks of his shaft in and out, burying himself in with each release of his seed, the long jets of cum coating her insides more violently than the man before him. She clutched him to her as he reached his zenith, holding him deep within her.

When finally the thrusting came to a slow, tapered finale, he grunted and wavers on his arms, lowering himself down then taking hold of her before flipping them both over, pulling her on top of him as he still lay within her folds.

Clutching her, he rested, eyes still shut, as the weary half-breed looked ready to doze off immediately. Despite that though, he raised a hand to her head and pulled her in, kissing her again, murmuring a fond string of words.

She smiled as he rolled her on top of him, looking soft and sweet atop him before he dragged her to his lips. Briefly her mind wandered back to the human, wondering when he'd leave his post and what he'd do when he saw the half fiend in his room, exposed as he was. She figured that, worst case scenario, it'd be best to have Glaurakos' cock... hidden from view, glistening and magnificent though it was, and she struggled from him, buttoning it up with quick fingers and moving to grab their blanket, pulling it over them and holding herself to him.

With a shift of his bulky frame, he clung to her tightly, not seeming to like her removal of his shaft from her confines though being too near to sleep to object further. His unnatural heat was strong beneath the covers, though he was unbothered by it and seemed unwilling to relinquish her from the hold despite any sweaty discomfort. She wasn't used to the heat and found herself growing slick in the confined room, warmed by their lovemaking, but staying curled to him nonetheless.

"Sweet dreams," she wished quietly.

Reclining, he gave a low, barely audible grunt in response to her greeting before murmuring her name affectionately, his strong face outlined by his black horns and golden-orange hair.

CHAPTER 26

"We'll stick to our strengths," Glaurakos reassured the avian softly.

They stood on the outskirts of the refugee camp, talking in whispered tones lest one of the guards overhear them.

He'd told her that the cold weather was too hard on her and scouting out the location of the portal and the dragon hoard would not be easy or fast. "So you will stay here and tend to camp for us. Establish us within the refugees and get together what supplies and information you can. I'll seek out the lay of the land and return when I have more to report."

Lilah's face was sour, even as she agreed with him. Neither would admit how much they would miss the other when Glaurakos parted that afternoon in search of an escape for them.

CHAPTER 27

Lilah knew that Glaurakos was truly motivated with concern for her, but now she was in the tiny room they were "renting" all on her own, the evening approaching in the crowded monastery turned bustling town.

There were few things that Lilah hated more than being alone. Truthfully it was why she had lived with her father so long, long after he had taught her all he knew and given her all he had. Loneliness didn't sit well with her, and bad decisions were quick to follow. Still, though, she had agreed that she wasn't cut out for long travel in the snowy regions. She was too thin, disliked clothes too much, to be of much use, and knew she'd only worry him further if she went. She made him careless.

She stood, dressing and taking on the visage of the human woman she had adopted for the occasion, primping herself with some disdain. She figured this would be a temporary thing... a few days maybe. She missed her own body, her own face, and her wings. The weight was still heavy on her back and she tried to flutter them, but the spell rendered them nearly useless as well as invisible.

Still, she brought her periwinkle jacket around her shoulders as she set out toward the door in search of food.

The level of the monastery Lilah resided in was no less crowded and bustling than ever as she set foot outside. People crammed around fires and the entrances to tents, humans huddling together everywhere in the chill wind that blew down from the mountains. However, from up one of the massively wide stone stairways a large procession could be seen pushing through the masses. Even with how tightly crammed everyone was together, many seemed to cry out and try to rush out of the way of the group. It took a while before she saw them, and a man next to her grumbled fretfully, "Not them again."

She could see the group was an odd mix, not a human amongst them that wasn't scurrying out of their way. Half-orcs, half-breeds, even brutish half-trolls. All monstrosities of interbreeding, they were gruff and hard from a lifetime of discrimination. Neither the orcs nor the trolls cared for such intermingling, and the half-breed demons like Glaurakos were never welcomed with open arms.

The group moved in a procession, and giving stiff shoves to anyone in their way.

She looked to the man next to her with an incredulous gaze, her wide, expressive eyes opened in concern.

"Who are they?" she asked in a hushed tone before her gaze was drawn back to the procession. The body she took was that of a beautiful woman with blond, curly hair the colour of butter, glinting in the dimming light, her lips naturally pouted, her complexion giving her almost a permanent blush.

The man beside her was plump, despite the shortage of food and supplies. He was wrapped in worn old leathers and a scruffy fur hat. Without looking to Lilah he answered her question, "Some gang of misfits. They've got a lot of muscle, but they don't care for us humans, or even most full-breeds, to be honest," he said with distaste. "If they're up here it's no doubt to make trouble or take somethin'." The procession meanwhile stayed true as they shoved through people, the many various members of the mixed gang carrying weapons — actual weapons in some cases — as they moved off towards one of the larger tents.

She frowned, giving the man an appropriate nod, taking a moment to look around the area.

"Who's in charge?" she asked, a plan churning in her head, her eyes seeking some temporary respite from others' gaze.

The portly man raised a brow and looked over at her for just a moment. "In charge? Of them?" He snorted distastefully, "Some half-beast they say. One of them man-beasts. Though dependin' on who you ask, what *kind* of man-beast changes."

"I see. So he doesn't come with them?" Well, so much for that. Still, she doubted some cute-as-a-button human was going to beguile them away. She moved towards the nearest private spot she could find.

The man began to answer, but noticed her walking off. With a shrug of his heavy set shoulders he looked back to watch the scene at the large tent, the head of the procession seemed to be discussing something with a tall human man.

With the commotion, it wasn't terribly hard for Lilah to find a spare spot behind a tower or tent out of view.

Quickly she slipped off the disguise, enjoying the stretch of her white wings. Her clothing, too, had slipped from her and left her in her typical regalia of skirt and cropped top, her warm winter boots crawling up to her knees. She took flight, then, soaring for a moment before reaching the human, flittering down next to his side, looking for the rabble's reaction.

The head of the procession — a large, towering half-troll that seemed barely capable of talking coherently — was gruffly arguing with the tall human man, apparently some sort of military figure judging by his worn armour. All of them went quiet as the angelic figure fluttered down beside the captain, so many curious eyes wide and staring, red, golden, green, and blue. Finally the half-ogre called out, "What's this trickery?!"

"Why are you bothering these people?" Lilah let her voice raise confidently over the silence, not lacking her signature seductive tone, "They have nothing for themselves," she added, looking briefly over the mass of refugees doubtlessly trying to flee from the chaos of this realm's sorceress disaster, then back at the half-troll, knowing she wasn't likely to get an answer from him.

A small man with narrow, keen eyes and a sleek, bald head stepped from the gang's midst. He had markings down his smooth scalp, and his skin was pale grey. He hissed, "Why do you defend them? Are you some sort of saviour come to defend the bigots?" He wore a black, hooded robe that was cinched tightly about his waist. Though he looked human at first glance, Lilah soon realised he wasn't.

She looked at the man a long time, considering him.

"If they are bigots, who's to say they're wrong in this? You come and, what, extort them every few days? Weeks? And they grow sore toward those that don't look like them? You're just feeding their misperceptions," she leaned forward, her sleek form on view, "These people are not unkind, but they are stressed, they are worried, they have lost much, and you seek to bleed them for every bit they haven't lost? Of course they're upset with you!" she said softly, her voice wrought with compassion, "There must be another way. A better way."

The grey-skinned man hissed at her distastefully, the whole group of them all reacting with irritation and anger.

"Oh shut it up," someone said from in back. A scaly-skinned orc-like man spoke up, "This is dumb.

Some victims these humans are, who expelled us all to the lower reaches in the first place to starve. They're forcin' us to group up."

The half-ogre grunted loudly, his oafish, booming voice resounding, "Yeah, shut up little woman."

The human captain just sort of looked around awkwardly, not sure what to make of the odd interruption.

Her eyes narrowed as she looked at the rabble, "What more do you expect from them? For both groups to starve to death? Then you'll be happy?"

The smallish, hissing man spoke softly beneath the din of angry voices, "You don't know what you're involving yourself in if you're here to side against us. You'd be wise to move along."

"Yeah, well, I can't. I'm stuck here, and I'd rather not have to be hiding from your lot for the rest of my stay here," she affirmed, looking at the man, unflinching but for the ruffle of her wings, "And I wish to speak to your leader about what arrangements can be made to ensure this will remain amiable."

The lumbering half-ogre reached a large hand out to shove the lithe avian out of the way, his strength immense. The gesture was but a small twitch of his muscle to him.

"Then bring the dumb girl back, am finishing business first!" he exclaimed.

The human captain and the rest of his refugees did nothing in support of her, either afraid or unconcerned, though a half-orc moved to catch her and keep her from falling.

She let out a light cry of shock, her wings twitching against the half-orc as she caught her balance, offering him a smile.

"Thanks," she replied softly, looking properly admonished, waiting for the argument to be over. She really had no good deal of love or compassion for the humans at the monastery, but it was a meeting spot and she'd like to keep her place here.

The half-orc had only a nod for her in return, lifting her up and giving her a push towards the back of the group. The throng of mixed beings absorbed her and she found herself quickly surrounded away from the front, from then on only able to hear the occasional loud bellowing of the half-ogre. Pressed so tightly amongst them all there would be no way for her to take wing. Though the small bald man, looking somehow young and fit, cropped back up beside her, hissing, "You are a fool to intervene so. You have no idea what you're getting in to."

"Probably not," she admitted to him, her eyes moving to the sky as she shifted slightly. She smiled, trying to seem unfazed, "But I suppose I'll soon find out, won't I?"

The grey-skinned man looked displeased before pushing back through the throng. The negotiations didn't last much longer, and soon the group was moving back around to where they had come from. The push of so many large and strong bodies around her kept her moving with them, no real room to resist the flow as they set off down the wide stairway.

CHAPTER 28

From out of the crowd a young man with an oddly thick mane of wheat-gold hair, and abnormally flat nose with almost feline eyes wrapped a sharply nailed hand around her upper arm. In a firm voice he said to her, "I'm taking you to the chief."

"I'm the one that asked to see him. It's not like I'm going to turn heel now," she frowned, trying to shake off his hand, "Besides, it's not like I'm going anywhere, even if I wanted to," she added on for good measure, "You needn't mar my skin while we're being friendly."

The man seemed unmoved, his strangely exotic features still and firm as he dragged her along with the gang. He didn't respond to her, but as they descended into the lower reaches of the monastery, he separated from the gang and into the crowd. There, other various half-breeds and 'lesser' races milled about much as the humans did above, though there were fewer tents and buildings available. Her captor dragged her toward a large building.

As they separated from the crowd, Lilah took longer strides and fluttering her wings. She plastered a look of steely confidence on her face, and was actually pleased for the lack of cold, cutting wind. She didn't see why they'd be so upset about having to live below, all said, even though she had to blink a bit to adjust her eyes to the dark.

Leading her onward, he marched her past some mix of guards and into the main building. What was once a storage place for the monks was now divided up into residences, many of the inhabitants crowded around various rooms. Finally he brought her past two more guards and into a small chamber, crammed with crates.

"Wait here," he instructed, waiting for an answer from her.

"Wouldn't rather be any other place," she chirped with a smile, avoiding the crates lest they give out beneath her and cause another kerfuffle. She really thought this one through, she mused bitterly. Squaring her shoulders, she flickered her wings and settled in to wait.

The man finally let her go and left the room. He left her there for a while. It was ten minutes or so before a secret wooden door along the back wall opened up.

"Come in," a mysterious voice said gruffly.

Lilah made her way through the new entrance — after spending her waiting time preening her outfit and her hair. She walked gracefully, a warm smile on her lips for whomever first she saw. She felt good about this, she thought, and planned to be back in her roommate's bed before dawn.

Lilah found herself in a makeshift office, stairs leading up from the entrance to a higher level. A desk sat beneath a high window; wooden shutters opened to the cold air outside. There were shelves with scrolls and books upon them on one wall, a bed on the other, and another door to her right.

The only other inhabitant of the room was a man that looked a great deal like the oddly feral fellow who guided her there. However, this one seemed older, his hair thick and golden, swept back behind him and around his shoulders, framing his face. He had narrow, almond-shaped eyes with dark rims around the edges, almost like a natural mascara. He had a flat nose that gave him a feline appearance; he was quite certainly not a full human. He wore a suit of specially crafted ceremonial armour, mail beneath a black outer layer with intricate designs stitched into the fabric. His skin was smooth and a deep golden-brown, he was standing behind the desk and observing her with a curious gaze.

She returned his gaze and took another step in.

"Good evening, Sir," she greeted with a bit of a curtsey, dropping her gaze for a moment. "I don't wish to waste any time of yours further than need be," she said, raising her eyes to him once more, "Thank you for meeting with me."

He kept his position, studying her a while longer.

"What are you?" he asked finally, in a deep, rolling voice. He had no pretence for formalities.

"Whatever you want me to be," she offered, taking a step towards him, eyes looking away from him and then back, "But was that why I was brought here?"

His eyes narrowed and he took a deep breath.

"What are you?" he repeated, not seeming to be in much of a mood for coyness, "You weren't brought her for games, so just tell me what you are, and then we can get to why you're defending those vermin up there."

She sighed and rolled her eyes.

"A half-breed," she stated, meeting his eyes once more. "And I defend those up there because I need a place to stay, and they let me in once I... altered my form. I'd rather not starve, though, or have the people around me in more dire straits so that I can be assured a comfortable, happy vacation." Though her words were laced with sarcasm, she spoke truthfully.

The man, a good six feet tall, she approximated, furrowed his brows and looked her over again.

"You're telling the truth, aren't you?" he asked. Sizing her up, he stepped around the desk, his clawed feet bare beneath his armoured legs. "So you hide amongst the humans pretending to be one of them so they'd let you have a place to stay, and you're causing trouble with us for THAT?"

She smiled up at him, though she was only half foot shorter than he, offering him a small shrug.

"Call me a pacifist, I guess," she dodged through her pouted lips, "Plus I was curious what was happening around here."

Looking at her darkly, he circled her, tilting his head as he inspected the lithe half-breed and her scantily clad form.

"You investigate what's happening by blindly choosing a side against your own kind in defense of some humans who'd never have let you stay knowingly?" he interrogated, growing irritated.

"I didn't choose a side. I got attention, and I got to come speak with you, didn't I? Who told you I picked a side?" She smiled up at him, not bothered by his scrutinizing gaze, "I just assumed there to be a better way to deal with this so that both sides would win. Wouldn't that be nice?"

Arching a brow he stood before her.

"So it was all a ploy, ridiculing us and speaking against us? Just a means to get to see me, is that what you're saying?" He snorts lightly, "To negotiate between us? You don't even know what's going on here, do you?"

"Not the slightest. And are you telling me you'd just as likely see me if I were some mindless winged thing that joined in your fight?" She rolls her eyes, "In my experience, half-breeds would rather rape then discard a potential ally, but I had hoped they'd at least let me see you if I was figured to be an enemy. You'd want me interrogated, to see if I was alone, just how deep my treachery ran, right? And then the raping and the killing, but," she shrugged her shoulders, "I got here in once piece and I'm having a lovely conversation with you, so it's best not to think on the whys and hows, and focus more on the whats. You know. What's happening. What's going to happen."

His hands still clasped behind his back, he huffed in a light laugh at her words. With a slow shake of his head, he looked her over once more.

"What a strange woman you are," he shook his head, licking his lips and displaying his sharp fangs before reaching up to stroke his smooth, dark hued chin, "If you had just come to us we would've given you a place to stay with your own kind, without the pretense. We don't turn away our own here, no matter how bad things might be." With a low rumble in his throat, he gave her a long stare, "That's our way."

"To be fair, Sir, I didn't know you lot were here until after I had secured a room. And now, well, I have a friend that's set to meet me there in... well, I'm not sure how long, but in a while. I'd like to be there, in one piece, in order to be found. What are you raiding for?"

"Raiding?" The strange, feral man furrowed his brows and looked to her curiously. With a snort he huffed and turned to his desk, unfurling his hands and waving them dismissively, "Is that what you think you witnessed? A raid?"

She shrugged, looking over at him, "Why else would you send such a force to grunt at a human?" she asked, honestly not following him. She took a tiptoed step forward, "I just imagined it was for supplies. And women." Her shoulders shrug.

Snorting at her words, he turned his head back to look at her, "Women, huh?" He looked her over then shrugged.

"We have our own women here, you'll see," he dismissed, tapping a nailed finger on the desk. He paused before continuing, "Those men were sent up to collect a payment owed. Nothing more, or less." Curling his upper lip slightly, he continued, "They killed one of ours. And in exchange they insultingly offered supplies to appease our rage. I talked my men into it to keep the peace, but then the mongrels hadn't even the decency to deliver all they promised, and we had to go remind them of the debt owed."

Her lip curled slightly, "Ahhh," she sighed, "Well then, why did they kill them?" she asked, curiously.

"They claim," he began, his upper lip still curled, "that they mistook her for a monster, about to attack the encampment." He spat into a corner of the room, "She was unarmed, and carrying a bundle of sticks!"

She frowned, giving him a sympathetic look, "I see. Then... is there a way for me to be of assistance to you?"

He scowled before moving to his seat and thudding down into it. "If you haven't the self-respect or decency to consort with those who accept you, at least stay out of our affairs and quit your meddling. You're lucky Ofrish is gentle for his kind, or he could've broken some bones, or worse."

She looked at him blandly before nodding, "Of course. Am I to be dismissed, then? Is that it?"

Giving a snort, he looked away, "I'm not some commander. And these aren't troops. They're just a gang of desperate folk who do what they have to survive." He turned a hard eye toward her, "You've got what you wanted, yes?"

She gave him a small shrug, "I suppose," she stared at him for a moment, "I did offer my help," she added lightly, "But if you don't wish it, I won't infringe on your collections."

Reclining back into his seat at an awkward angle, he looked her over again. "Good," he said before continuing, "And what kind of services do you offer to me and mine then? You say you can change your shape, yes? Not something completely unique amongst us, but useful none the less."

She crinkled her nose. Not unique, she thought, pah!

"There's hardly a male around that can resist me, should I so choose it. Surely that holds something unique, in combination with my other skills."

Before her eyes, the feline man sat a little straighter, his skin beginning to tremble, until his feral features melted away and he sat before her looking like a regular, dark skinned human with a thick head of hair.

"You make quite a boast," he noted.

Her eyes rose as he assumed a human form. She was uncertain what his true form really was. She folded her arms lightly under her chest.

"Yes, well, be that as it may," she paused, looking over his features more keenly now, her interest piqued, "I'm not one to boast above my means to deliver."

Reclining back in his chair, he looked for a bit like some haughty male commander, his jaw strong, eyes still retaining a hint of their dark outline making his gaze look intimidating. "Szezreck," he purred.

She assumed that was his name.

"Lilah. A pleasure," she replied, curtseying again. She was almost always between the limits of over-formal behaviour and downright tawdry, she thought, often blending the two, as she did then. Certainly a curtsey didn't befit a woman wearing barely more than a slip of clothing around her privates.

Gesturing to her with a human looking hand now he said, "I can have some clothes fished up for you to keep you warm in the climate, Lilah. As I said, we don't have much but we do tend to others like ourselves. Half-breeds and misfits."

She offered a smile, shaking her head.

"No, thank you. Clothing is constraining to one of my kind." She bowed her head, "It's kind of you to offer, though." Her eyes flit to his once more, holding his gaze, "How did you come to lead them?"

Reclining back he tugged at the waist of his armour, securing it snugly as he nodded, "Very well. You know what you need better than I. As for how I came to lead them?" he shrugged, "They needed a leader to keep them not only safe and orderly, but to keep them from exacting painful vengeance on the humans for expelling them. And though my sons and myself could hide amongst the humans, we chose not to. It was the right thing to do."

She stared at him, seeing his point but still not liking the implication, "We're not intending to stay long. We're looking for a few components and then we'll be gone again." She held her gaze upon him, "I understand your cause, but..." but what? She wasn't entirely certain, she thought. "Well, I hadn't any idea before this night of any of this, truly."

"We're?" He returned, his nose twitching slightly as he watched her, "Who else do you have with you then? Others of your kind, hiding amongst the humans above? And where will you go from here? There is little else out there, and few live to search far beyond this place."

"I told you. I'm waiting for someone. And from here?" she paused, "I plan on returning to Sho'ar."

"Sho'ar?" he said with some surprise. He laughed, chuckling at her expense as his features shifted back to the way they were when she entered, "You must be either new or crazy."

"Maybe," she conceded, folding her hands beneath her breasts, "but I'll die before I surrender myself to this fate. If I have to deceive some humans to do so, then I'm willing to, Szezreck."

Taking a deep breath he added, "A shame. You must do what you will, but you could be a great addition to our makeshift clan. Despite my earlier words we have, sadly, few women. And shape shifting is still rare, only my sons and I are capable, really. You could be an asset to your own kind here, and earn respect and admiration amongst them."

She watched him as his features began to shift almost imperceptibly.

"I have some time before my companion returns," she said after a long pause, "Though I must, at least, ensure there's a place for him to go back to. I'm sure, should you have any imagination, you can figure out how I'm paying for the room, and I'll be expected back shortly. However," another pause, "if there's something I can do in the meanwhile to help you, I'm all ears."

Arching a brow at her, he stared a while, "A shame," he finally repeated. "You could've stayed amongst us for free and given the rest freely in return as gift as well. And been more appreciated for it." His nose twitches and he reached up, scratching at his chin.

She laughed, smiling at him mirthfully, "Yes, well, if I had known, that might have been how it'd be," she said, her words soft and seductive before looking away, "But what's done is done, and I won't know more until I check in with my new roommate."

Reaching to his desk he plucked up a copper ball, and tossed it casually from one sharply nailed hand to the other idly, "And lest you have a fancy for mundane humans, you'd no doubt have enjoyed it far more with us. Our rank and file stretch from the exotic to the very bizarre. A much more interesting pool amongst whom to mingle."

"I feel no real affection for any but for the guard who took me in," she said after some moment's pause, looking at him with a curious, raised brow. "You seem rather... hopeful that I stay, aren't you," she looked at him, giving him a small, cocky grin, "And I wasn't even trying."

Wrapping his fingers about the copper ball he stopped to toss it, looking to her with a sigh, "I've enough sons already. But as I said, you could've been of use to this group." Placing the ball back on his desk he reclined, "But if you wish to help us, go on ahead. Find some way to make yourself useful. There will be no shortage of those in need."

Her brows furrowed, "I'm not some brood mare, you know," she argues, annoyed. "And what do you mean, rewarded well?" She stared at him a few moments longer, getting uneasy, though she wasn't entirely sure why.

Shrugging his shoulders slightly he responds casually, "Very well, as you wish. And I mean," he starts, looking to her again, "we reward those who help the collective with good lodgings, food, wealth... respect and authority. We see to it the best, most contributing and brightest move up in everyone's eyes."

She listens closely as he replied, nodding, "Very well. I'm sure you'll hear from me again, Szezreck," she paused, looking back to the room she came from, "Am I to see myself back, then?"

Raising his brows up at her, he looked a little confused, "What? Did you wish an escort out? You look capable of handling a walk through the halls on your own, I'm sure." He cracks a wry smirk at her then.

She nodded in agreement.

"Very well. It is a pleasure meeting you, then," she said, unease striking her hard, "I hope your night goes well."

CHAPTER 29

Born from the chaotic union of an elf and a demonic dragon, Glaurakos burned with a deep inner fire that stood against the snowy storm. Yet, without his new companion, he was troubled. For the first part of his journey he wasn't even sure of what was troubling him, yet the longer he soared without her the more he grew to realize it was her presence he missed.

Thoughts of her lithe frame soaring through the sky behind him distracted him from the unpleasant realities of the freezing mountains, so he almost didn't notice when the storm abruptly died off.

The unnatural shift in climate ultimately roused him from his daydreaming, however, and he studied his surroundings closely.

The high winds were tempered there, the snow gone. The temperature was higher, yet there was no real reason for it that he could see. Glaurakos was still far up in the mountains, and places lower still were still experiencing the high winds and blowing snow with which he was being assaulted.

It took him some time, but he finally figured it out: the portal had to be nearby. The bleeding effect from their realm was warming the closest area, and had to be what was causing the unnatural change climate. It had to be.

Swaying on the air, he beat his leathery wings and made way toward a nearby ridge along the mountainside. He couldn't see over it from his vantage point, but he didn't want to risk giving away his position to anyone that might be there if his hunch was right. So he landed a distance away, then approached the crest of the ridge on foot.

His caution was rewarded when he peered over, for he had indeed found the portal, nestled in a green field that seemed to have expanded considerably since he and Lilah had first passed over. More noteworthy than that were the angelic figures in glimmering mithril armour that still lingered about it, apparently guarding the site, though one seemed to be busy trying to understand the portal itself.

Judging by the magical implements that were set up around it, they were trying to do more than simply understand the gateway.

Glaurakos' mind reeled. The five of them were either trying to seal the gateway, or destroy it for good.

He couldn't be certain of that fact, but somehow he just felt it.

As he brushed his thick golden hair back, he tried to formulate a plan.

Yet how could he take on the five of them by himself? He and Lilah, together, had fled the last time.

We had been unprepared, he told himself.

That was right. They were caught unawares. Now, though, Glaurakos had them in his sights, and they were not ready for him.

There would be no time to get Lilah. Not if his suspicions were correct.

Their escape would hinge on him alone, he told himself.

CHAPTER 30

Night fell upon the mountains, and even the relatively temperate climate of the portal area grew chill. Glaurakos watched as the angelic figures set up a fire for the night, just as he'd predicted they would from the signs of a flame pit.

All the better, he assured himself, as it would lessen their sight in the dark.

He had hoped they would send out some scouts during the day, so he could pick them off in smaller groups, but it appeared they were more afraid of the dragon detecting them than of being caught unawares. That had been the key to his catching them, though it proved a frustration.

With the daylight hours spent preparing, however, he set in motion his plan.

Drawing his cloak around him, Glaurakos took a moment to initiate his spell, shrouding himself in the darkness. Only the workings of the arcane could mask the towering fiend from sight, leaving him an apparition in the dark, and he used it to stalk close to the angelic figures.

They were a perfect mystery to him, for they looked to be full-blooded, unlike Lilah. Yet they were beings known for their peaceful innocence; delicate, fae beings of good, with pacifistic tendencies. Then again, there they were before him, armoured and arrayed for holy war, it would seem. He had only heard of such a thing in passing before, such winged beauties being claimed as arbiters of a deity's justice.

It should have given him more pause, the thought that they bore the good will and blessings of an actual god, but Glaurakos had no time for reservations. He stalked one of the angels that walked a perimeter around their makeshift camp.

The first pounce was so swift even he barely heard a thing. The crack of bones couldn't be heard over the chatter of the three by the flames.

It wasn't a satisfying feeling. Beneath their armour they were delicate, and all Glaurakos had to do was get his blade in between his helm and hauberk to finish the job.

The second one on patrol took a while to circle around to Glaurakos' direction, then she, too, joined the first.

The half-dragon began to find himself getting cocky. They were hardly worth the worry at all, he surmised. Why had they so readily fled from these beings?

That left only the three at the campfire, and he rejected his plan to wait for one of them to break away, or go in search of the missing patrols. They didn't seem worth the effort.

So instead, shrouded in the blackness of his ritual spell, Glaurakos approached the three of them, sword in hand. He could take out one of them before they could respond, then it would be two to one. He liked those odds.

Or he did, before the great flash of light that burnt away his magic shroud and blinded him.

There were no words from the angels, but once Glaurakos had regained his sight he saw nothing. No sign of them, just a bright light from the fire that filled the meadow around them as though it were midday and not midnight.

An arrow split the air, and he heard it in time. That was, if not for the holy energy that imbued it with unnatural speed. So instead of dodging out of the way, he felt the tip of the arrow pierce his armour and gouge a furrow in his side.

Such a flesh wound wouldn't have phased the seasoned spellsword, but that holy energy seared his tainted blood and made him cry out.

"A demon-spawn!" cried one of the angelic beings as it rushed toward him.

Metal tore through the air, and before he ever saw it, Glaurakos managed to raise his own blade and block it in time. Though when he kicked out to knock the assaulting angel away, he instead found her armoured fist in his face.

She could not have been that strong, but her blow was empowered by some holy force that sent the half-dragon reeling, though the momentum thankfully helped him avoid the next arrow that came his way.

It also bought him enough time to let his eyes adjust to the bright light and gauge the position of his enemies.

In the air above, two of them flew, pearly-white wings unfurled as one chanted a prayer and the other knocked his bow. While before him a tall woman — broad for her kind — came at him with a flurry of her blade.

He had underestimated them, and was now stuck in an unpleasant situation, caught between their holy justice from above and righteous fury below.

His best chance lay with surprise.

Glaurakos shot his sword up in the air, sacrificing a maneuver against the oncoming woman as a bolt of lightning struck his blade. A discharge of electricity around him shot out and stung her, though as the power coursed through him too, and his own wings unfurled. They burst out of his clothes as he ascended into the air, now charged with lightning speed.

An arrow pierced through one of his leather wings, and he couldn't help but cry out in rage. Yet it wasn't enough to impede his assault as he soared toward the two angels.

With a slash of his blade he had cut the bowman in half, while the arc of his sword sliced through the wing of the cleric, sending him spiralling down in a flurry of feathers and his own cry of anguish.

The victory was short lived however, as the furious swordswoman was back upon him. They dueled in the air, her fast motions barely deflected or blocked in time by Glaurakos' heavier blade.

He fell back, and to the side, again and again, her assault relentless. She had true zeal, and her tenacity more than made up for his superior strength.

When his own strength and skill with the blade failed him, he turned back to his sorcery. Poised in the air, another bolt of electricity surged through him from the dark sky above, and each blow she struck that landed against his blade sent a painful shock through her.

Yet still it wasn't enough.

It didn't even succeed in slowing her down, and instead only heightened her rage, driving her on to attack faster, more furiously.

A strike with her sword very nearly sliced off one of his hands, and Glaurakos knew he had to finish it with her. Soon.

The electric current in the air grew as their dance of swords continued, and their hair began to stand on end as the static charge filtered through them. The sharp stabs of pain did not deter the assaulting angel, her teeth gritted together as she spun and attacked mercilessly.

With a heave and a lunge, Glaurakos put his bulk behind his weapon and pushed her sword away. She fluttered and twirled, but her majestic wings brought her back on course so quickly — quicker than he could've managed — and she renewed her assault with a battle cry.

The dragon-kin's eyes went wide in shock, though the swordsman misread it.

The sky overhead broke open, and a bolt of lightning surged from above. It struck Glaurakos with a bang just a split moment before their blades touched again.

Realization sprang to her mind quicker than she could express it, her sword making contact his as the explosion of energy went from the conduit of the fiend into her.

The half-demon let loose a mighty roar that shook the mountainside, and she screamed piercingly as her flesh was fried and seared by the power coursing through her.

An explosion of feathers filled the air as the last of the heavenly energy dissipated, and one charred body fell limply to the ground.

Glaurakos himself lurched in the air, though his powerful wings managed to recover. They were weary, suffering from the remnants of the electrical spell.

Breathing heavily, his eyes began to focus slowly as the bright flash of his spell was replaced by the gloom of night in the mountains. Far below, he saw one of the angelic figures still persisting.

The beautiful male cleric, whose wing had been severed, was on his knees. Praying.

The half-demon was exhausted, but the work wasn't done. He surged down towards the dainty figure. Mere moments before he reached his target, a holy glow emanated from the man, forcing Glaurakos to have to shield his eyes with his forearm and come to a stop.

It was a defensive posture, not sure what sort of holy assault it might have been upon him. When nothing more occurred and the bright burn subsided, Glaurakos opened his fiery gaze to look down again upon the figure. What he saw surprised him deeply.

The lost wing was restored. In full. The beautifully bright feathery appendage looked as though it had never been lost in the first place.

There was no time to appreciate the miracle, however, so Glaurakos landed down upon the grassy clearing with a thud. The angelic priest glared, but made no move against him.

"You cannot free her," he declared zealously.

To which Glaurakos backhanded the man reflexively. No defeated foe dared tell him what he would or wouldn't do. Though as the dainty male reeled away, the question of what he meant rang through in the half-demon's mind.

He would have to wait for his answers, as the delicate looking man was knocked unconscious.

CHAPTER 31

"Why do you try to stop us from escaping?!" Glaurakos demanded, splashing the ice-cold water on the angel's face.

A flutter of his wings straightened the angel's posture as he nursed his battered jaw. "It is our holy duty to guard the prisoner," he declared in his melodic voice, even after so abruptly awaking. "And none shall stop us from keeping her bound and the world at large safe."

Glaurakos snarled and stepped towards the pious man, though at last the angel's demeanor broke and he stepped away reflexively to avoid another blow. "My partner and I are going to get out of this… whatever it is! And none shall stop us! Not you! Not your damnable god either!" And he struck at the man again, eliciting a yelp.

"You mean the one you came here with?!" he asked in a startled voice, looking fearful of the half-dragon that threatened his very life.

"Of course I mean her!" snarled Glaurakos.

"Then… you aren't here to free the dragon-queen?"

Glaurakos stopped in his tracks, the question an utter surprise to him. "That thing in the mountains is a queen?" His heart skipped a beat, for in all the realms known to him, there was no more fearsome a creature than a dragon-queen.

A demi-god that could stride upon mortal realms, such beings gave birth to nearly all the evils of the worlds. Including him. Though that didn't make it any less frightening, "You bastard! I need to get Lilah out of here immediately then!"

He raised his hand to strike the angel but the petite man cried out. "Wait!" It stilled the angry half-demon's hand a moment. "We only acted because we thought you were here to let her loose upon the world!"

Glaurakos smacked him anyhow, though the slap merely stung. "The hell good does that do us now that you've delayed us?!"

"It's too late now! The dragon-queen broke out of her prison, but before she could reclaim her pearl of power, our Lord ripped the land from out of time and space as a failsafe to keep her in check. You… you two broke that seal, and now she will eventually claim what was hers and return to the mortal realm as powerful as ever!"

Glaurakos wanted to hit him again. What did it matter what this dragon-queen did? As long as he was far away from her, not at risk to be enslaved by the empowered will of such a vile creature. Though perhaps it was pragmatism telling him that she'd pursue through the same hole he'd escape through that made him pause. Or more likely it was that mention of the pearl.

"She doesn't have her pearl?" The implications were grand. The great dragon-deities bound immense powers in such baubles; it was the housing for their souls, or as close to a soul as such a foul demonic thing could create from arcane magic. Without it they were but raging beasts in search of their essence. Albeit raging beasts with an immense size and physical strength.

"If she gets it there will be no stopping her," intoned the angelic man. "We need to seal this place off again, rip it back out of time so that she cannot reclaim it and the world outside remain safe."

"No deal," growled Glaurakos. "I am getting out of here one way or the other, and I shall not sacrifice myself for the purposes of this stalling tactic your god has concocted."

"But —"

The half-demon slashed his blade in the air.

"Listen to me," he commanded menacingly, his mind working at a frightening pace. "I can do you better than just stalling her."

"H-how?" the look of disbelief on the angel's face unmistakable.

"I can take the dragon's pearl and take it far from here. She will have no way to escape this magical prison without the consciousness and power inside it, and you will be free to gradually lead the survivors here out of this hell and back to the real world." It was the most powerful thing in the dragon's arsenal, and he knew it wouldn't be easy. It'd require a lot of precision and, unfortunately, trust.

Hope flickered across the delicate man's face, but it was short lived. "How?" he repeated.

Glaurakos licked his full lips, "You will distract her for me. Lead her away so that I can get past her to the pearl. Once I have it, I will go and leave, never to come back."

"A fine plan, except how can I distract her for so long a time? And besides," he said, standing up rigidly despite the bruise across his jaw, looking defiant to the last, "I meant how can I trust you?"

"Lure the dragon to the nearby monastery," he intoned firmly, "leave the rest to us." Glaurakos slid his blade into place in the hilt down his spine. "As for trust? Does your god not tell you if I speak truth or no?"

The zealous priest stiffened at the words, though less in outrage and more in surprise at the realization. Shutting his eyes he muttered something, a prayer Glaurakos reckoned. When he opened his eyes, the surprise didn't fade.

"It's a rare thing to meet demon-spawn of your ilk who speak truths." He took a deep breath then nodded, "I can lure the dragon-queen to the monastery, and little else. But I do it for the good of all, not you," he remarked in an accusatory fashion, eyes narrowing. "Your judgement is yet to come for all of this that you have wrought."

Glaurakos turned and walked away, back towards the gateway. "I'll be ready when it does come," he said grimly, lowering himself down to a kneeling position as he prepared to cast his spell.

CHAPTER 32

Lilah wore the visage of a simple human woman, but beneath the illusion beat the heart of her normal half-breed self, the fiery passions, the fickle yearnings. Already she was growing bored of the dingy monastery-turned-refugee camp. The people lost in such a strange land, ripped out of time itself and turned to such dull desperation.

Something tickled the back of her mind, reminding her of Glaurakos, her partner, gone from her for seemingly so long already.

She hated how much she missed him. She'd promised herself she'd never love another man as long as she lived. She'd loved her father, dearly, yet what she'd done to him... what she had to do to him, she chastised herself.

Still, the longer Glaurakos was away, the more she yearned for him, and the more she yearned for him, the greater her fear grew. Fear of what would come between them.

He was a half-breed, a demon. Spawn of evil and never to be trusted.

So why did she trust so deeply in him? Perhaps because some trace of her father's dark taint still remained in her, sullying her roots from her mother.

She paced the small room, trying to work out her conflicted emotions as they swirled within her, but it was impossible.

Love could not be out-thought.

The memories of him grew stronger despite her attempts to resist, until finally it was a slight burning. It dawned on her then that it wasn't just idle fancy that was driving her, some schoolgirl style yearning for a man, but a magical sending.

She should have realized it sooner, she chastised herself, but she was so caught up in her feelings of frustration and loneliness that she missed the telltale signs.

Moving onto the sleeping bag, she got down upon her knees and shut her eyes, closing out the world as she attuned her senses to the arcane.

The practiced meditative stance was like hovering in a void, and his familiar rasp carried to her from across great distance. The harsh husk. So masculine. So delicious. It tickled her ear even though she heard it only with her mind.

"I have found the gateway. And taken it," he said to her, his voice so reassuring.

She never doubted he would be able to, even in the worst of her worries.

"Is it safe for me to find you?" she asked.

Through the magical link they shared, she could almost feel him, his ethereal heat seeming to tingle her back.

"There is something I need you to do for me first," he said. "One final task to take care of this dragon before we make our escape, Lilah."

"What? The dragon?" Fuck, was it blocking their exit? What hope did they have if that was the case?

"I have a plan, but we must act fast, and you must trust me." He hesitated, and Lilah swore she could almost feel his breath against her ear as they communicated across the snowy mountains.

CHAPTER 33

Lilah had some difficulty shaking Aphim so she could leave the upper reaches of the monastery. Yet once she did, she managed to slip into a dark alleyway and drop the illusory disguise. She still drew stares from the half-breeds and misfits with her angelic figure, but they were no longer angry as they would be for seeing her as a human.

"Take me to Szezreck, I have urgent news," she told the guard outside the bosses building.

With a cursory look over her — and a tinge of interest, she noted approvingly — the thuggish looking half-orc turned and escorted her inside.

The place was cramped and hot, so many people shoved into the tiny area, showing that even their leader didn't get much space to himself most times.

The tedious formalities of the guard heading in, stating the nature of the visit, then emerging to let her know she could enter all dragged on.

She entered into the now-familiar room, the feline-looking man standing behind his desk, looking over some documents with what she assumed was one of his sons.

"I was told this was urgent," he remarked without looking her way, though she couldn't have said the same for the younger man, who was staring at her rather intently. "I suspect this isn't just about you changing your mind about my proposal?"

"Not just, no," she agreed. Lilah didn't fancy being ignored by him, though, and slid closer to his desk. "There are things I wish to discuss that I figured would be of interest to you. I'm assuming, since you saw me so promptly, that you trust my instincts."

The almost stately looking demi-human gave her the attention she sought. He pushed his shoulders back and gazed at her intensely. "When I get word of urgent news, I take it seriously. My personal ego shouldn't stand in the way of what's best for the folk of the lower reaches here." Szezreck folded his arms over his chest and waited.

"Your ego," she purred, finding his partial confession to be charming. "Well, I'm sure they're all grateful to you. I came as quickly as I could, once I saw... well. I'll start from the beginning, I suppose. When I was up top, after you and I spoke, I began to notice things. Things that I hadn't before you opened my eyes up to the reality of the situation. I became suspicious, and did some investigations of my own."

Lilah sat, perched atop the corner of her desk, her angelic wings fluttering nervously as she spoke, "Szezreck, they were arming themselves. Preparing for a surprise attack."

Those feline eyes of his and his son's went wide with some surprise, though Szezreck masked it better. "They're terrified of us up there, why would they act so foolishly?" though she could detect the doubt on his voice. He was ready to believe, he just needed that extra nudge.

"Terrified people behave foolishly, and after your display..." Lilah's gaze dropped to the floor, her expression turning introspective. "It's no wonder they're trying to attack. They figure you're far more capable in battle, so they'll likely try to hit you when and where you least expect it. Here."

That did it. Lilah could tell it was exactly what he needed to hear to sway him, and his eyes dropped then slid over to their son. "Go, spread the word. Get ready to defend ourselves. Take up positions as practiced."

Lilah shook her head, adamantly, and her dark hair bounced off her fair cheeks. "Defense? Szezreck, I know you feel you have a home advantage down here, but you don't. The space is too limiting. You should take the battle to them, make sure not a single spy sets her eyes on the layout down here."

"If what you say is true, we don't have much time," Szezreck argued.

His son spoke up, "We can make a show of force and maybe ward them off from a full on assault.

We've got more weapons and tricks up our sleeves than they realize."

"We might prevent them from making a fatal error. You're right." Szezreck looked back to Lilah as his son raced out of the room, rallying all the demi-humans he could. "You can take shelter here with us, or join in the fight. We could use all the help we can get."

"You'll have my help, but I'll serve you better as a spy. I'll return above and act as your ears and eyes. I will let you know what they're planning." Lilah slipped from his desk, her graceful feet keeping her poised like a dancer even in such an urgent time.

"When next we meet, it will be on the path to victory, Szezreck. Don't under estimate what you'll be up against. There will be panic, and the panicked are brutal in combat."

Had she overplayed her hand? There was a look of hesitation on the man's face, but he gave a resigned nod as she left.

CHAPTER 34

Aphim's hand shook, "You were right," he muttered, turning away from the outlook in the tower over the whole of the monastery. "They really are gonna come up here and conquer us," he gulped, his Adam's apple bulging. "Or worse."

From the lookout it was hard to miss the flood of armed demi-humans in the streets below. The other scout had already taken off down the tower in a mad rush to relay word of the impending assault.

"We have to get ready to fight, Aphim. There are good people here, people who need you to protect them." She was pleading with those wide, human eyes. Once more she was disguised, and she found herself hating the illusion more and more. She'd never had that problem before. Looking like someone else was always a welcome relief from the gaping stares, and she knew it was the same here.

But damn it, she just wanted to look like herself again.

She couldn't wait for the battle to be won. Though, of course, the battle isn't the one that either side was expecting.

The young human was shaking, and had to take slow steps down the stone stairwell. "M-maybe we should…" He was so nervous, and the prospect of an actual fight seemed to have rattled him considerably. He looked to her with wide, fearful eyes, "Maybe we should run until this blows over. Go hide somewhere or make our way to another camp."

Her heart broke for the weak little man, but she pushed those feelings away. She barely knew him, but his innocence stirred something within her and she had to force herself away. "Aphim... It's better to die in battle than to die a coward. These people... I need you. I need you to fight what comes next. To be strong."

She needed everyone to be strong. If what Glaurakos said was true...

The wide-eyed young man looked away, and she could only reckon it was embarrassment. "You should go hide out in my room then until this blows over. It won't be safe for you out around anymore."

"Aphim... promise me you'll be careful." Lilah gave a small smile, the back of her fingertips grazing across his jawline. "You're so sweet. You deserve so much good."

How had she become so soft again? She thought that side of her had been locked up tight, hidden and suppressed for so many long years. And somehow a demon manages to stir it all up again?

Of all things...

CHAPTER 35

Glaurakos could hardly believe the daring of the frail-yet-resilient man. Only shortly before the half-demon had lopped off one of his wings, now he soared through the sky with such grace and bravery, fueled only by the power of his faith.

Keeping the lead, the half-demon had to peer back to see those feathery wings so far behind. The looming threat of the mother dragon, despite being a mile or more in the distance, was still clearly discernible.

He thought back to their last conversation. The angelic priest questioning him, "Why would you challenge one of your own dark deities, demon? It makes no sense."

Glaurakos didn't need to think on it much, but he did anyhow.

"My people are beings of power and chaos," he responded simply. "I embrace power. I seek it. But chaos?" He sneered at that time, unable to help himself. "Let this act against the Dragon Queen be my tribute to chaos for all time. May it please her so," he said derisively.

It hadn't taken much from the angelic priest to rouse the ire of a demonic queen of dragons. Certainly not when she was so mindless and instinctual as this. He only hoped they could outpace the thing long enough while still maintaining her interest.

CHAPTER 36

Lilah stalked the monastery during the night from the parapets above. She could see the many watch fires lit around the upper and lower reaches, dark forms around each one of them. Their attention had been all turned against each other, which made her worry. They weren't watching the exterior as they should be.

An idea began to form in her head and she quickly moved into the belly of the building. Finding a secluded space, she settled down upon the hard ground. Rummaging through her bag she removed a few reagents and began to work, urgently. The ritual would still take time to cast, and that was not in the abundance.

If a war truly did break out between the two factions, all would lose.

Lilah took a deep breath and began to chant.

Illusion magic was something she was intimately familiar with, and the last few days had kept her in good practice. However, conjuring such a large one was a challenge, especially while on a time limit.

As the incense burned and her chanting continued, her own personal illusion flickered then faded. She knelt there in her true visage, her wings extended as she brought the illusion to shape in the casting.

It was when she heard the mighty roar of the faux-dragon above that she finally cracked a smile. Her work was a success. Even from inside she could hear the clatter of boots and weapons.

The illusion wouldn't last long before it soared off into the horizon, providing a new worry for the locals to focus on in anticipation of the real one's arrival.

As Lilah brushed herself off and went up the steps to see her creation in action, she didn't notice the slight form of Aphim in the shadows. The young man had receded into the corner, eyes gleaming with revelation at the sight of her spellcasting.

CHAPTER 37

The sun was about ready to rise, its orange glow spreading across the sky slowly. Lilah had awaited Glaurakos' arrival for over a day, though she knew the travel time had to have been long. His plans took time. Still, she was getting antsy, and the nervous folk of the monastery had turned their attentions to the skies more than each other. Or at least as much as.

Her display had been brief, but the job was done. They were now manning the rooftops, bows and whatever other ranged implements they could muster at the ready. They were no professional army all amassed together, but they would have to do.

It was all they had.

The casting had exhausted her, despite how short the display lasted, but she persevered, even without the needed rest. She catnapped when she could, but she couldn't trust herself to fully sleep. Not when everything had to be perfect.

Everything was so deceptively quiet, until she heard the approach of footsteps. She turned and saw it was Aphim again.

"I know I should be inside," she began, but he cut her off.

"Take me with you," he said firmly. "I need to get out of here. You can't leave me here for whatever is coming." There was no sadness or anything pitiable about his demeanor, it was like he was another person.

Speaking like another person.

It gave Lilah pause as she studied him closely. Her fingers flexed, the instinct to run burning through her legs and hidden wings.

"I'm not going anywhere," she replied, but her tone was no longer honeyed. It was hard, and a bit distant, almost challenging.

The young man peered over her shoulder towards the horizon, his eyes widening. "Tell me what's coming," he insisted. "I need to get out of here with you, whatever it is. Time has run out."

She turned to the direction he was facing, and saw it there. A dark shape in the distance, approaching closer. It was small, indiscernible from where they were, but it had to be large to be seen at such a distance.

"What's coming..." she started, her usually strong voice a bit weaker. "The dragon is returning."

The colour seemed to drain from his face right before Lilah's eyes. "If you don't help me get out of here, you'll regret it."

From out of the mountains a cold wind blew past her, like a foreboding portent of the calamity about to strike the monastery. It chilled her to the bone, and before she could recoup to respond, the leather flap of wings beat heavily nearby.

She turned to see the familiar, looming visage of Glaurakos above her. His approach had been masked by the shrill and chilling wind, but there he was, right before her, and she swore she could feel the ethereal heat of his body reaching out to her.

"We must go. Now," he stated, reaching out to her with his clawed hand. She swore she even detected a faint glimmer of a smile there, some small, nearly unnoticeable sign of relief at seeing her yet again.

He looked even better than she remembered, and Lilah didn't hide her smile from him. He made it all worthwhile. The demon's presence distracted her from the way her skin prickled, how tight her stomach felt.

Why couldn't she shake the idea that she was leaving these people to their doom?

Probably because it was, at least in part, true. She didn't have the luxury of over thinking it, though, and her gaze went to Aphim. The human wasn't a fighter. Hell, he was barely into manhood, and she couldn't deny the pity she felt for him.

Yet there was no way to grant his request. They had to fly, and Lilah shook off her disguise, stretching her now visible wings.

"I'm sorry, Aphim," she apologized sincerely.

The young human was about to protest, and he reached out to grab her hand. Instead, Glaurakos took hers in his, that familiar heat rushing through her flesh as he pulled her up into the air with him.

For one brief moment the dashing demon held her to his hard chest and gave her a tender smile, but their reunion was impromptu and rushed. "We'll have time to reunite properly once we're out of here," he husked deeply.

Her fiery lover had blocked out the sounds of the protesting Aphim, pulling her off on their hurried errand. She didn't hear the plea to just accept his spell, nor saw the young man's true form. She was too busy staring where Glaurakos pointed her, the growing silhouette of the approaching dragon queen startling to behold.

"It took us a while to lay our traps, to lure her where we wanted. The trip back to the mountain fortress will be briefer. Hopefully brief enough," he said, still holding their hand as they soared together once more.

Her heart pounded with such excited pleasure.

He'd returned for her.

It startled her just how much she had feared he wouldn't, that this was all a trick to get rid of her somehow, but it wasn't. The affection she felt at that moment was purer than she could have ever remembered knowing, and she wanted to revel in it.

To cover herself in his body, to feel that inhuman heat surround her.

Yet she still had her wits about her and forced herself to move faster than she'd ever gone before. Her muscles burned, her lungs gasped for air, and her flesh called out for her lover.

They soared away from what would be the scene of what would decide whether they returned home or died a fiery death in a lonely world. A single angel and a horde of struggling refugees facing off against a demonic queen, all to buy some time to end her reign for good. Yet it was not their part in the grand tale.

CHAPTER 38

The scene of that monumental peak was still familiar to them both. They'd come by it so soon after arriving on the forlorn land, and it had been immediately marked as a point to avoid. Yet now they soared towards it, the sharp winds, the dagger-like ice shards all trying to throw them off course, to beat them back from their goal of the icy-black fortress.

The whole of the way there, Glaurakos had told her of what he'd learned. Of his plans to claim the dragon's pearl and return to their world triumphant. To know they were even playing some role in the defeat of such a force of evil was a bit comforting after the sacrifices they had made.

"We have to keep pushing!" he called to her through the winds, the two of them having to shield their faces from the ice shards even as they bit into their two sets of wings. They had stalled out, and had to put so much more of their strength into the act of flying to simply avoid being caught up and tossed about in the maelstrom.

It bit into their flesh, though Lilah was the worse off. Her pale skin had grown almost red from the pelting, even with what protection she wore from the cold. It still wasn't enough to combat the wind as it whipped the hood from her head once more.

Through the bite of the weather's assault, Glaurakos reached out and grasped her wrist and hand. That tight hold was such a comfort, unlike anything she could have imagine a simple holding of the hand could be. With his support to her, he pushed ahead, their two sets of wings beating furiously as they pushed through.

A loud, bellowing roar came from the half-demon as he fought the wind and ice, some act of resistance against its furious assault.

Together they pushed and pushed on, and when their wings felt like they might fail them, the thought of each other and the fate that awaited them should they relinquish their struggle for even a second — a dizzying tumble into the maelstrom and inevitable death — brought them through.

Glaurakos struck the icy-black surface of the fortress first, and he clung to it with all his might. His sharp claws digging into the nooks and crannies as best as they could as he pulled her in with him.

"Don't lose your hold!" he yelled as he pulled her in beside him, shielding her from the wind and securing her place.

She could hardly hear him but she knew what she had to do. Even as her fingers struggled, her nails digging painfully into the rock wall, she wouldn't fail him.

Not in this task. Not with something so important on the line.

Facing the perils of the mountain top, they struggled to look around as they secured their position as best they could. Though something began to sink in. "There's no entrance," growled Glaurakos. "It's just a stone tomb!"

It made sense. The angels put the pearl there to keep it out of the dragon queen's grasp, and no other reason. They couldn't destroy it, so they simply sought to separate her from it for as long as they could. "Tell me you know some spell to break through magical stone," he breathed in exasperation, looking to her with his glowing-ember eyes, arm about her tightly.

"Aren't you in luck," Lilah managed out through gritted teeth and raw throat. "My father used to try to... hide things from me."

The half-demon tightened his hold about her, keeping her securely in position. The stone would have heavy enchantments to protect the dragon's pearl, intricately cast. He knew Lilah's counter-spell would require great concentration and focus, and she couldn't give that if she were worried about being swept off the top of the mountain by an errant gust of wind.

Doing her best to shut out the weather, Lilah focussed her consciousness upon the task. Despite her bravado with Glaurakos it wouldn't be an easy casting. Taking on the stone itself would've been fine, but the fact that it was magically imbued made her task far more challenging.

Normally it would've taken the better part of an hour, but she didn't have that. So instead she reached her powers into the stone, probed it. Felt the strands of arcane energy within, sussed them out and explored their properties as much as she dared. They were not simply arcane, but spiritual, a blending of the both. Which made a daunting task seem impossible.

Her delicate brow furrowed, she was about ready to curse and shout her frustrations as the ticking of that imaginary clock counted down in the back of her mind. It was then, though, that an idea occurred to her.

Licking her puffy, wind-blasted red lips, she took a chance.

The tendrils of her power wound into the magical thread. A pluck of a chord here, there…

Beneath them the stone simply… melted. Hard obsidian coated in at least an inch of ice seemed to vaporize like water over a fire. The two of them fell inward with it, into the dragon soul's icy tomb. The hard landing that awaited them both was cushioned when her burly protector clutched her to his chest and twisted, impacting the stonework with his shoulder and back, sparing her the brunt of the force.

She let out a tiny ooph before trying to shift and give him room to recover. Her lungs stung from the cold but still her concern was for him. "Are you okay?" she blurted out quickly.

Glaurakos looked a bit stunned, but he shook it off, and the damp traces of the ice that littered his fiery hair with it. "I'm fine," he grunted, though she knew such a fall had to have hurt him more than he let on. With a few blinks he asked, "How'd you cave it in so fast?" She could detect the surprise and respect on his voice, for the magical swordsman respected nothing more than such sorcerous prowess.

She stood, her limbs still numb from the cold and a bit shaky from the flight. Everything in her body felt so exhausted, but she still had a small smile for her demon lover. "There was a kill switch. Laying a trap with multiple and contradictory types of magic... It was begging to collapse. It just needed the right touch."

Of course it wasn't that simple, turning the two threads of magic -- spiritual and arcane -- against one another was no easy task, and he obviously recognized that despite her modesty. Now he saw why the pearl was still unmolested--such a feat would be nigh impossible for the cumbersome arcane magic of the dragon, but certainly feasible for the likes of an angel. "Well done," he growled, standing himself up and brushing away the ice and debris.

The two of them looked about, for though there was no outside entrance, within it had carved out hallways, twisting and turning. The search for the artifact would be tiresome, but Glaurakos seemed to detect something. "It's this way," he said, pointing down one direction, and Lilah, too, realized she felt some faint tug, as though some power was calling out to her.

Lilah's legs trembled as they walked hand in hand, and she blinked away the exhaustion she felt. "Do you really think this will work? Those people..." She'd left them to a dragon. To die, all for her chance to return back to her home and do what?

"It'll work," he stated firmly, the towering Glaurakos pulling his enchanted blade from his sheath and taking the lead. He had no time for doubts, or anything but their successful capture of the pearl.

The tunnels went on in a seemingly endless maze of twists and turns, with numerous dead ends. It felt like they were retracing their steps, wandering over the same path over and over again. Though the further they followed that faint aura, the stronger it became. Lilah began to feel the pull of that dark force kindling some desire in her. She'd not been affected by the lust for its great power as Glaurakos had before, but the further they went and the more the frustrations of false paths mounted, the stronger she felt it.

It seeped into her very soul.

"Dammit!" cursed the broad half-fiend, slamming his fist into another dead end wall. "Is there even an end to this?!"

Lilah felt her own frustrations rising, but through the buzz she felt some reason pushing through. She could use her magic upon the wall as they had against the exterior, and simply push their way through to their destination.

It was so remarkably clear, and she didn't even bother explaining. She moved to the stone and felt for those now familiar chords of magic. It was so... close. So tantalizingly close.

And it snapped, giving way to her careful assault.

The wall melted away before them, but only gave way to the sight of yet more corridors. Through them they went one by one, pushing onwards as the call of that pearl's power pulled them forward. Yet all the while it was as if the tick of a death clock sounded like the beat of the dragon queen's wings.

Glaurakos fidgeted, tensing his grip upon the blade hilt as he watched Lilah work. She could even hear him grind his teeth with his anxiousness, almost feel the words of urgency that he so barely suppressed.

When the last wall came down, their frustration was swept aside by an overpowering wave of energy that crashed over them both.

Peering into a dark chamber, lit only by a pale green glow, they both gazed across a dark abyss and onto a pedestal where lay the dragon's pearl.

Though the room was dark, the pearl itself seemed to devour even blackness itself. It was a void that consumed even nothingness, yet exuded such a promise of greatness.

It was Glaurakos who climbed through first, the call of that power too much to resist for the half-dragon.

It made Lilah's heart skip a beat, and a warning sounded in her mind. "Don't!" she pleaded with him insistently. The powerful brute paused and looked back at her, though she could see in the flickering flames of his eyes that even that delay was a struggle for him. "It's too much like your demonic half," she explained. "It'll consume your identity and make you a dragon whole!" It was as if the words came unbidden, uncontrolled by her, and she couldn't be sure if they were the product of her worries for her lover, or from some greedy pull of the dragon's that was making her act for the pearl herself.

Maybe it was both.

Either way, Glaurakos' only response was to bare his teeth and growl before kicking up and beginning to fly across the chasm.

Whatever her motivation, Lilah felt she had to act or lose it all.

With a running start, she kicked up into the air and let her feathery wings lift her over the dank chasm. The exhaustion and chill that penetrated her frail bones melted away in the face of such urgency.

The ancient air, so long sealed off from the world filled her lungs so stagnantly and carried her as if it resisted doing even that.

Glaurakos had a moment's head start, but she managed to pick up speed quicker. "Don't!" she cried out again, feeling the doom of that pearl drawing them both in.

"It's mine, Lilah!" he growled. "And when I have it, I'll take you away and carve an empire for us!" Even in his lust for power he promised to stay with her, but it was getting so jumbled. So difficult to keep track of what was happening and why, the motivations of Lilah's own mind hard to work out.

She'd managed to catch up with him, but though she picked up an initial burst of speed quicker due to her light frame, in the long run she knew she couldn't outrace him by much. Her wings fluttered and she only eked ahead of him so agonizingly little.

The pearl would be hers though! That is, she thought so until she felt the tight, heated grip of his hand upon her ankle and calf.

"Don't betray me, Lilah, not now!" he snarled, and she saw that trembling sword hand of his. He was resisting the call of the pearl, telling him to cut her down and claim his prize. She knew it was so, for even she felt it, and she did not share the blood of a demon dragon within her.

Her breath hitched, and time seemed to freeze as she awaited his action. The blade never came though. He stilled his quavering and held back the weapon. Instead he pulled back on her calf, using his brute strength to tug her out of the lead.

Something had to be done, and she moved her slender digits towards him as they flew. "I'm sorry, Glaur," she murmured, sounding distraught.

The powerful half-fiend took it as an admission of defeat and he pushed ahead, but when her hand touched his wrist he froze. Completely and utterly he was locked in time, suspended over the chasm.

With a twist of her delicate wrist, she freed herself and zoomed ahead. Her spell wouldn't hold long, she realized. She had to claim the pearl before he could, and that uniqueness of his personality was consumed by the soul of the queen demon.

It was like the beat of those draconic wings were all around her, about to bear down and make her food for a brood mother. Yet, she didn't waver. She soared to the end and the instant before her fingertips touched the pearl she heard Glaurakos' roar carry out and shake the foundations of that ancient tomb.

The rest was darkness.

Lilah felt the raw power of a demon queen surge into her. It blotted out all light and she felt blind. Rivulets of void matter snaked across her skin — beneath her skin! — infusing her being, polluting her very soul!

She managed to resist. Though she was no longer aware of her physical self, she shook as she fought the corrupting influence on her soul. Her young adulthood was spent seeped in such darkness, and she'd managed to persevere.

Not unscathed, however.

Her lifetime of sorcery, of twisting the dark arts to her will, was put to the test. She had to avoid the intrusion, divert the power! Turn it to her own uses without becoming slave to it.

Her whole body convulsed — a war of magic, cunning and willpower — as all that was *her* battled to retain its independence — its uniqueness — against the essence of an immortal demon goddess. It raged within her, her body and soul the battleground.

"Lilah!" came the faint sound of his voice from across the no-man's land of her consciousness.

Something odd happened. She knew it was Glaurakos calling her, beckoning her back, but she was not responding to it. Well, not entirely. Part of her, long buried and forgotten, had awoken.

So many years ago, darkness had taken her. Stolen her from her innocent, avian life.

Her father.

The corrupted parts that he had awakened in her were willing and even eager to assume the power. But that pure, avian blood still pulsed within her, responding to Glaurakos' call. How did he touch such an innocent and frail part of her? How could a demon reawaken the delicate and radiating love within her?

How could so many long years of living such a dark life be washed away by someone just like her?

The first glimmer of reality eked back in, and she realized that no longer was it her own body shaking, but Glaurakos that was shaking her. He held her in his grasp, knelt by the pedestal as he cradled her delicate form, precisely as she knew it on the outside, but brimming with such intense new power within. Power the likes of which she'd never envisioned.

Tears stained her cheeks but urgently she pressed her full, chapped lips to his. Never had she connected with another on so many levels. Never in her life had all the complicated facets of her bloodline, of her history, been so matched by another.

And she was certainly not going to throw that away. Not for anything in the world.

She could sense his frustration. Even with the pearl claimed, he wanted the power independently. Yet she couldn't help but be relieved to know he set aside that bitter jealousy to kiss her back and hold her.

The sweet press of their lips was short-lived, however, for more acutely than ever she was aware of the approach of the mindless dragon queen. Her power was taken from her, claimed for Lilah's own, but her consciousness had been driven off, separated. And freed.

Some tether connected them now, Lilah and the dragon queen, For they were one in the same. Time had run out. *She* was nearly returned, and *she* would have what was hers or tear the worlds apart trying.

"We have to get to the portal." Lilah was already moving, even as she gasped for breath. Fear drove her to tug him along. "She's coming. Now." The avian's eyes were wide as her wings brought her up into the air and she began to fly.

The ceiling was in their way, but with the new power freshly coursing through her Lilah had no issue dissolving the stone barrier. It melted away and created a gaping hole that was several stories thick through to the cold winds outside.

Glaurakos flew up beside her, and she caught a glimpse of the awed expression on his face. The surprise and appreciation for her new power overwhelmed any jealousy. At least for now.

As Lilah carried out into the biting storm, she extended an aura of heat to battle the storm. Ice shards became water, and the water was pushed away and dissolved into the air so that they coasted on a warm current towards their destination.

"Such majesty," he gaped, amazed.

Lilah pushed forward harder, but she wasn't ignorant to his compliments, or his pain. "I didn't take it to hurt you." There was so much more she wanted to say, but she hadn't the time to do it justice. "I would never betray you, Glaur."

They soared along in silence, but he gave a brief nod to her in understanding. Under the circumstances, it seemed to be enough.

When they touched down near the portal, she saw the bodies of the other avians — the holy angels — left in scenes of peace. They had been neatly but hurriedly arranged, some sort of last rites performed over them.

"I'll need to focus," she said, for even with her new powers, making the gateway complete could not be accomplished so abruptly. Though no sooner had she said it than she could feel the dragon queen's voice echo in her own mind. It was simply laughter, mocking Lilah for her foolishness because there would be no time. The dragon queen would be there before she could finish the gateway.

"What's the matter?" asked Glaurakos, his warm hand upon her shoulder, so comforting. So familiar.

Lilah looked to it, and a thought occurred to her. "Do you trust me?" she asked, as he had so similarly asked her to trust him just over a day before.

Her answer came with little delay. "I do," he responded solemnly, and she felt the tingle of something odd pass between them. Trust was not for their kind. Never for their kind. Yet they gave it to one another freely.

"Be my Dragon Knight," she declared breathily just a hair of a moment before she grasped his neck and mashed their lips together in such a passionate frenzy. Their tongues met in molten hot passion, so ill fitted to the situation. Yet it had its purpose.

The knowledge of what was happening wasn't something she knew of. Not before she'd touched that precious and powerful stone, at least. Now, she knew intimately what she had to do.

Lilah's nails scratched along his ruddy skin, over his bicep and along his neck. They sunk through his skin, and finally made him wince but she kept his mouth locked with hers. The dark tendrils of power coiled up from her and entered into him. It was as if his blood became replaced with black oil, and the veins jutted out from his body.

Breaking their kiss, he lurched back as he felt the power she bestowed enhance his self. Before her very eyes he bulged and swelled, growing taller, stronger, but still... Glaurakos. His fangs and claws extended, and he took on more monstrous proportions, more like the dragon that had spawned him.

Her gift to him.

"Go," she beckoned him with a lick of her lips. "You can't destroy her, but you can buy us time while I work."

He looked down over his own form, the leather robes strained and torn by his transformation. Yet he nodded to her, holding back any shock. "I'll hold the line," he promised.

She didn't give herself permission to lust for his improved form, but her body responded of its own accord. Lilah forced her gaze away even as the blood pounded between her ears, her face red with desire as she set to her work.

She had to concentrate, to flush those desirous thoughts from her mind. They were something so innate, so ingrained in her being that it was not so easy, however. Even as he took off, her mind buzzed with distracting thoughts and she had to force it back to the matter at hand.

Finally her pulse returned to normal, her breath still shallow, but she was able to concentrate once more. She had to do this right.

The rest lay with her knight.

CHAPTER 39

Glaurakos flew, no longer protected by her aura. He still was possessed of an enhanced preternatural heat. It resisted the icy cold as he pushed toward the oncoming dragon queen, somehow knowing where she was even before her dark shadow became visible in the snowstorm.

She was immense, enough to fit his previous form into her mouth and devour him whole. Even still, larger and more powerful he may have been, he wouldn't prove more than two mouthfuls for her maw.

Pulling his sword from its scabbard, he felt that blade — intrinsically linked to his own soul — grow in size to match his new proportions. The magic that linked them made it keep pace with him, and he noticed a curious new design to it. It had odd curves, strange etchings, draconic yet suggestive.

He pushed that aside and flew toward the gaping jaws of hell itself as her roar carried through the mountain peaks towards him.

Her booming voice was returned to the dragon along with her consciousness, set free by their bravado in the fortress-tomb.

"Insolent whelp! Corrupted spawn of my loins!" Her ire was raised, and she beat those massive wings of hers with a fury, "I'll consume you, her, and claim every morsel of my power back with but three bites!"

Glaurakos gave no immediate cry back but narrowed his flaming gaze upon her as she became clearer in the storm. It wasn't until they were nearly upon one another that he dared speak ill to the goddess of darkness. "Your queendom will be hers!"

They collided. Glaurakos crashed into the dragon's neck as he narrowly avoided her snapping jaw. Her scales were like metal plates, and the impact would have broken his shoulder, were he in his smaller form.

Now, though, he was more resilient.

His great talons dug in between her scales, pierced her flesh as he hung onto her long neck. The demon queen spun and twirled, the whole world a dizzying mess to Glaurakos, but he lifted his blade, cramming it under a scale and sliding it into the more vulnerable flesh beneath.

That elicited a cry from the creature, but little else. She snapped for him, twisting her neck about and lunging. He sprang away, his own large wing-span twisting in the wind as he was barely aware of what way was up or down.

Black, oily blood flowed from her throat, and as he surmised the damage, he realized that she suffered more than the wounds he'd already inflicted. One of her eyes looked seared shut, doubtlessly by holy magic from the brave priest. Her wings had countless holes through them, yet none were enough to hinder her in any real way.

Her voice boomed out, rasping and outraged. "You have dared wound your own mother. I condemn you to the pits of my own personal hell, ill-gotten spawn!"

With a great fury she retaliated, but it was more than Glaurakos had thought possible for such a large creature. She moved so fluidly, so fast as she lunged for him, battering him against her hard, scaly chest as her four claws lashed out at him in a flurry of assaults.

It was too much to dodge or guard against, and so many of those sword-like claws struck true upon Glaurakos' torso.

His leather robes shredded and tore further away, blood poured from his wounds, yet... what should have torn him to fibrous shreds, instead merely left him bloody and battered. The power Lilah had bestowed upon him made his flesh nearly as hard as the dragon queen's scales, and the demon goddess did not expect that.

She nearly recoiled in surprise. "She's made you her champion?!" she bellowed in shock. "That fool!"

Glaurakos had no way of understanding the demon goddess' shock and rage. Why that realization was so surprising to her.

He had little time to contemplate it, for before he could recover from the savage mauling she snapped at him. Her mouth clamped down, and where her claws were mostly repelled, those massive fangs sank true, piercing his flesh.

Glaurakos could not suppress the scream of agony that came from him as the dark former demigod bit into him.

She clamped her jaws shut tighter, and he felt the power — and his life — flicker from him. Thoughts of his last kiss from Lilah, the faith and power she bestowed on him flashed through his mind.

There was no way to be certain where the knowledge came from, but in that moment, he had some glimpse of what it meant when Lilah had bestowed the knighthood upon him. She had shared the power she had claimed in a more intimate of manner than they'd ever had in all their carnality.

There were no words appropriate enough to express it fully, but he understood and was touched.

A flame of life reignited in him and he summoned his own magical powers back to him. From out of the sky all about them, a charge of electricity built, coursed through the dragon queen and into him where it built up continuously.

She could no longer clench her jaws tighter as she struggled against the pain of it, but managed to hold him in place.

Her stubborn resistance was her undoing though, for Glaurakos lashed out with his blade. Her tongue was severed into a bloody, oily mess and she opened her mouth to cry out in agony.

It was enough to escape, or would have been, if the newly minted dragon-knight were not speared upon her bottom fangs still. He had to rip himself from those dagger-sharp pikes, his own blood pouring forth as he fought on, bitterly.

With a slash of his electrically charged blade against the roof of her mouth, and a stab, he thrust with all of his bodily power and pushed the sword through the back of her throat.

Exaltation filled him as he put all his muscle into trying to saw open the beast's neck, heedless of Lilah's warning that she could not be killed by their power.

With a mighty fury, the dragon queen exhaled a purple gout of flame that sent Glaurakos reeling through the air, their two bodies spiraling away from each other.

CHAPTER 40

She was done.

This was it.

After months of being trapped on this island, locked away from time and space, she'd opened that mysterious portal once more. All of the memories of their time there, of the fun they had, of the cold nights in the cave that Glaurakos held her tight overwhelmed her.

Part of her didn't want to go, but she knew they didn't belong in this place.

They didn't belong anywhere.

She stood on her exhausted legs, took a deep breath in, and put the call out to her Champion to return. It was time for them to go home.

CHAPTER 41

Bloody and battered, Glaurakos stabilized himself with some effort. His ripped chest bled, the tatters of his robe dangled from his waist burning and his breathing was ragged. The punctures of the dragon queen's fangs had hurt him worse than he let on, and he could not possibly keep up the fight much longer.

The summons came then, Lilah's call out to him through the bond they now shared. He had to get back to her, but his sword still lingered with the queen as she clawed at the edge of the mountain, trying not to fall down its cliffs.

Holding out his hand, he summoned the blade back to him.

It didn't come right away.

The dragon queen snarled and roared, shook her head from side to side, and after her futile fight ended, the blade pushed through the back of her neck and spun through the air towards Glaurakos. He caught the hilt in his hand, greasy with her dark blood, and began to fly away, back towards the portal.

The deposed queen was not done, however. She rose back up into the air and bellowed her rage as she pursued. Even the hole in her throat was not enough to keep her from coming after her prey!

Glaurakos beat his wings as fast as he could, but the muscles ached, and he felt singed and battered. He didn't dare look back, but simply felt the change in the air as she exhaled her plume of dark fire at him again.

With a bob and a weave in the air he avoided its searing blast, then swung his blade in a smooth arc, casting a spell that sent a bolt of sparkling lightning down against her in retaliation.

It wasn't strong enough to cause her any serious harm, but it did distract her, set her to swaying in the storm a bit more.

Every moment felt like an eternity, but Glaurakos pushed on as the queen drew closer. Lilah and the portal came within sight as he neared that clearing, her tall elegant figure his beacon in the blinding snow.

"Go through!" he bellowed out as loudly as he could, his voice marred by the blood he coughed up with each word.

The snap of the dragon queen's jaws behind him came as an all-too-near threat.

He watched as Lilah hesitated, but she followed his command and all of a sudden she was... gone.

Glaurakos dived in the air, avoided a blast of purple flame as best he could — receiving further burns upon a single wing — and trusted the rest to gravity.

The piercing cry from behind him shook the mountains and he dove through the portal, coming out the other end with a crash.

The old ruins they had not so long ago left were welcome reprieve, but as Glaurakos thudded and rolled across the hard floor it was not over.

Too small to fit the whole of her, the dragon queen's head lunged through. Snapping, blood-spattering jaws went for them both.

"Shut it!" wailed Glaurakos in his damaged voice, edging to his knees and backing away as he did his best to shield Lilah.

The dragon queen reeled back, and he knew what was to come: enough hellfire to flood the room a dozen times over.

Lilah reacted quickly, and though it took so long to open the portal, to shut it was another matter.

A few deft flicks of her wrist and the new power she commanded caused the portal to become unstable and begin collapsing.

It wasn't happening fast enough though, and the dragon queen let loose her belly full of fire. It spewed forth, and Glaurakos pushed himself to his feet, lunging before Lilah and shielding her just mere moments before the flames consumed the entire room.

EPILOGUE

The freedom of flying never quite grew old.

Lilah could soar and enjoy the feel of the air beneath her feathery wings each and every day of her long life, and it still provided some thrill. Swooping, looping, somersaulting and diving. It was what her mother's kin were made for, and it passed through to her.

Her dark hair tendriled behind her, sweeping into her face and tickling her fair skin. Her cheeks were rosy and her green eyes were bright, but her smile wasn't there. Despite her joy and serenity, there was something missing.

Flying alone no longer held the same appeal to her that it once did.

Now it was a sore reminder of the long journeys with Glaurakos by her side, the relatively lumbering man a firm and steady companion. He did not have her grace, none of the delicacy of her lineage, but that had made things special in its own way.

It made her other companions pale by comparison. They didn't understand or titillate her the same. To quite the same degree.

They hadn't given her the adventure of a lifetime, with spoils that promised eternity.

Her trip to the hills was over, and she landed back to the ledge of her tower. It wasn't the sprawling manor she inherited from her father, but it would do for the time being. Until she was ready to return home, triumphant.

Bare feet carried her in through the gently wafting satin curtains, the warm summer breeze following her on in past the empty canopy bed. She sensed the serenity in the air, but she didn't feel it. Not truly.

She went to the adjoining room, and began to mix the berries and reagents she acquired. Her old craft had a familiarity to her. The smell of the normally poisonous berries breaking open and mixing with the other ingredients had a pleasant tang that tickled her petite nostrils.

The concoction prepared, she poured it into a decanter then carried on down the stairs to the lower levels. She had few reasons to go down there, and preferred her aerie in the upper reaches of the tower, but she had work to do.

As she reached the main floor, she hesitated. Her foot pausing less than an inch from the stone as something seemed… off.

Had someone followed her back from her journey for ingredients?

She had little reason to fear anymore, not with the power she had claimed. So she pushed ahead, at the ready for mischief.

The most curious thing she saw was the front door ajar.

Before she could react, arms were about her. That familiar, heated body crushed against her and Glaurakos' lips stole their kiss from her passionately. Savagely.

His injuries from their escape were extensive, and his wings still had not healed, but he was looking hale and hearty otherwise. The powerful half-dragon groped at her rear as he twisted her about and mashed her against his chest.

In his low, gravelly voice he rumbled between kisses, "I could smell your cunt returning from a mile away." Judging by the press of his stiff male organ to her stomach, he wasn't lying.

Considering how little she wore, it was understandable. Now that they'd escaped the wretched north she was able to go back to her old, familiar outfits. A skirt barely covered her ass, its gossamer material nearly transparent as it pooled around her upper thighs. A light, airy top draped across her modest chest.

With his health returning, she felt all that smoldering passion she had to deny herself rise up once more.

When he'd risked his life to save hers, she knew she'd never find another in her lifetime. Not like him.

Who had ever heard of a demon more concerned for his lover's life than his own? Yet he'd done it, he shielded her from the blast as he used his powers to teleport them from the room and being utterly consumed by the flames.

That tenderness, though, was still expressed in the most carnal manners as possible, and she tasted him hungrily. Her teeth bit into his lower lip before her mouth trailed down, licking the masculine taste from his neck as she purred her own pleasure.

He swept her up off her feet, her slender form weighing near nothing in his arms. With a spin it felt like she was soaring again as he suckled her earlobe and let his sharp nails dig into her pert ass up in under her skirt.

The effects of her initial power-sharing had worn off on him, but she had plans in that regard. His large, muscular form was arousing enough as is, anyhow, she assured herself as he bit and suckled his way down to her neck, grinding his throbbing cock into her lower belly. "I need you," he growled, "now."

"I noticed," she teased. It felt so good to... joke with him. To know just how endless their time together would be.

Their long adventure was behind them, but the world held so much more in store. It gave her the time and patience to truly enjoy this. Him.

The way his flesh warmed hers, the way his skin tasted, the masculine scent that surrounded him. She brought her fingers to his hair, scratching the back of his neck as she kissed him. It was hard and passionate, thankfulness at being alive seeping out of her.

Together they were so ravenous, and he wore just as little. A pair of trousers bulged obscenely from his arousal. The whole of his hard, muscular chest was on display as they lived freely in their secluded tower retreat.

Her legs lifted and wrapped about his waist as he carried her up the stairs, and out to the balcony. Her deft fingers reached down and rubbed over his package before freeing the thick member from its confines.

She never grew tired of its heat, so much stronger than other men's. Since she'd taken on the dragon queen's mantle, she felt that desire even stronger somehow. As if their bodies were more suited than ever. Doubtless some left over part of the dragon's nature now resided inside her.

Glaurakos hoisted her up where her wings could billow and flap in the air freely, so that she was suspended over the ruddy-dark crown of his manhood. His mouth was eager to move down her neck towards her chest, where he gnawed and tore to get at her teat.

The pain only made it better and she cried out. Months ago, she'd bartered with him for her freedom.

Now she realized she hadn't even understood what that word meant. The thought of her old, lonely life as being free was pitiful. Never had she felt so alive and glorious as she did then.

Her puffy, pink nipple prodded out towards his tongue, her feminine scent thick in the air. Her pulse quickened as she ground against him, begging her demon lover to lower her further, to let her feel that sweet, delectable kiss of his dick against her cunny.

He didn't leave her waiting long, as he lowered her body and his mouth. The warm wetness of his lips and tongue devoured her stiff teat as he let her slick cunt swallow whole his thickness, consuming its veiny shaft down to the root as he let loose a loud, rapturous groan.

Never did he grow tired of her, her flesh, her kinky nature. He growled as his fingers sank into her thigh and ass, raising her body then pushing it back down, pumping his girth into her with an insistent motion that betrayed the depths of his desire with each increasingly loud smack of their loins.

She lusted for him even more than the day she first met him. Their relationship had blossomed into something wholly unexpected, but what surprised her most was what it did to their sex.

To the way they fucked.

From an outsider perspective it looked like the same ravenous, hungry act. But they knew better. It didn't need to be spoken of for them both to understand the little motions that differed, the emotions that had shifted.

She bit into his neck, lavishing his heated skin with her tongue as she moaned so wantonly against him. She was so warm and wet with wanting, and her nails dug into his shoulders as they fucked.

Those tight, black-leather clad ass cheeks of his tightened, rock hard as he thrust up to meet her body with his lifting motions. He pounded up into her with increasing intensity, meeting and exceeding her passion at each step, just as she did his. The two clamoured to match and surmount each other in their display of love and lust.

The break of alabaster skin beneath his claws as he mauled her ass, the sore sting of her nipple as he sucked and bit so hard, it was all ravenous, savage and beautiful to its core. Her angelic figure fluttered in the air as she was fucked by a monstrous half-demon, his leathery wings unfurling for the first time in months as he claimed her, and she him.

Neither of them knew how they could have gotten so lucky as to find one another in the darkest of situations, but both were equally grateful for it.

She gasped as he struck her so deep, that combination of pain and bliss coalescing so wonderfully as to bring her to that peak of pleasure. Her orgasms had gotten so intense, as if her father's demonic blood was strengthened by it, bringing out the hedonist in her.

Rewarding the hedonist in her, more accurately.

Her angelic wings went rigid as they stretched out, her nerves spasming as she sucked in air and then let out a loud scream.

Meeting her cries came his grunts, louder and louder, with each hard thrust of his veiny cock up into her. He was a beast in heat with her, more and more, nothing held back in his mad rush to have her, to claim her again and again.

The tensing of his muscular form, each sinew straining across his hard pecs, rigid abs, bulging biceps as he impaled her upon his steely-hard girth and unleashed his flood of virile seed. The bestial manner in which he unloaded such a torrent of creamy cum was so perfectly raw and masculine. Her puffy, slick pussy siphoning each and every last spurt of its essence up into her.

Her cry warbled like a beautiful bird, praising him over and over again as her cunny milked him of his cum. Her grasp was so tight on him, despite all the bruises and marks he left on her.

Perhaps this was how they could love. How they could let everything go and just enjoy one another for what they were.

Two corrupted hearts.

NOTE FROM THE AUTHORS

Thank you so much for reading and purchasing our story! We hope it made you squirm. Once you recover, sign up for our newsletter at http://jmkeep.com/newsletter and check out the rest of our catalogue at http://jmkeep.com.

Did you enjoy yourself? Take a quick second to tell your friends in a review on Amazon and Goodreads! Reviews are a great way of helping other readers to find our work and make it so we can write more frequently!

We love connecting with our fans! You can find us here:

Website: http://jmkeep.com/

Twitter: @jmkeep | @jekeep

Facebook: http://www.facebook.com/jmkeep

Remember, though. The best way to find out what major projects we have in the work is through our newsletter at http://jmkeep.com/newsletter! You'll get a free book just as a thanks for signing up.

MORE BY J.E. & M. KEEP

Erotic Novels:
The Vixen Torn
The Vixen Arises
Magic Academy
When Dreamers Wake
The Warlord's Concubine
The Mistress
Vile Wasteland
Forgotten Thrones
Erotic Novellas:
In Her Dreams
Brutal Passions
Brought the Stars to You
Bound as the World Burns
Her Master's Madness
Led Into Temptation
Outcast
Outcast 2: Her Survival
Bound by Forbidden Love
Bad Wolf, Be Good

Collections:
The Ultimate Erotic Horror Collection – Contains Her

Master's Madness, Bad Wolf, Be Good and Led Into Temptation

BIOGRAPHY

Joshua and Michelle Keep combine fantasy, scifi, horror, romance and mystery into exciting and titillating books.

As long term, loving partners in a very happy relationship, they love to torture their characters. Dark romance wraps its way around all of their stories, corrupting both characters and readers alike.

Some of their work contains dubious consent and erotic pain, so it's not for the faint of heart. Their stories are often called twisted and arousing — at the same time.

Joshua and Michelle have been writing fantasy erotica for over 10 years from their home in St. John's, Newfoundland Canada. They are the owners of Darknest Fantasy Erotica, a forum dedicated to adult fantasy and video games.

Newsletter: http://jmkeep.com/newsletter
Patreon: http://www.patreon.com/jmkeep
Facebook: http://www.facebook.com/jmkeep
Youtube:
http://www.youtube.com/user/JMKeepSFF/videos
Twitter: http://twitter.com/jmkeep |
http://twitter.com/jekeep
Email: admin [at] jmkeep [dot] com